LAST
DAY
ALIVE

BOOKS BY J.R. ADLER

Dead Woman Crossing

LAST DAY ALIVE

J. R. ADLER

bookouture

Published by Bookouture in 2021

An imprint of Storyfire Ltd.
Carmelite House
50 Victoria Embankment
London EC4Y 0DZ

www.bookouture.com

Written by J.R. Adler

J.R. Adler has asserted her right to be identified
as the author of this work.

ISBN: 978-1-80019-240-9
eBook ISBN: 978-1-80019-239-3

To my family

CHAPTER ONE

I didn't realize what I had done until I saw the blood on my hands. Sometimes things just happen… The blood was thick like honey or maybe I just thought of it that way. It made it easier to wash it from my hands when I pictured sweet, sticky honey. It was actually comforting to look at the little girl after the life had drained from her. She didn't yell. She didn't try to get away. She didn't scream for help. She just laid there peacefully. If I hadn't known any better, I would have confused her for an angel, a sweet, sleeping angel. Her hair was blonde like butter, falling just below her shoulders. I held her for a long time, brushing her hair, braiding it, unbraiding it. It was so soft and feathery. My fingers were rough and calloused, so occasionally a strand would get stuck on cracked skin, pulling from the little girl's head. I retied her tennis shoes, loop, swoop and through. Then I tried the bunny ear method, because I assumed that was how she would have tied them. I caressed my hand against her rosy cheek until her skin turned cold. I couldn't decide whether I wanted her big blue eyes opened or closed. No matter where I moved around the room, they seemed to be staring at me. At first, I liked it. Like she was paying attention to me, like she was listening. But then I didn't like it. It felt like she was mocking me, taunting me, judging me. So, I closed them but maybe not all the way. Just a little bit, so she was still peering at me. I wanted to keep her forever.

CHAPTER TWO

"Mom! Have you seen my baton?" Kimberley tied her long, dark hair back into a low ponytail. She bent down beside the bed, flipping up the skirt to look underneath. Nothing but dust bunnies and random toys Jessica was no longer interested in filled the space. Kimberley blew out her cheeks as she stood back up. She raked her hands down her tired and pale face, pulling at it. She was beyond exhausted. That was life as a single mother with a two-year-old.

"Did you leave it at work?" Nicole yelled from the kitchen.

Kimberley shook her head but then thought for a moment. Maybe she did. No, she wouldn't have. Before exiting the small bedroom, Kimberley took one final look around. It had become more crammed over the past year thanks to Jessica's crib being switched out for a toddler bed, complete with pink sheets and loads of stuffed animals. The vomit-green shag carpeting still covered the floor but Kimberley had taken care of the popcorn walls by covering them with wood paneling, giving the room a more rustic farmhouse feel. It wasn't pretty, but at least it wasn't dangerous anymore. She didn't expect to live here as long as she had, but with everything that had happened, she knew her mother needed her. She exited the room and started down the hallway. In the living room, Kimberley found her police baton in the hands of her mischievous daughter. Of course Jessica would have the baton rather than the dozens of toys that were spread all around the floor in front of the television. Kimberley walked around the plaid couch and floral chair.

"Jessica," she said in the sternest voice she could muster.

Her two-and-a-half-year-old daughter was the spitting image of Kimberley. Big blue eyes, a heart-shaped face, and long dark hair.

"Uh-oh," she said with a giggle as she placed the end of the baton in her mouth. Her daughter was at the age where everything ended up in her mouth. From fireflies to rocks to the wheat grass that seemed to take up every square inch of the state of Oklahoma, even working its way through the cracks in the asphalt.

"Uh-oh is right," Kimberley said, marching toward Jessica. She bent down and gently pulled the baton away from her grasp.

As soon as the baton left her little hands, Jessica erupted into a torrent of screams and cries like a volcano. A volcano would be much easier to handle, Kimberley thought to herself. Tears ran down her red face and her shoulders shook. Telling a two-year-old 'no' was about the worst thing you could do.

"What did I say about taking things that aren't yours?" Kimberley slid the baton into her utility belt, giving Jessica a stern look.

Jessica cried harder, but Kimberley chose not to give in and coddle her. Instead, she bent down so she was eye level with her daughter. Never negotiate with terrorists, she thought to herself.

"Jessica, what did I say about taking things that aren't yours?" she asked again, tilting her head.

Her daughter huffed and puffed, wiping her wet eyes with the back of her hands and sniffling to regain control over her breathing. The tears slicked back her soft, brown hair.

"Don't do it," she said just above a whisper.

"That's right, sweetie." Kimberley nodded. She hoisted Jessica up onto her hip as she stood, planting kisses all over her cheeks.

"Momma," Jessica said in between fits of giggles.

Like an Oklahoma tornado, the tantrum had passed quickly, and Kimberley was grateful for that. Dealing with hardened criminals paled in comparison to dealing with Jessica's outbursts at times.

"The punishment for your crime is one hundred kisses." Kimberley laughed, planting little pecks all over Jessica's forehead, cheeks, and neck.

They walked through the dining room into the small kitchen that had a bar top counter and a couple of stools. Her mother had attempted to make the place her own by installing floral curtains that clashed with the tacky rooster backsplash—almost as though the present and the past were colliding.

"Your turn, Momma," Jessica said, kissing her mom on the cheek.

Nicole stood at the stove, pouring several cups of oats into a boiling pot of water. She turned and smiled at Kimberley and Jessica. Her face had grown a little brighter and a little rounder over the past year. She looked younger, happier, and more vibrant. Kimberley knew that feeling. It was the feeling of getting rid of dead weight in your life. And that dead weight was her husband, the one that cheated, lied, and murdered his mistress. Kimberley had gotten rid of dead weight before, but not like her mother. For her, it was a boyfriend that wanted nothing to do with fathering his own child.

"Found your baton?" Nicole asked.

"Yes, this little stinker had it." Kimberley tickled Jessica.

"You're the steeeeen-ker," Jessica said.

She was also at that age where she repeated everything she heard, so Kimberley had to be extra careful as to what she said in front of her parrot of a daughter. She placed Jessica in her high chair, while Nicole set some cut up fruit in front of her.

"I want oat... meal," Jessica whined, slapping her hands against the tray.

She was also at that age where she knew exactly what she wanted and knew that tears and whining could be used as psychological warfare against her mother and grandmother.

"Sweetie, I'm making you oatmeal. You have to be patient," Nicole said.

"Don't wanna be pat-tent," Jessica said, trying to copy the word.

Kimberley shook her head as she poured herself a cup of coffee. "It can't get worse than the terrible twos, right?"

"Yes, you have her teenage years to look forward to," Nicole said with a laugh.

"Oh goody." She took a sip. "So, today's the day?" Kimberley raised an eyebrow.

"Yes, the divorce is finalized." Nicole nodded as she scooped a spoonful of oatmeal into a bowl and sprinkled brown sugar on top of it.

"And when's yours going to be finalized?" Kimberley cocked her head.

She didn't understand how her mother could have possibly still been married to her stepfather, David. He was a monster, a cold-blooded one at that. He murdered Hannah Brown. A single mother who had fathered his child during an affair. Kimberley had become friends with her briefly before her life was taken. David had killed her to keep his affair and love child hidden. When Kimberley was closing in on him and his lies, he threatened Jessica's life. When Kimberley discovered the truth, he attacked her and tried to take his own life. After all of that, how in the hell could her mother still be married to him?

"I'm working on it. Divorce takes time and money." Nicole set a bowl and spoon in front of Jessica who immediately dove right into it.

Kimberley had accepted that answer for the first three months, the first six months, the first nine months—but now it had been a year. A year since David had been arrested. If her stepsister, Emily, could find the money and time to divorce Wyatt who had lied and illegally sold moonshine, her mother could find the time and money to divorce a murderer.

Nicole filled another bowl with oatmeal and held it out for Kimberley. She shook her head. "I've lost my appetite."

"Is that the example you want to make in front of your daughter?" Nicole looked at Jessica while she scooped another spoonful into her mouth.

"Eat, Mummy." Her mouth was full of sticky, sweet oatmeal.

Kimberley let out a huff. Every time she tried to have this conversation with her mother, Nicole used Jessica as a shield in some way.

"I'm watching the grandkids tonight, so you can spend time with Emily."

"Yeah, a little divorce soirée." Kimberley raised her brows. "Can't wait to celebrate yours."

Nicole refilled her mug with coffee and took a sip, ignoring her daughter's comment.

"I'm glad you two can be there for each other. Emily's been having a hard time."

Kimberley took a bite of oatmeal and washed it down with some coffee. "I would be too after what's she been through. Her father's serving a life sentence for murder, and her ex-husband who nearly lost the family farm is now galivanting around town with a new woman before the divorce papers are even signed."

After everything that had happened, she thought for sure Emily would blame her. After all, it was Kimberley that had discovered Wyatt's illegal moonshine making business. And it was Kimberley that had solved Hannah Brown's murder. But somehow, it had brought them closer. It didn't happen overnight, but it did happen.

"Have you seen Wyatt with that new girl?" Nicole pursed her lips.

"A couple of times at The Trophy Room." Kimberley brought her bowl to the sink and quickly washed it out.

"Such a shame."

"It is," she said, drying off her hands on a floral printed hand towel, another one of her mother's touches.

"How's work been?" Nicole asked. Kimberley figured she was trying to change the subject before it got back to 'why the fuck are you still married to that murderer?'

"Good. Aside from dipshits at the local bar causing trouble."

"Dip… shits," Jessica repeated.

"Damnit," Kimberley said, slapping a hand over her mouth.

"Damnit," Jessica repeated. Her face scrunched up into a smile, followed by a fit of giggles.

"Kimberley," Nicole said with a stern voice.

She immediately felt thirteen again, her face turning red in embarrassment.

"I'm sorry." Kimberley walked to her daughter and placed her hands on her cheeks. "Jessica, we don't say those words."

"Dipshit." Jessica giggled again.

Kimberley took a deep breath. "Yes, that's one of them. We don't say that. Mommy shouldn't have said that. Do you understand?"

Being a mother to a toddler had challenged her more than almost everything else Kimberley had endured in her life, and she had endured a lot. She even figured an army of toddlers could do more damage than any other world power or at least that's what came to mind just before she fell asleep some nights after battling with Jessica for bedtime.

"Mommy. I won't s-tay dip… shit." She smiled a devilish grin.

Kimberley looked up at Nicole. Her face said, 'please help me.'

"Ouch!" Nicole cried, grabbing at her ears.

"Grandma, owweee!" Jessica pushed out her bottom lip.

"That's right. Every time you say those naughty words, it makes Grandma's ears hurt. You don't want to hurt Grandma, do you?" Nicole made a sad face at her granddaughter.

Jessica shook her head vehemently. "Please, Grandma. Don't hurt."

"I won't as long as you don't say those naughty words." Nicole tilted her chin.

"I won't. Promise." Jessica held out her tiny pinky finger.

Kimberley wasn't sure where she had picked that up from, but she wrapped her pinky around hers anyway. "Good girl," she said, giving Jessica a kiss on each cheek before standing upright.

"Alright, I've got to head to work." She glanced at the watch on her wrist and then back at her mother.

Nicole looked at the bird clock on the wall. "This early?"

"Yeah, Barb called and said Sam wanted me to go in early to discuss something. Can you take Jessica to daycare?"

Nicole nodded. "Of course," she said with a smile.

CHAPTER THREE

Kimberley took the backroads to work in her police-issued SUV. Driving through Oklahoma was like going to visit the Wizard of Oz, following the yellow brick road. Except all the yellow was wheat and sunshine and Oz didn't actually exist. She didn't mind the dryness nor the heat nor the mundaneness of it all. Kimberley had learned that she got used to everything around her as all people do. Whether it was a waterfall, a skyline of skyscrapers or miles and miles of rolling wheat. Eventually the extraordinary became the ordinary once she'd been around it long enough. She just got used to Oklahoma quicker than usual. But she knew she needed a little change of scenery, a break from it all. Kimberley hadn't taken a day off of work since she started at the Custer County Sheriff's Office a year ago, but that would change soon as she had a vacation planned in a couple of weeks at Gloss Mountain State Park. Her mother and her stepsister, Emily, and Emily's boys were going to join her and Jessica. She was very much looking forward to it, and it came highly recommended from Sam, her boss, who had vacationed there many times with his family. Kimberley had thought for sure she'd have more time to spend with her daughter after relocating from New York City to Dead Woman Crossing, Oklahoma—and she did to an extent—but she was still a single mother with a demanding job trying to make ends meet.

Pulling into the Custer County Sheriff's Office, she immediately realized something was off. All of the deputies' vehicles were already there as well as Barb's minivan. Had something happened?

It had been quiet since the murder of Hannah Brown occurred a year ago. Just traffic violations, drugs, disorderly conducts, and domestic violence. Run-of-the-mill type of stuff that would happen in any small town in Middle America. Kimberley sprang from her vehicle, quickening her pace to a jog as soon as her feet hit the asphalt. Something bad had to have happened for everyone to be in this early. She threw open the first set of doors and the second and expected to see Barb sitting at her desk knitting something. But she wasn't at the front desk. She was always at the front desk unless she was delivering coffee or baked goods. She threw open the doors to the floor that led to the deputies' desks and her and Sam's office. But what she found was darkness and silence. Not the rows of desks with a couple of deputies sitting at them entering in reports. Not Sam sitting in his back office looking through the glass window that overlooked the deputies' floor. Just blackness.

"Hello?" Kimberley said. It wasn't a question of who was there. It was a warning. Her voice was full of authority and confidence. Seven years as a NYPD detective had taught her that. Never enter a strange room with any sort of apprehension.

A slight shuffle in the back grabbed her attention. Her neck jerked in that direction, and she willed her eyes to adapt to the darkness quicker. All of a sudden, the fluorescent lighting turned on.

"Surprise," a group of people yelled.

Kimberley jumped backward, squinting her eyes. Standing in front of her were deputies, Sheriff Sam Walker, and Barb wearing birthday cone hats, while Barb held out a homemade birthday cake. She could see the colorful balloons and streamers all over her office. Barb was petite with gray, curly hair permed on the top of her head. She wore linen pants and loose-fitting blouses, always covered in some sort of pattern from flowers to birds. She was like a grandmother to everyone at the station.

"What? It's not my birthday," Kimberley said. She took a couple of deep breaths, regaining control of her racing heart.

Barb smiled and stepped toward Kimberley. "I know. It was two weeks ago. Your mother told me a few days ago. Trying to pull a fast one on me, aren't ya?"

Kimberley couldn't help but smile. She looked over at her deputies and Sam who were all laughing. "You told me if I didn't tell her, she wouldn't do this," she said to Sam.

"Barb knows all. There was no sense in trying to hide it." Sam grinned back.

"It's true. I do." Barb nodded.

"I'm just not into celebrating my birthday, and it was two weeks ago."

"Celebrating a birthday is like saying I'm happy you're alive and in my life. And we're all happy about that. So, you're into it now." Barb set the cake on a desk and began slicing it up.

"This time last year when you swooped in and took my job, I wasn't happy. But you grew on me, King," Deputy Bearfield teased. His long, silky, black hair was tied back in a low ponytail. He brought his hand to his sharp jawline and rubbed it as he chuckled.

"Ha-ha," Kimberley mocked, flicking her wrist.

"You know I'm just messing with ya," Bearfield said, plopping his large hand on her shoulder and giving it a small shake. His smile was wide and completely contrasted with his piercing, dark eyes. They had gotten off on the wrong foot when Kimberley joined the force as she had been hired on as the Chief Deputy, the job Bearfield had applied for. But she quickly earned his respect and his friendship. Kimberley was grateful that she had a good team and people she genuinely enjoyed working with, minus Deputy Craig Lodge. He was the only one not wearing a birthday hat, and his crooked smile was clearly forced, like there were two hooks in his mouth being pulled in two different directions. Despite never being in the military, he sported a buzzed military haircut.

"Mind if I hit the road, boss?" Deputy Lodge asked Sam.

It was obvious he didn't want anything to do with this celebration, and Kimberley was happy to see him go.

"No cake?" Sam asked, tilting his head.

"Nah, gotta watch my weight," he said, patting his abdomen. Lodge was a small man, only around 5'9", but he walked around like he was seven feet tall, a true Napoleon complex.

"Alright, yes. Feel free." Sam waved him off.

Lodge gave a slight nod and a tight-lipped smile at Kimberley as he hurried out the doors.

"Where is he rushing off to?" Deputy Burns asked. Burns had been on the force for a year now, so he wasn't a rookie anymore. Kimberley had noticed with each month, his presence and confidence got stronger. He had light blond hair and hazel eyes with soft features that were almost feminine. He was the opposite of Lodge in nature, but that made him an even better deputy.

"Why does he still work here?" Bearfield slightly shook his head.

Sam shrugged his shoulders. "He completed his substance abuse counseling, and he and Sarah are going to marriage counseling."

Kimberley twisted up her lips. How the hell did a sworn-in officer keep his job after physically abusing his wife and getting charged with domestic violence? She never believed in second chances when it came to violence.

"Here you are. First piece is for the birthday girl," Barb said as she slid a slice of double chocolate cake onto a plate and held it out to Kimberley.

"Thanks, Barb. Did you make this?" Kimberley immediately dove a plastic fork into it and tossed it into her mouth. The chocolate was rich and the cake was moist, making it melt as soon as it hit her tongue.

"Of course. Store bought is for the people I don't care for. This was made with love," Barb said with a smile.

"Hey, you brought in a Dairy Queen cake for my birthday." Officer Burns squinted his eyes.

Barb handed him a piece of cake. "I standby what I said." She chuckled.

Burns shoveled a bite into his mouth.

"Barb, you're cold," Bearfield said with a laugh.

"Well, he would have gotten homemade, but he let my plant die when I was on vacation. I asked you to water it, Bryan. I came back and it was bone dry and dead. And I know you had the time, just hobbling around here like a bouncing sack of potatoes." Barb scrunched up her face.

"I'm sorry, Barb. I'll buy you a new one. Better yet, I'll plant it myself and grow it for you. Homemade." Burns gave a small smile.

"Then you'll be back in my good graces, my dear," Barb said with a nod.

"Load me up." Sam held out his plate.

Barb sliced off an even bigger slice for him. It was no secret that Sheriff Walker had a sweet tooth.

"Whatcha doing for your birthday?" he asked Kimberley. Sam's eyes grew wide just as a fork full of cake entered his mouth.

"It was two weeks ago." Kimberley took another bite and half sat on one of the desks. "I worked."

"You've been here a year and haven't taken a single day off." Sam arched an eyebrow.

"Yeah, you're making the rest of us look bad," Bear teased. He rocked back on his heels just as Barb handed him a plate with two slices of cake. Bearfield's name was appropriate for both his size and his appetite, so Barb always gave him extra.

"Well, I'm heading up to Gloss Mountain State Park in a couple weeks, just before school starts up, so my mom, and Emily and her boys can join Jessica and me for some camping and hiking," Kimberley said with a smile.

She had never taken a real family vacation in her entire life. Growing up, the last thing on her father's mind was quality family time, as alcohol took center stage and scorched earth seared through anyone trying to block that goal, usually Kimberley's mother. Living in NYC, where she'd been before Dead Woman Crossing, a vacation for Kimberley and her daughter was spending an hour or two in Central Park for a picnic. She never had the time nor the money to get out of the city. But now that Jessica was a little older, and they were living in a small town with significantly lower living expenses, working a job she could actually get away from, a vacation was possible.

"You're taking my recommendation? You're going to love it there," Sam said. His smile was bright but his eyes gave it away. Sam had told Kimberley about the park when she'd mentioned needing a change of scenery and a getaway. It was the last place he had vacationed with his wife and son before they passed. So, Kimberley could see why it was important to him. Some people might think that the pain in his eyes that was radiating out, drowning the whole room, if for just a brief moment, would fade over time. But Kimberley knew better. Some wounds never heal. Every happy memory he had was followed by a swift reminder of why they were just memories now.

Kimberley nodded.

"I'm glad you're taking the time off. You certainly deserve it." Sam grinned at Kimberley and then returned his focus to the chocolate cake.

"Anything pressing for me to dive into before I bounce in a few weeks? Anything that has a nice twenty-one-day expiration date on it?" Kimberley joked, trying to embrace the idea of her leaving her work, instead of dreading it. Work had made up most of her identity. When she stepped away from it, it felt like she was losing a part of herself.

"Oh, not really. Things have been rather quiet since... well, you know. Just routine stuff. You can get cracking on any little thing you like," Sam said with a mouth full of cake.

"Will do." Kimberley looked to Barb. "Thank you… for all this. It was… very sweet." She wasn't used to having people do nice things for her, so it was hard to get the right words out.

"It was my pleasure, Chief Deputy King." Barb winked at Kimberley.

The phone at Barb's desk began to ring, so she quickly set down her plate and hurried to answer it.

"Custer County Sherriff's Office, Barb speaking, how may I help you?"

Kimberley had heard that line hundreds of times now, and it was somehow pleasant and soothing every time. It was as if Barb knew how…

"Ma'am! Ma'am! I need you to calm down, okay? I'm right here with you and we are going to talk through this. So, tell me again what you know." Barb's eyes grew wide. "Uh huh… Yup… And how long has she been missing?"

Barb nodded as she scribbled down on a piece of paper what the person on the other end of the line was telling her. Kimberley glanced at the other deputies and then at Sheriff Sam Walker. Sam and Kimberley exchanged a look, the same one they had exchanged a year ago when Hannah Brown was brutally murdered. Sam and the deputies tossed their plates into a garbage can, not finishing the rest of their cake, and wiped their hands, while Kimberley made a beeline for Barb's desk.

"And where was the last place you saw her…? Okay. Edna, is it? Edna just stay on the phone with me, and I'll get some more details but I'll send some deputies out to you immediately." Barb pulled the phone away from her face and covered the mouthpiece with her hand. She turned to call for someone but Kimberley was already there waiting.

"Did I hear missing girl?" Kimberley asked.

Barb nodded and then spoke into the phone again. "I'm right here with you, and I'm going to stay on the line until our officers arrive. Tell me where you live?" She scribbled down an address and handed it to Kimberley.

"Whatcha got?" Sam stood beside Kimberley, while she quickly read over Barb's notes.

"Little girl missing. Edna Chase, her grandmother, is on the phone. Been missing since this morning. They live in Dead Woman Crossing, north of Deer Creek," she said all in one breath.

North of Deer Creek was the forgotten side. The houses were a little smaller and a little older. The few businesses the town had were south of Deer Creek, which split the town in half. Kimberley lived south of the creek and rarely ventured to the other side of it.

Kimberley hoped the little girl was only missing. Missing meant she could be found… alive.

Sam turned back to Bearfield and Burns who had formed a semicircle just behind him, waiting for his command. Their hands were clasped together right in front of them, feet shoulder width apart like a row of soldiers. They knew when to joke around and when to take things seriously. It was why Kimberley enjoyed working with them.

"Kimberley and I are going to go speak with Edna and find out more. No need to panic yet. Carry on with your daily duties. Be ready to join us if we need additional help." Sam nodded, letting them know his instructions were over.

"Shouldn't we set up a search and rescue? The first twenty-four hours in a child's disappearance are critical." Kimberley looked to Sam, raising an eyebrow.

"Let's get over there and talk with Edna first. Kids run off all the time. I don't want to cause a panic by jumping the gun too fast." Sam nodded and proceeded through the double set of doors.

She looked over to her deputies and gave a tight smile, before turning on her foot and following behind. Kimberley hoped Sam wasn't making a mistake by not acting quickly enough. In situations like this, seconds could be the difference between life and death, and she was all too familiar with those seconds.

The memory sprung to the front of her mind like a camera flash.

She could instantly smell the musty, mildew scent that was attached to that moment. The squeaks of rats. The cobwebs that grabbed onto her face as she walked through the basement. A flashlight the only source of light. Kimberley wanted to stop it, but it kept playing in front of her eyes. The feet covered in small burns and cuts. The legs equally inflicted as though her flesh had been scored. She was stripped bare, no clothing, no jewelry, nothing, except for a paper bag that covered her head.

Kimberley shook the memory from her mind. She didn't need to relive it again, not right now. She had relived the night she was too late a thousand times already. The night she found her partner's dead body. She carried the guilt of not being able to save Detective Lynn Hunter everywhere. And she carried the determination to never let another killer get away. She had made that mistake before. She wouldn't do it again.

CHAPTER FOUR

Kimberley sat in the passenger seat while Sam sped from Arapaho where the Custer County Sheriff's Office was located to the north side of Dead Woman Crossing. It was a twenty-five-minute drive and every minute felt like an eternity. She tried to keep her eyes on the road ahead and the golden blur of wheat all around them, but Kimberley couldn't help watching the time tick away on the dashboard clock. They didn't know much, just that Edna's grand-daughter had gone missing sometime today. Sometime wasn't a good time in a missing person's case. Every minute that passed was like a punch in the gut. Were they too late? Would they find her? Was she lost? Had she been taken? Or maybe it was something less nefarious? She was at a friend's house. Lost in a wheat field. Kimberley had learned a lot about wheat in the past year and one thing she knew was it could grow as tall as four feet. The little girl could definitely get lost in a wheat field, Kimberley presumed. Especially on a day like today. It was dreary and overcast, the sun opting not to make an appearance. A sheet of gray hung low in the sky, so low it felt as though it could fall at any time, suffocating everything below it. Perhaps it already had.

Kimberley looked at the clock again. It was nearly nine thirty in the morning. Right as she was going to ask how much further, Sam turned his SUV and pulled into a blacktop driveway. It led up to a modest white ranch home with red shutters and a screened-in porch. A two-story home sat across the street and then nothing but woods and wheat for miles. Getting out of the vehicle, Kimberley immediately noticed the front door was partially open. Sam looked to her, and she pointed toward the open door. He nodded, and they proceeded toward the home. She noticed the outside of the house was well kept. A fresh coat of paint on the siding. Trimmed bushes lined the outside. Shutters were pristine. Even the driveway was spotless as though someone had power-washed it. It looked like a clean chalkboard. The porch was tidy with a bench, two rocking chairs, and a small table. Everything seemed ordinary minus the open front door and the child that had not returned home. But was it too ordinary? Too clean? Too spotless? Kimberley's brain was like a freight train: once an idea started, it took off in one direction. She knew she needed to stop it before it went off the rails. She took a deep breath.

"Hello. Custer County Sheriff's Office," Sam called out into the home.

His voice was met with silence, then pounding footsteps. An elderly woman with dark brown, shoulder-length hair entered the living room. She was pale with bloodshot eyes that gave way to the fact that she must have been crying.

"Oh, thank heavens, you're here. Come in. Come in," she said, beckoning with her hand. "Sit down. Sit down." She motioned to the brown leather couch. "Arthur. Arthur. They're here. Come. Come."

Kimberley knew the woman was panicked. Everything she said, she said it twice, almost as if her brain hadn't registered it the first time.

"Edna, why don't you have a seat, so we can talk?" Kimberley gestured to the couch. She needed her to be calm before they asked her any questions. A panicked person was never a reliable witness.

"Yes. Yes," Edna said, taking a seat on the couch. She placed her palms on top of her knees and took a couple of deep breaths, or at least tried to. Her left leg bounced, and Kimberley could see she was pressing her hand down on it firmly to stop if from shaking. White crept across her hands.

Another set of footsteps echoed throughout the home, and an elderly man emerged from a doorway off of the dining room into the living area. Glasses hung at the end of his nose, and he quickly pushed them back up. He was tall and lean, and his skin was as pale as Edna's.

"Hi, I'm Arthur Chase," he said, extending his hand out. He shook Sam's first and then Kimberley's. "Thank you for coming so quickly."

Kimberley noticed a couple of beads of sweat sat at the top of his receding hairline.

"Why don't you take a seat, Arthur?" Sam suggested.

Arthur nodded and sat down next to Edna, placing his hand on hers.

Kimberley and Sam each took a seat in two wingback chairs that sat kitty-corner on either side of the couch. Edna looked to Arthur with wild eyes, then back at her shaking leg. The inside of the house matched the outside, in the sense that it was immaculately clean. The coffee table in front of them had a small tray decorated with a vase of flowers, a Kleenex box, and a stack of coasters. The fireplace mantle was full of framed photos of a little girl with blonde hair and blue eyes. She presumed that was their granddaughter. Kimberley pulled out her notepad and pen and looked to Edna and Arthur. Edna's leg had stopped shaking, so she knew she had calmed down enough to give a statement.

"Tell us what happened." Kimberley started with an open-ended statement. It was best to let a witness tell their story in their own words, before asking the specifics needed in order to fill in all the blanks.

Edna took a deep breath, letting it exhale through her nose. "Piper, our granddaughter, left last night after dinner to go and stay at her friend Miley's house. They've been attached at the hip since they went to summer camp together the first week of summer. They play at Miley's house and then spend a lot of time riding bikes over on Black Heart Lane and playing in the woods."

Sam cleared his throat.

"Black Heart Lane?" he said.

Kimberley wasn't sure if it was a question or not, but she noticed a tightness in his eyes and his lips folding as if he was trying to contain the words just behind them.

Edna nodded. "Yeah, that backroad they repaved with blacktop a few summers back. It winds through the woods. Kids like to ride down the hills, since they get good speed. It's just about a mile away, and then another mile to Miley's house."

Kimberley took notes as quickly as possible only pulling the things she thought were pertinent.

"She's been missing since last night?" Kimberley raised an eyebrow.

Edna burst into tears throwing her head into her hands. Guilt.

Arthur cleared his throat. "We didn't realize she was missing until this morning when Miley called the house and asked to play with Piper."

A parent's or, in this case, a grandparent's worst nightmare. Thinking they know where their grandchild is and realizing they weren't where they thought they were.

"What time was that?" Sam asked.

"Just around eighty-thirty." Arthur rubbed at his temple.

Sam leaned forward, squaring up his bent knees with the Chases'. This was how Kimberley knew things just went from minor to serious.

"What time did Piper leave the house last night?" Sam asked.

"Five fifteen." Edna lifted her head. "We eat dinner at five and Piper was so eager to go and stay at Miley's that she inhaled her food."

Kimberley jotted down the time. "And Miley's house is a couple miles away?"

"Just about." Arthur rubbed at his eyes and pushed his glasses back up the bridge of his nose.

"How old is Piper?" Sam asked.

"She's only ten years old." Edna erupted in tears again.

"Is it normal for Piper to go off on her own?" Kimberley asked. She couldn't imagine ever letting her daughter out of her sight, but then again, Jessica was only two and a half. Maybe she'd feel differently in eight years time.

"Yes, of course. Since she made friends with Miley they always go for bike rides, play in the woods, have sleepovers," Arthur explained. "When Piper's head isn't in a book, she's outside playing. She's an outdoorsy girl and kids need time without adults around. That's how I was raised. Playing outside from sunup to sundown."

It felt as though he was trying to convince himself more than Kimberley and Sam. Guilt, Kimberley presumed. Was it guilt because he had done something wrong or was it because he hadn't kept a close eye on his granddaughter and blamed himself? She'd get to the bottom of it.

"And you said today that Miley called here asking if Piper wanted to play? That's when you realized your granddaughter was missing?" Sam rubbed at his chin.

Arthur and Edna nodded. "I nearly dropped the phone," Edna added.

"And you said that was around eight-thirty this morning?" Kimberley asked.

Edna nodded.

"I took the phone from Edna and got Miley's mom on the phone to confirm Piper never came over last night," Arthur added.

"What's Miley's mom's name?" Kimberley asked, making notes.

"Linda. Linda Baker."

"Do you two know Linda well?" Sam asked.

Arthur and Edna looked at each other for a moment and shook their heads. "We've never really spoken aside from our phone call this morning. Miley and Piper became friends this summer like we said," Arthur explained.

"And what did she say to you?"

"She said Miley didn't know about a planned sleepover, and that she wasn't feeling well yesterday, so she was home all day." Arthur wiped at his eyes again.

"Does Piper have any other friends?" Kimberley asked.

Where else could Piper have run off to? Had she lied to her grandparents and had plans of her own that they wouldn't have approved of? Kimberley felt ten years old was too young for those type of shenanigans. She associated that type of behavior with teens. But these days, kids seemed to grow up faster than when she was a kid.

"Not that we know of," Edna said. "Before Miley moved here at the end of the school year, Piper didn't really have any friends. We were so happy she'd made one."

Arthur squeezed Edna's hand.

"And you don't know Miley or Linda Baker all that well?" Kimberley asked.

Edna looked to Arthur. They both shook their heads.

"And you two are her grandparents?" Sam asked as he repositioned himself in his chair.

Arthur and Edna pressed their lips firmly together and nodded. Their reaction told Kimberley there was family drama involved. She could pick up on that sort of thing, because she knew family drama all too well. Perhaps, their family issues had something to do with Piper's disappearance.

"Where are Piper's parents?" Kimberley tilted her head.

"Well." Edna cleared her throat. "We never met her father, and we got custody of Piper a couple of years ago… back when our daughter, Shana, couldn't take care of Piper any longer." There was sadness and anger in Edna's eyes as she spoke.

"Is Shana in the picture?" Sam cleared his throat.

"We haven't seen her in nearly a year," Arthur cut in.

"What happened with Shana?" Kimberley asked, getting straight to the point. She didn't like this beating around the bush and felt like they were wasting precious time. Time that could be spent looking for Piper. But she knew that she and Sam needed all the details. Because looking for a missing child without any clues as to where the child was would be like looking for a needle in a haystack—damn near impossible.

"She got into drugs and drugs got into her." Edna shook her head. "We tried getting her help so many, many times. But she kept relapsing. We petitioned the state for custody of Piper and became her legal guardians six years ago. Shana showed up a year ago demanding her daughter back. We don't want to keep Shana away from Piper. We offered to let her stay with us as long as she was clean and develop a relationship with her daughter… and maybe someday, she could be her mother again. Well, she's always her mother." Edna shook her head again. "But her real mom. Shana only stayed a few days before she took off. Piper was devastated." Edna wiped her tears as quickly as they poured from her eyes.

Arthur put an arm around her, trying to offer some comfort. He looked over at Sam and then Kimberley. "Do you think Shana took Piper?"

Kimberley pursed her lips together and took her time before speaking. She had to be careful as saying the wrong thing could jeopardize the case. "We can't say for certain. But we'll find out if she did."

"She wouldn't do that." Edna dropped her head back into her hands. "Shana has her problems, but she would never take Piper. She always wanted the best for her daughter, and the best for her daughter wasn't her."

"Where does Shana live?" Sam asked. He was now sitting on the edge of his seat, and Kimberley could tell he was eager to get going.

"Somewhere over in Weatherford. I don't think she has a permanent address. Just bounces around." Arthur rubbed Edna's back as her shoulders slightly shook.

Weatherford was a bigger town, fifteen minutes south of Dead Woman Crossing. They had their own police department, so the sheriff's office pretty much only patrolled the highways that ran through it, U.S. Route 66 and Highway 54. Occasionally, the Weatherford Police Department would request additional support from the Custer County Sheriff's Office, but it was rare, and it hadn't happened in the time that Kimberley had worked as chief deputy.

"Does Piper have a cell phone?" Kimberley asked.

Edna lifted her head revealing a crumpled-up face. "No," she cried. "She wanted one, but I said no. I said she was too young to have a cell phone. If she had one, you'd be able to find her, wouldn't you? Wouldn't you?" She raised her voice more so at herself than anyone else in the room. More guilt, Kimberley thought. They'd never stop blaming themselves.

"Not necessarily," Sam cut in. "Let's not go down that route, Edna. It won't help. Let's just focus on finding Piper."

"How? How will you find her?" Edna pleaded.

"Let us worry about that. Do you have a recent photo of her?" Kimberley asked.

Arthur nodded and stood from his seat. He walked to the fireplace stiffly and scanned the photos above it. Finally, he took hold of a gold frame. Before he took the photo out of the frame, he gazed at it, running his fingers over the picture. His hands shook as he removed it and placed the empty frame back on the shelf. Turning toward Kimberley, he handed the photo over before retaking his seat next to Edna. Kimberley's eyes scanned over Piper Chase. She was thin, with blonde hair that fell just below her shoulders. Her eyes were big and blue like the Oklahoma sky, and her smile was infectious. In the photo, she was standing on the porch wearing a graphic tee and jeans. A backpack was slung over her shoulder. The picture was surely taken on her last day of school before summer began.

"Do you remember what she was wearing before she left last night?" Sam asked.

"White tennis shoes. Jeans. There were holes in the knee area, and a pink T-shirt," Edna recalled.

"And she took her pink bicycle. It has white tassels on the handles and an old plastic crate strapped to the front." Arthur wiped his eyes. "She asked me to put a basket on her bike this summer."

Kimberley nodded. "Anything else you can tell us?"

Edna's eyes bounced from Sam to Kimberley. "Piper's a good girl. She's shy, so she wouldn't have just gone off with a stranger. Someone must have taken her. She loves to read. Harry Potter is her favorite. She loves to ride her bike. We've replaced the tires on it twice already because she rides that thing into the ground. She's kind of a tomboy in that sense…" Edna paused, then looked at Kimberley. Her eyes were wide and glossy and pleading. "You'll find her, right?"

Kimberley stood from her seat, giving a reassuring look. "Don't worry, we're going to do everything we can to locate Piper. We just need you to stay here in case she shows up and near the phone in case she calls. In the meantime, I'll send a deputy over here to sit with you. Okay?" Kimberley folded up her notepad and placed it in the front pocket of her shirt.

Sam stood quickly from his seat. "We'll find her," he said with a nod as the two of them exited the house, closing the door behind them.

CHAPTER FIVE

As soon as Sam and Kimberley were in their vehicle, they let out a deep breath, the one they'd been holding in since they heard a little girl had been missing for over sixteen hours. The first twenty-four are so critical in child disappearance cases, and sixteen had already been burned up from not knowing their child was missing. Kimberley could understand the mix up on some level, but on another, she thought how could they not know? Sixteen hours… sixteen minutes didn't pass without Kimberley knowing what Jessica was doing.

Sam pulled his radio from his uniform and held it up to his mouth. "Officer Burns."

Seconds later Burns answered. "Yeah, boss."

"I need you to get over to Arthur and Edna Chase's house. Sit with them until we know more about their missing granddaughter, Piper. If she shows up, I want to know right away. If they get any calls about her, I want to know right away. Understood?"

"Yes, sir. Heading there now."

"Thanks, Burns. Just keep them calm."

"You got it."

Sheriff Walker reclipped his radio to his shirt and looked over at Kimberley.

"Shouldn't we start looking for her? Search and rescue?" she asked.

He nodded and put the SUV in reverse. "Get Bearfield on the phone. Tell him to call in night shift and get everyone over to the

Chase house. They'll need to start the search and rescue there. Bring in the canine unit too. Because for all we know, she never left that house."

Kimberley's eyes widened. "You think Arthur and Edna had something to do with it?"

"I can't say for sure. But they were the last ones to see Piper, and they didn't report her missing for sixteen hours. We'll go and talk to Linda and her daughter, Miley, and see if they can tell us anything more. Once we can establish Piper left that house, we'll widen the search, send out an Amber Alert, and bring in volunteers."

Kimberley could see how Sam had come to that conclusion. The story Arthur and Edna had was too neat. The timing was questionable and a bit neglectful. And, so far, they had no one else to verify that Piper had left their house on her own. Kimberley found Linda Baker's address and typed it into the navigation system on the dashboard. As soon as the directions pulled up, Sheriff Walker backed out of the driveway quickly all in one clean arch. Before he took off, Kimberley glanced over at the two-story yellow house across the street. The only nearby neighbor. Perhaps they saw something, she thought as Sam sped off toward Linda's home.

It was less than ten minutes before Sam shut the vehicle off in the short driveway leading to a small gray ranch home. The grass was patchy and brown. It clearly needed a good watering. The house didn't appear to be well kept on the outside, chipped paint and broken shutters. It looked like most houses in Dead Woman Crossing, like a cliff face bracing against a raging sea, the façade being broken away, wave by wave, before its inevitable collapse. They walked to the front door, and Sam quickly rapped his knuckles against it. They had no time to waste. They could hear commotion inside, footsteps, and items moving around. A minute passed before the door opened, revealing a woman with long, scraggly, jet-black hair and heavy makeup. She was no more than forty, maybe younger. Kimberley couldn't tell if she was older or if life had aged her beyond her years.

"Are you Linda Baker?" Sam tilted his head.

"Yes, that's me. Is this about Piper?" she asked, her dark eyes zipping back and forth between Kimberley and Sam like a pendulum.

"Yes, it is," Kimberley said. "I'm Chief Deputy King."

"And I'm Sheriff Walker."

Sam reached out his hand but Linda didn't grab for it, instead hiding herself partially behind the door.

"Did you find her?" she asked, skipping the formalities.

"Not yet," Sam said.

Linda pressed her lips firmly together and rubbed at her forehead. "Poor Edna. Oh my God. When Arthur got me on the phone this morning, I could hear Edna in the background. She was hysterical after I told him Piper never came over last night."

"Can we come in?" Kimberley asked.

"Oh yes, of course. Of course." Linda opened the door allowing them room to come inside. She gestured them in with her hand. "Excuse the mess. I've been doing some reorganizing since I've been home from work with Miley. She's been under the weather."

Kimberley and Sam crossed the threshold walking into a messy and small living room. Pillows and blankets strewn about. Balls of Kleenex and water cups spread out on the coffee table. The television had on an old episode of *Lizzie McGuire*, and a small girl lay on the couch, wrapped up in a blanket watching the TV. Kimberley presumed that was Miley. Her skin was pale, and large dark shadows hung under her eyes. Her hair was black and stringy like her mother's, but her eyes were hazel, a nice contrast. She glanced up for only a moment before returning her attention to the television and missing the small smile Kimberley had given her.

"Like I said, Miley's been sick since yesterday," Linda added. "Can I get you two anything to drink?" She turned her body as though she was going to leave for the kitchen, but Sam and Kimberley shook their heads and told her no. They didn't have time for hospitality. The clock was ticking.

"Edna tells us she thought Piper was staying here last night. That Miley and she had planned a sleepover," Sam said. It wasn't a question. It was a statement.

Linda shook her head vehemently. "I don't know why Piper told her grandmother that. Miley wasn't well yesterday. She was here all day and so was I. She didn't see Piper."

"And she's still sick today?" Kimberley asked, glancing at the little girl on the couch who was trying to make herself as small as possible.

"Yes."

"But she called Piper this morning asking to play, right?" Kimberley tilted her head.

Linda tightened her eyes. "Yes. She thought she was well enough to go out and play. You know how kids are. I didn't even realize she was calling over to Miley's house until she said Arthur wanted to speak with me."

Sam and Kimberley nodded.

"Do you know Arthur and Edna well?" Sam asked.

"Not really at all. I've seen them a few times in town. We just moved here at the end of the school year, so we've only been in Dead Woman Crossing a few months," Linda explained.

"Where'd you move from?" Kimberley asked.

"We just moved from Weatherford. Not far at all. I was renting there and got a great deal on this house. It was in foreclosure. I still work at the Walmart Supercenter, so it added ten minutes to my commute, but I wanted a house with a backyard for Miley, not a crammed apartment." She nodded.

"Do you mind if we ask Miley a couple of questions?" Sam asked.

"Of course." Linda walked to beside the couch and sat down. "Sweetie, are you up for answering a few questions from these officers? They're trying to help find Piper." She pushed the hair out of her daughter's face and helped her sit up on the couch. Miley looked at her mother and nodded. She glanced up at Kimberley and Sam. Her lip quivered and her eyes immediately bounced away from them.

Kimberley kneeled so she was eye to eye with Miley. She hoped the little girl would look at her, but it was clear she was uncomfortable. She looked very ill. Kimberley wanted to place her hand against her forehead to feel for a temperature. It was a motherly instinct. She stopped herself.

"Miley, did you see Piper yesterday?" Kimberley asked.

The little girl looked down at her lap, fidgeting with her fingers. She shook her head.

"You didn't see Piper yesterday?" Kimberley asked again as she wanted a verbal confirmation.

"It's okay, sweetie. Answer the nice officer," Linda encouraged while she wrapped an arm around her daughter and rubbed the side of her arm.

Miley looked up at Kimberley, hesitating for a moment before she spoke. "No, I didn't see Piper yesterday."

"And you weren't aware of Piper's plans to have a sleepover?" Kimberley said in her most comforting voice. She knew this was tough on the little girl. She was sick and her best friend was missing.

"No, I didn't know she was going to sleepover," Miley said just above a whisper.

"Do you know if Piper has any other friends she'd have a sleepover with? Maybe someone she met at summer camp?" Kimberley asked.

Linda rubbed her daughter's shoulder telling her it was okay.

"Not that I know of," Miley said, pushing out her bottom lip.

"Did Piper ever talk about her mom, Shana?" Sam cut in. His arms were folded across his chest. Miley looked up at Sheriff Walker and nodded.

"What did Piper say about her mother?" Sam unfolded his arms and bent down beside Kimberley.

"She said… she said… she missed her and wished she could be with her mommy again. She was really sad when she left." Miley's bottom lip quivered.

"Do you know if Piper spoke to her mom after she left?" Kimberley tilted her head.

"I don't know. She didn't say, but… she did…" Miley paused.

"She did what?" Sam asked.

"She did say her mommy left a note for her when she left."

Kimberley's and Sam's eyes widened.

"When was this?"

The little girl looked up at the ceiling as if she was trying to remember. "This last time she visited."

Kimberley knew from Edna and Arthur this last time was nearly a year ago.

"And what did the note say?" Kimberley asked.

Miley hesitated. She looked at her mom. Linda nodded encouragingly, telling her it was okay to answer. The little girl glanced up at Kimberley. Her hazel eyes were wet, and she swallowed hard before she spoke.

"It said… I'll come back for you."

CHAPTER SIX

Kimberley stepped out of Linda's house first with Sam following behind. Linda waved them off and told them she'd contact them if she learned anything else, before closing the door and locking it. In a small town, people didn't lock their doors. They would now, Kimberley thought. The sheet of gray had lifted revealing the sun set high in the sky. They were losing precious time.

She looked back at Sam, stopping so he could catch up beside her. "What do ya make of that?"

"Well, the little girl, Miley, looked awfully sick. She was a bit skittish. But she's ten, so I'd expect that. Based on what Miley said about the note Shana left for Piper, she could have very well come back and got her." Sam nodded as he walked. "Regardless, I'm issuing an Amber Alert."

Sam clicked the call button on his radio and spoke into it. "Bearfield." Radio static followed for a moment.

"Yeah, boss."

"I need you to request an Amber Alert on Piper Chase. Last seen leaving her grandparents' house at approximately five fifteen last night, presumably on a pink bicycle. Ten years old. Get a recent photo and description from the Chases to distribute via the media and local agencies in the surrounding areas." Sam tightened his lips as he let his thumb release from the call button.

"Will do. The team is here at the Chases' home now. Haven't uncovered anything yet. I'll put in the alert immediately, sir." Bearfield's voice was hurried.

Kimberley gave Sam an approving nod. If it were up to her, she would have requested the Amber Alert the moment they received the call from Arthur and Edna Chase, but she knew things were different here in Oklahoma. Kids went outside and played, ran off with friends, snuck out at night. Danger didn't seem as imminent here as it did in other places. They climbed back into the SUV.

"I think you're right," Kimberley said as she blankly stared through the windshield at the small, gray house.

"Right about what? I'm not used to you saying that to me," Sam teased, trying to lighten the mood just a little.

Kimberley gave him a small smile, but it quickly disappeared. She could never enjoy herself when a case she was working was unsolved, especially ones that involved children. "We need to establish that Piper left that home." Kimberley still felt uneasy about Edna and Arthur Chase. How could sixteen hours have passed before they reported Piper missing, before they even noticed she was missing? Everyone made mistakes, but was it a mistake?

Sam turned on the vehicle and started backing up. "Let's head back over to the Chase house then."

"But the Amber Alert was the right move," Kimberley added.

"Better safe than sorry." Sam bobbed his head.

Kimberley slid her cell phone from her pocket and selected Barb. She picked up on the first ring. She always picked up on the first ring.

"Kimberley, what can I do for you? Did you find the little girl?"

"Not yet. I need you to contact the Weatherford Police Department and have them put out an APB on a Shana Chase," Kimberley said into the phone.

"I'm on it."

"Give them my number and have them contact me as soon as she turns up."

"Your wish is my command."

"Thanks, Barb. Talk soon." Kimberley ended the call sliding her cell back into her pocket.

"Good thinking, King." Sam gave an approving nod of his head and drove the same route back to the Chases' home.

Pulling into the driveway of Edna and Arthur Chase's house, Kimberley and Sam could see that Bearfield had done a great job of starting the search. Several deputies scoured the garage off to the side. They could see movement through the windows of the home. Kimberley and Sam were quick to jump out of the vehicle and enter the house again. Inside, Edna and Arthur sat on the couch. Edna clutched a cell phone in one hand and a cordless telephone in the other. Her fingers had turned white from how tight she was holding them as if it would make them ring. Arthur watched Deputy Burns search the living room, lifting up items, pulling books from bookshelves. Arthur's eyebrows were knitted together in confusion. When he noticed Kimberley and Sam, he rose from his seat.

"What are they doing? Why are they searching our home?" Arthur gestured with his hand around his living room, which was tidy when they were there earlier, but not anymore.

Kimberley gave Sam a look that said, 'I'll handle this.' She knew it was important not to let Arthur and Edna know that they were considering them as suspects. During investigations, everyone was a suspect until they were eliminated.

"Arthur, our officers are looking for any clue that would indicate where Piper went. Maybe a note from a friend or something like that. We just spoke with Linda and Miley, and they said they had no contact with Piper yesterday. Our canine unit should be able to pick up her scent, so we have an idea of what direction she headed in. Do you understand?" Kimberley said in her calmest voice.

Arthur stammered and when he tried to speak, his voice cracked. He pushed his glasses back up his nose and wiped his eyes with the back of his hand. "Just… just please bring our granddaughter back home to us."

"We've put out an APB on your daughter, Shana. Do you have any contact details for her? Address, phone number? It would help us locate her quickly," Sam said.

Arthur scratched at his head. "No, like we said before, she doesn't have a permanent address, and we haven't seen her in nearly a year."

"And was that the last time you spoke with her?" Kimberley pursed her lips.

"Yes." Arthur nodded. "We haven't been able to get a hold of her. She's been doing this since Piper was a baby. She shows up and disappears." Arthur blinked rapidly as if he was trying to blink away what was happening.

"The phone… the phone. There was an alert for Piper," Edna said, staring off at the wall. Her eyes were so wide, they looked like dinner plates. Her voice quaked. Her body was stiff and rigid.

"Yes. That's right," Sam said. "We just issued an Amber Alert for Piper."

"Does that mean she's in danger? Isn't that what those are for?" Edna's voice shook.

"We don't know that yet. But we need all the help we can get to find her. This will give us a better chance of locating Piper sooner rather than later. Everyone with a cell phone in the surrounding area will have seen that alert. The media will broadcast it. All that means is we've got more eyes looking for your granddaughter," Sam explained.

Edna nodded her head slowly. Her lips parted, but nothing came out but a gush of air.

"Thank you. Thank you both," Arthur cut in and sat down again next to Edna.

"Sheriff Walker. Chief Deputy King," Bearfield's voice called from down the hall.

Kimberley and Sam headed down the hall to the back bedroom to find Deputy Bearfield holding a piece of paper. The room was small and pink with a twin-size bed, long dresser, bedside table and a pink shaggy rug. A stack of Harry Potter books sat on the bedside stand. A jewelry box with a spinning ballerina and a couple of knick-knacks and little rocks were on the dresser. The rocks were all different colors and they looked to have been collected by Piper like little outdoor prizes.

"Whatcha got?" Sam asked, closing the distance between him and Bearfield.

Kimberley continued to scan the room. The closet was closed, so she walked to it and opened the door revealing dozens of hung up T-shirts and a few dresses that looked almost brand new, as though Piper wasn't the type of girl that wore dresses. On the floor sat several pairs of worn sneakers and a laundry basket half full of clothes. Kimberley looked at the bed where a stuffed teddy bear sat and a couple of decorative pillows. The teddy bear immediately reminded her of Jessica's stuffed elephant. Her heart sank into the pit of her stomach.

"It's a letter she wrote to her mother," Bearfield said, holding it up.

Kimberley walked to Bearfield and Sam, looking down at the child's writing.

Dear Mommy, why did you leave? I want you to come back. I want you to be with me. Please come back, Mommy. Love, Piper.

How could a mother not want her daughter? Kimberley closed her eyes for a second and took a small deep breath. She knew the feeling. Like a dagger to the heart, she knew it well, for her father hadn't wanted her and Jessica's father didn't want her. It was something she could never ever understand. She looked to Sam. The pain in his eyes was clearly visible, the pain of wishing he could still have what this woman just walked away from. He blinked a few times, pushing the grief back down into its tarry pit.

"Do you think this was in response to the note Miley said her mother left for Piper?" Kimberley asked, trying to push forward before she lost Sam.

"It would definitely seem that way."

"What note?" Bearfield asked.

"Miley said Piper's mom left her a note that said, 'I'll come back for you.' Have you found that?" Kimberley looked to Bear.

"Negative. This was the only thing I found that was out of the ordinary. Our canine unit should be here momentarily. Amber Alert has been issued."

"Excellent. Hopefully, we find her quick with that alert. But we'll need something with a strong scent from Piper," Sam said with a nod.

Bearfield folded the note back up and dropped it into an evidence bag. Kimberley walked back to the closet. She slipped on a glove from her utility belt and pulled out a graphic T-shirt that was in a crumpled ball on top. Holding it up she read the letters on the shirt, '*This girl believes in magic*.' Kimberley hoped all the magic that that little girl believed in would help them find her alive and well.

"This will work," Kimberley said, holding it up.

Sam and Bearfield nodded.

"Canine unit is here," Officer Burns yelled from the living room.

Outside, Officer Hill approached with a seventy-five-pound German shepherd on a leash. The dog walked right beside him, eyes straight ahead. Since Hill had filled out, he now looked like he walked the dog rather than the other way around. Hill's hair was well coiffed, and he was clean-shaven with a pointy nose. Now that he was able to start working out again, he had gone from tall and lanky to tall and fit. After shooting himself in the foot during a routine traffic stop, a little over a year prior, Hill hadn't been allowed much exercise for six months and was moved from night shift to day shift. Ever since then he had been trying to work his way back up and get in the good graces of Sheriff Walker and Chief Deputy King. Kimberley didn't mind him at all. He had made one horribly embarrassing mistake, and he had paid for it with months and months of physical therapy and endless teasing from his co-workers. But he was hungry to prove himself, and Kimberley loved that. Him being there was another example as Kimberley knew he had used vacation time to take the day off. But here he was, ready to work, ready to prove himself.

Kimberley, Sam, and Bearfield stood right outside the front door.

"Whatcha got?" Hill asked.

Kimberley held out a clear plastic evidence bag that contained Piper's worn T-shirt.

"Alright, Winston. You ready, boy?" Hill said to his canine. Winston looked up at him and sat down, while Hill grabbed the bag from Kimberley. He slipped on a glove and pulled the shirt out of the bag, holding it out for Winston to smell. The dog sniffed and sniffed and sniffed.

"You got it? You got the scent? Let's go. Find it," Hill said. The dog took off in a controlled frenzy, sniffing the ground and walking to the front door. Hill and Winston disappeared inside the home.

"That's not a good start," Bearfield said.

"Give it time. He'll sniff her scent all over the house and hopefully it leads him outside and away from this property," Kimberley explained.

"You two think she's here somewhere?" Bearfield folded his arms in front of his chest and raised an eyebrow. Kimberley had noticed that he was always good at picking up on what she and Sam were thinking.

"Maybe. She could just be hiding. Wouldn't be the first time. It ends up being a big waste of time and resources but it is certainly a preferred outcome," Sam said, scratching at his chin.

"The team's just about done searching the house and garage. Their property is around nine acres according to Arthur. Want us to start there?" Bearfield shuffled his feet.

"No, let's wait on what Winston finds. If he can pick up her scent leaving the home then we'll widen the search and continue on in the direction she left. We've also got Weatherford checking on the girl's mom, Shana Chase," Sheriff Walker said with a nod.

"Best case scenario is she's with her mom," Kimberley said.

"Worst case—" Bearfield started.

"No worst cases. Not yet," Kimberley cut in, giving a slight shake of her head.

CHAPTER SEVEN

When I got the Amber Alert, I knew I couldn't keep you any longer. They would find you, not the way they wanted to find you, but they would. And I couldn't have them discover you here with me. I made the most out of our final hours together. I laid with you for a long time, even fell asleep with you in my arms. You were cold like ice, so I wrapped you in a blanket. I watched your skin change colors from blotchy to yellow to blue and to gray, your final color. You were stiff like an old porcelain doll, hard to move. I knew I had until nighttime. They would call off the search and it was then that I could begin mine... Locating the perfect spot to place you. Before that, though, I had to make sure your ice-cold body wouldn't lead them to me. I considered dismembering you, burying you, tossing you in Deer Creek. But I couldn't bring myself to do that. I also thought about pouring bleach all over you. The bleach would eat your skin along with any evidence I may have left behind, but you looked too perfect to ruin. Instead, I carefully washed your exposed skin with soap, water, and a rag. I wrapped packing tape around my hand, sticky side out, and took my time pressing it against your head, shirt, and pants. The whole process was tedious and took hours, but I enjoyed the time we spent together, and I think you did too.

When night falls, I will say my final goodbye to you, and by that I mean, until we meet again.

CHAPTER EIGHT

Officer Hill looked to Kimberley and Sam as he stood on the side of the road with Winston sitting beside him. They were a quarter of a mile down the road from the Chases' house. The German shepherd looked up at Hill, a sign that his work was completed, and he had done all he could for his owner.

"He lost the scent," Hill explained, giving Winston a pat on the head and an ear scratch.

"So, what's that mean? She got into a car?" Sheriff Walker shuffled his feet and crossed his arms in front of his chest.

He glanced back at the house and then forward at the long black road that seemed to go on and on for forever. Over the curve of the earth, dropping off into eternity. The wheat fields on either side of the road swayed back and forth in the wind, almost as though they were waving at them saying, 'this way' or at least that's what Kimberley imagined. They had lost the scent, but the only good thing was they knew Piper had left her grandparents' house. It didn't rule Edna and Arthur out completely, but it made them a little less suspicious, at least to Kimberley.

"Could have. Or she was walking her bike and then got on to ride it?" Hill explained. "Or she was riding it slowly and then took off."

Kimberley pulled out her phone and went straight to Google Maps, then she zoomed in on her location. She noticed there was a crossroad up ahead a quarter of a mile, called Nerge Road. A quarter mile down that road was Black Heart Lane. Now that they had established Piper had left the home, if she really were on the way to Miley's house, that's the route she would have taken.

"Whatcha looking at, King?" Sam asked.

Kimberley held up the phone, showing it to Sam. "If she was going to Miley's house—and the Chases mentioned Black Heart Lane is where Piper and Miley met and played—this is the route she'd take."

"But Miley and her mother said they didn't have plans to meet up with Piper." Sam scratched at his chin.

"Maybe Piper was going over there to surprise her," Kimberley said as she brought the phone back into her line of sight, following the red line on the map. Her eyes scanned over the words 'Black Heart Lane' several times. Something in her gut told her that was where they needed to be looking, but she slid her phone in her pocket, letting the feeling fade away.

"Maybe," Sam said, looking out at the horizon.

"And we got nothing on the mom yet?" Sam asked, already knowing the answer.

"Negative," Kimberley said, following Sam's line of sight to the horizon. She thought about the missing person cases she had worked at the NYPD. New York City was large and sprawling, filled with millions of people, thousands of buildings… but this felt scarier, bigger. The nothingness of it all. Wide open spaces.

"Mind if I give Winston here a break? Get him some food and water before we start again?" Hill asked.

Sam and Kimberley looked down at the dog. Long strings of drool hung from his jowls as his mouth opened and closed in little pants. They both gave him a pat on the head, telling him he was a good boy.

"Yeah, go ahead," Sam said. "Make it quick, though."

Hill nodded. "Come on, boy," he said to Winston as the two walked off back toward the Chases' house.

Sam and Kimberley stood in silence for a moment. Kimberley mulled over the facts of the case internally. Piper had left the evening before at around 5:15 p.m. with the story that she was going to her friend Miley's house, whom she had met at summer camp earlier in the summer. Miley had been sick and they'd not seen Piper. That was all they had. The facts repeated in her mind, flipping and twisting, rearranging... trying to make sense, to get the pieces to fit together differently. The problem was, there weren't enough pieces.

"I fucking hate these types of cases," Sam said, interrupting Kimberley's train of thought.

Kimberley knew what he meant. With every other case, you had something; a victim, a body, which could tell you a story, a story that would help solve the case. A missing person's case was like an Adlib word game, where you had to fill in the blanks and hope the story would make sense when you read it back.

"I fucking hate these types of cases too," Kimberley added.

"We've had some drunkards go missing in the past here. Usually found them passed out in a wheat field or in the woods. We once had a woman go missing. Turns out she ran out on her husband and was found safe and well a few towns over. But never a child. Not in my time here." Sam rubbed at his forehead and ran his hands over his cheeks.

"We're going to find her," Kimberley assured, trying to make her voice as commanding and as confident as possible. Deep down, she wasn't sure, though... Not with the fact that nineteen hours had passed since Piper Chase was last seen.

"Sheriff Walker. Chief Deputy King," Bearfield yelled as he ran toward them down the side of the road. For a large man, he ran quick, his footsteps thundering and kicking up loose gravel and dust behind him.

Nearly out of breath, Bearfield got out the words with what was left in his lungs. "Barb just rang. The Weatherford police picked up Shana Chase, and they are holding her for questioning." He tightened his low ponytail, smoothing it out.

Kimberley and Sam's eyes went wide.

"Why didn't Barb call me?" she asked, remembering she requested she be contacted right away.

"Said your phone was off."

Kimberley pulled it from her pocket and sure enough it was dead. Jessica had surely unplugged it from the charger. Now that she was in her terrible twos she got into anything and everything, making destruction and terrorization a game. Her favorite game was unplugging her phone from the charger.

Kimberley gave a slight nod.

"Want me to head over there and take a statement?" Bearfield asked, always willing to step up to the plate and help in anyway possible.

Sam looked to Kimberley and then back at Bearfield. She appreciated that he treated her like an equal.

"I think you and I should," Kimberley spoke up.

Sam nodded. "Yes, King and I will go and question her. Bearfield I want you to start the search team from this point and make your way to Miley Baker's house going the route of Black Heart Lane. For now, just our team. If we gather from Shana that she's not involved, we'll bring in volunteers."

"Shouldn't we do that now?" Kimberley raised her chin.

Sam scratched the back of his neck. "No. I don't want to over-react if it turns out Shana came back and got her daughter, and we've got the Amber Alert out."

"But underreacting could cost this girl her life," Kimberley argued.

"King's got a point," Bearfield spoke up.

"Would you take that risk if it were your kid? I know I wouldn't with Jessica." As soon as the words left her mouth, Kimberley immediately regretted them. How stupid and insensitive, she thought to herself, forgetting for a mere second that Sam had lost both his wife and his son.

"Enough." Sam raised his voice.

"I'm sorry, Sam," Kimberley said just above a whisper. Her eyes grew wide in embarrassment. "I wasn't thinking."

Sam ignored her, looking at the floor, kicking up gravel with his boot. "We've got the Amber Alert out. Volunteers will start showing up, I'm sure. But I don't want to call on the town yet. There's no sense in causing a stir when we don't have all the facts, and right now Shana is a strong lead given the letter Piper wrote to her and the letter Miley mentioned."

A loud exhaust caught their attention and they looked down the road to see a big black pickup truck approaching. The truck pulled up beside them and the driver's side window rolled down revealing Deputy Lodge, or as Kimberley liked to call him Deputy Dipshit.

"What's going on?" Lodge asked.

"Nice of you to join us. Where the hell have you been?" Sheriff Walker tightened his eyes.

"Patrolling, and I broke up a nasty fight over at The Trophy Room." Lodge gave a smug look.

Sam looked at his watch and shook his head. "Get down to the Chases' house. We're starting a search and rescue. This is top priority. Officer Burns and Officer Hill will catch you up."

"Actually, see that house across the street." Kimberley pointed at the two-story yellow house.

Lodge followed her finger and nodded.

"Make sure someone interviews them. They're the only nearby neighbor. Maybe they saw something." Lodge looked to Sam.

"Good thinking. Do as King says, but have Burns and Hill fill you in first."

"You got it, boss," Lodge said with a slight smirk as he revved his engine and sped off the quarter of a mile to where the Chases' ranch home was.

"Ready?" Kimberley asked looking to Sam. He said yeah, and they took off toward the SUV with Bearfield following behind.

"I want updates every twenty minutes," Kimberley said over her shoulder.

"Sure thing, boss," Bearfield said. "But get your phone working, otherwise I'll be sending them via carrier pigeon," he added, letting out a deep belly laugh.

CHAPTER NINE

"Good afternoon," the policewoman at the front desk greeted as Sheriff Walker and Chief Deputy King entered the Weatherford Police Department. She was slim with short brown hair, a pointy nose and dressed in full blues, sitting at a desk behind bulletproof glass. A locked door was off to the side. There were several people sitting in the waiting area. Weatherford was a bigger town with a better equipped police station. Most residents of Dead Woman Crossing and the smaller towns surrounding made trips to this area for shopping and entertainment as they had a movie theater and a Walmart.

"We're from the Custer County Sheriff's Office." Sam motioned to Kimberley. "Chief Deputy King, and I'm Sheriff Walker. We're here to speak with a Shana Chase. Your guys picked her up after we put out an APB on her about an hour or so ago."

The policewoman nodded. "Yes, we've been expecting you." She rose from her seat and walked over to the glass door. Scanning her badge, the door buzzed and clicked and she pulled it open for Sam and Kimberley to enter. "Right this way," she said.

They passed through two more doors that required her badge to be scanned. Kimberley admired the security and thought the Custer County Sheriff's Office could use a major upgrade after seeing the security here. After all, Barb was their first line of defense. But Barb was feisty, and Kimberley had recently learned she had a conceal and carry permit. She kept her Glock in her top desk drawer when she was working and then had it holstered on her hip, underneath her flowery, flowy blouses when she was off the clock. She had named it Helen. When Kimberley had asked her why the name Helen? Barb had replied, "Because Helen was an ex-friend that stole my famous chocolate chip cookie recipe, and she was a real bitch. It seemed fitting."

Kimberley had laughed for nearly an hour. Barb was always surprising her.

They entered the office area that was filled with desks, just like the one at the Custer County Sheriff's Office, but it was twice the size. Many officers sat at their desks fielding calls or filling out paperwork. Several looked up and nodded at Kimberley and Sam as they passed through following the policewoman. They walked to the back where a large office was located. The door was closed and the nameplate read Chief Halsey. The policewoman rapped her knuckles against it.

"Come in," a deep voice bellowed from behind the door.

She pushed it open, revealing an office twice the size of Kimberley and Sam's with an executive desk and a fifty-year-old man with a potbelly and a thinning hairline sitting behind it. He quickly rose from his seat, walking around his desk.

"Sheriff Walker and Chief Deputy King are here from Custer County about the Chase woman," the policewoman explained.

Chief Halsey nodded. "Yes, yes." He extended his hand out first to Sheriff Walker shaking it.

Old boys' club, Kimberley thought.

After shaking Sam's, he shook Kimberley's.

"We got your APB, and my boys picked up Shana Chase at the Motel 6. We've got her in a holding cell," he said to Sam and Kimberley proudly, but then diverted his attention to his officer.

"Reynolds, get the Chase woman moved to interrogation room one," Chief Halsey commanded.

The policewoman nodded. 'Yes, sir," and immediately left the office.

"What do I got to do to get you to call me sir?" Sheriff Walker whispered to Kimberley, attempting to lighten the mood. There was always a shred of light even in the darkest of times, Kimberley had learned. And she appreciated that Sam knew that too.

"Build a time machine and take me back to the nineteen-fifties," Kimberley teased with a small smile.

Sam bumped his shoulder against hers and grinned.

Chief Halsey turned back to Sam and Kimberley just as they straightened out their curved mouths. "You were saying?" Sam said.

"Yeah, so my boys picked her up at the Motel 6. Got real lucky finding her as she's a bit of a floater. We've had a lot of run-ins with her. Anyway, when y'all put out that APB, we knew of some of her hangout spots, where she goes to score drugs or prostitute herself for drugs. We found her as she was coming down off of something, probably heroin, so she should be good to talk now. We got her food and water, so she'd be more coherent for you all. From my understanding, y'all got a missing kid. We got the Amber Alert here as well. You say the word, and I've got two dozen men at your disposal." Chief Halsey spoke like he was giving a lecture or a speech.

"Thank you," Kimberley said interjecting, knowing this was the type of man that would go on forever if you didn't interrupt. "You say she's good to talk?"

"Yes, ma'am."

Ma'am. Kimberley nearly rolled her eyes but stopped herself. "Have your officers questioned her at all?"

"No. Like I said she was coming down when we picked her up. Even if we wanted to, probably, couldn't get much out of her." Chief Halsey nodded. "Let's walk and talk." He led them out of his office and through the desk area, checking in on each officer as he passed.

"You got that report?"

"How are we doing on the Williams case?"

Kimberley wasn't sure if any of the questions he asked of his officers were pertinent or if he was just trying to establish himself as the man in charge for his guests.

"Was there a young girl with Shana? Around ten years old. Blonde hair?" Sam asked as they followed behind him. Chief Halsey walked like he had just gotten down from riding a horse, his legs a tad bow-legged. She couldn't tell if he was built like that or if it was how he walked to assert his dominance, making room for his big swinging dick, so to speak. She assumed from what she gathered from Chief Halsey, it was the latter.

"Not that I know of. My boys couldn't even figure out if she was staying at the motel or not. They talked to the front desk and some of the guests and no one could confirm. Like I said, she's a floater. The front desk didn't have a reservation for her, but that didn't mean she wasn't staying there, if you know what I mean. We've found her at the motel on countless occasions, a couple of abandoned houses, known drug houses, on a park bench, passed out in a car that was unlocked." Chief Halsey shook his head in dismay as he spoke.

"Have your guys checked any of those other locations like the abandoned homes or the known drug houses she frequents?" Kimberley asked.

If she had taken Piper and then went on a bender, she could have surely left her at one of those places.

Chief Halsey gave a slight nod and lifted his radio to his mouth. "This is Chief Halsey. I need all available units on the Amber Alert that came in earlier today. I want the Motel 6, the abandoned homes and drug houses that Shana Chase has frequented searched. Pull her arrest record and search any other place she's been picked up in Weatherford. We're looking for a ten-year-old girl by the name of Piper Chase. This is top priority." Clipping his radio back to the front of his shirt, he gave a small smile. "Good thinking, Chief Deputy King. I've got my men on the case." He turned back and led them down a long hallway.

Kimberley turned to Sam and slightly shook her head. Sam delivered a smirk back. Chief Halsey was the man she expected Sam to be when she moved to Dead Woman Crossing the year before, and she was grateful he was not. She had run into men like Halsey many times back at the NYPD. They wore their manhood like they wore their badge, proudly displayed for all to see.

Sam and Kimberley walked in step behind Chief Halsey until he stopped in front of a closed door. An officer stood to the side of it, watching it like a guard dog. The officer straightened up even more.

"How is she, Officer Jenkins?"

"Coherent now."

"Good… good work. Why don't you go and get our guests here some coffee?" Halsey said, reprieving him from his watch duty.

"Yes, sir."

The officer nodded at his chief and then at Sam and Kimberley as he walked off in the direction that they had all just come from.

"You all want me to sit in with you?" Halsey lifted an eyebrow. "I've got a knack for getting people to talk." The corner of his lip popped up.

"That won't be necessary," Sam said. "Kimberley here came to us from the NYPD. She's got a knack for that sort of thing, too." He motioned to Kimberley proudly with a small smile. Even after a year of her being on the force, Sam still loved bringing up the fact that Kimberley was former NYPD. It was clear to her that he was beyond proud of her and her credentials, but she was also sure he just liked dunking on Chief Halsey.

"Impressive." Halsey brought his hands in front of him for a moment, patting his fingertips together almost as though he was deciding what to say next. "Well… I'll leave you to it." He took a step back clearing the path to the door. "Officer Jenkins will be back momentarily. Let him know if you need anything. If my boys find anything, you'll be the first to know."

"Thanks, Chief Halsey," Sam and Kimberley said in unison.

"And my offer stands… you need help over in Dead Woman Crossing, we've got you covered."

"We'll need all the help we can get if Shana can't lead us to her daughter," Sam said, reaching for the door handle.

He pushed the door open and crossed the threshold with Kimberley following behind. The room was brightly lit with the only darkness coming from Shana's presence. She sat at a table with her head lolling side to side for a moment. Her stringy blonde hair hung past her shoulders like wet spaghetti noodles smothered in oil. Her eyes were partially closed and it wasn't clear if the black circles around them were from her clumpy, smeared mascara or from her choice of lifestyle. A white tank top hung loosely on her frail body. Her arms were covered in open sores, track marks and poorly drawn tattoos that appeared to have been done by a child or a crackhead. If this was her now, Kimberley couldn't imagine the state she had been in an hour ago. She shut the door firmly with a bang, startling the woman. Shana jolted, the lids of her eyes springing open, revealing thick red veins covering the whites of her eyes.

Sam walked further into the room and pulled out a chair taking a seat across from Shana. Kimberley stood for a moment, still taking in the person in front of her.

"Who are you?" Shana spat. Her front teeth were cracked in several places and shaded yellow like kernels of corn. Saliva gathered at the corners of her crusty lips.

"Hello, Shana. I'm Sheriff Walker and this is Chief Deputy King." He gestured back at Kimberley. "We're here about your daughter, Piper."

Shana narrowed her eyes. But not in a mean or accusatory way. More in a way like she was trying to get her eyes to focus. A cup of water sat beside her. She brought it to her mouth and drank the whole thing in two gulps. Wiping her mouth with the back of her hand, she set the cup back down. The door opened behind Kimberley, and she stepped to the side. In walked Officer Jenkins, carrying three cups of coffee. He handed one to Sam and Kimberley and cautiously set the third one in front of Shana. He nodded as he quickly exited the room. Shana cupped the coffee with both hands and slowly brought it to her lips, inhaling the steam and then taking a quick sip.

"What happened to Piper?" she asked as she set the cup down. Her hands shook, a cue she was ready for her next fix.

"She's missing." Kimberley took a couple of steps toward the table and pulled out the chair. She set her coffee down and took a seat, squaring up with Shana.

"No, she's not. She's with my parents."

"No, your parents reported her missing this morning. She hasn't been seen since last night." Kimberley leaned forward in her chair.

"Ha. And I'm the unfit parent." Shana shook her head. She caught a glimpse of her reflection in the two-way mirror to the left of her. Her eyes went a little wide and she used the palm of her hand to smooth and comb out her wet spaghetti string hair. It was as if she had seen herself for the first time.

"Shana, did you take Piper?" Kimberley asked, struggling to keep the impatience from her voice.

The woman whipped her head in Kimberley's direction. "Take her where? Where the hell would I take her?" Her voice was dry and raspy as though she had a chunk of chalk in her mouth.

"Have you had any recent contact with Piper?" Sam asked.

"Not since I stayed with my parents, like six months ago, maybe more… I can't remember exactly. I wanted to stay longer, stay clean, but my demons are too big, too strong." Shana rubbed at her face and scratched at her cheek, leaving a bloody mark behind. "Didn't want her to see me like…" She looked down at herself with pity. "Well… this."

"And you left her a note…? Saying you'd come back for her. What did you mean by that?" Kimberley asked. "Shana," she added, hoping the woman would look at her. She needed to look into her eyes to figure out if she was lying.

Shana lifted her head staring back at Kimberley. Her eyes were cloudy like a murky pond, red snakes swimming around it. "What note?"

"The night you took off, you left Piper a note saying you'd come back for her." Kimberley tilted her head.

Shana looked up at the fluorescent lights as if she were trying to conjure up a memory that wasn't there. She blinked several times before refocusing her attention back on Chief Deputy King. "I don't remember writing a note."

"Could you have?"

"I don't remember a lot of things." Shana picked up the coffee and brought it to her mouth again. This time taking a long sip as the liquid had cooled off enough to drink it without getting burned.

"Where were you last night around five fifteen p.m.?" Sam asked.

Shana set the glass back down. "I don't even know where I was this morning."

Kimberley slammed her fist against the table, half standing. "Quit playing fucking games! This is your daughter we're talking about. She's been missing for nearly twenty-four hours. Do you understand that? If you want to help us find her, you need to start being straight with us. We are running out of time."

Shana's eyes went wide, and she slightly leaned back in her chair as if to put more space between her and Kimberley. She let out a raspy breath.

"I was at the motel with a guy named Tony. I do him favors and he does me favors."

"You fuck him for drugs?" Kimberley said with an icy tone. She didn't care what Shana did. She cared about finding Piper.

Shana nodded, hanging her head in shame. "I was there all last night." She mustered the courage to look Kimberley directly in the eyes. "I didn't take my daughter. I don't know where she is. I promise you that. I would never do anything to hurt her. That includes pulling her out of her home. Look at me. I'd be the worst thing for her."

"How are your parents...? I mean, as parents?" Kimberley asked. She still couldn't wrap her head around them not knowing their granddaughter was missing for so long. And after seeing what became of their only child, they must not have been as innocent as they appeared to be.

Shana knitted her brows together as if she were trying to understand the question and the implications her answers would have. Kimberley couldn't tell if there was any ill will between her and her parents. Edna and Arthur basically described their daughter as a stray dog that sometimes comes around.

"They were fine. A little too strict. But fine."

Sam tilted his head. "What do you mean by strict?" he asked.

"Not abusive if that's what you're getting at. Just strict. They had to know where I was all the time. I couldn't have sleepovers, couldn't go to parties when I was in high school, couldn't have a boyfriend until I was eighteen. So, I kind of went wild when I wasn't under their thumb any longer, a little too wild, I guess." She shook her head slightly.

"Do you think they're good parents to Piper?" Kimberley asked.

Shana shrugged her shoulders. "Better than I'd ever be. I can't even take care of myself most days, but I make it work... life that is." She paused, looking at Kimberley. "Like I said, I would never do anything to hurt my daughter and that includes taking her from her home. I promise you that." Her voice cracked.

"Let's hope that's true," Kimberley said, standing from her chair. Sam followed suit.

"Please tell me when you find her," Shana pleaded. Her eyes swam with tears as her face crumpled.

Kimberley walked toward the door and reached for the handle.

"She's the only one in the world that loves me... even like this." Shana's shoulders shook. The realization of her missing child and what that could actually mean finally hitting her. She dropped her head into her lap, collapsing into herself.

Kimberley turned back toward the sad woman. "Shana, I'll make sure you know when we know." Shana looked up at Kimberley, saying thank you over and over again. Kimberley gave her a small nod and a tight smile.

Out in the hall, Officer Jenkins stood at attention beside the door. "If you want to head back to Chief Halsey's office. He's got an update for you two."

"Did they find her?" Sam asked.

Officer Jenkins shook his head.

Kimberley and Sam exhaled a big breath and took off back toward Chief Halsey's office. Inside, they found him sitting at his desk eating a McDonald's Big Mac. He flopped the burger down on the wrapper and wiped the special sauce off his lips and cheek with a napkin.

"Come in. Sit. Sit." He gestured while he wiped his hands. "Sorry. Didn't get a chance to eat lunch earlier."

Kimberley and Sam took a couple more steps into the office but didn't take a seat. They needed this to be quick.

"Jenkins said you had an update." Sam cocked his head.

Halsey nodded. "Yes, I had ten of my guys out checking the places we've picked Shana up in the last year. We didn't find the little girl, but we did find the room Shana was staying in. With a man named Tony."

Sam and Kimberley nodded.

"He's not the most reliable witness as he's a drug dealer and has a rap sheet longer than my..." Halsey looked at Kimberley and let out an awkward cough. She knew what that meant... old boys' club. "Well, it's long. Anyway he said Shana was there with him all night. Didn't venture further than the parking lot of the Motel 6 until we picked her up."

"Sounds about right. From our conversation with her, that story about Tony matches up," Kimberley said, folding her arms in front of her chest.

"Good. Good. So, what now?" Chief Halsey asked.

"We'll head back to Dead Woman Crossing. A search has already been in progress in the surrounding area of the grandparents' house, the last place Piper was seen. I'd like to take you up on that offer of sending your officers to us to help with the search and rescue." Sam lifted his chin slightly.

"Of course." Chief Halsey stood from his desk. "I'll send them right away. Do you need me to join?" he asked eagerly.

"Sure, if you want to help us cover ground in the search. We've got miles and miles of wheat fields and woods to comb through," Sam said.

Chief Halsey hesitated, and Kimberley knew what that hesitation was. This was a man that liked to sit behind a desk and bark orders. This wasn't the type of man that enjoyed getting down and dirty when it was needed. "I've got a bad knee, so I'd probably slow you down, so I'll manage my boys from the command center," he said with a chuckle, gesturing to his ostentatious office. "Doc says I should stay off of it. But I'll try to get up your way tomorrow if you still haven't located the girl and see what I can do to help. But any resources you need that I can offer, it's yours."

Sam gave him a tight smile and extended his hand. "Thanks, Chief Halsey. Appreciate it." He gave a firm handshake and turned toward the door.

Kimberley shook his hand too. "We'll be in touch," she added, leaving the office.

"I'd like that," Halsey said with a laugh.

Kimberley clenched her fists. Be professional, she told herself over and over.

CHAPTER TEN

Sam took off out of the lot of the Weatherford police station, heading back to Dead Woman Crossing. Kimberley was tense, the facts of the case replaying in her head. They hadn't really changed since she had cycled through them before, except for the fact that Shana was most likely not involved. From what she could see on the map earlier, the woods around Black Heart Lane were sprawling, rather unnatural for the area. Perhaps that's why the children played there. They could climb trees, play hide and seek, and stomp around in the streams. It beat rolling around in wheat.

"You must feel pretty lucky?" Sam said with a small grin on his face.

Kimberley gave him a puzzled look. "What?"

"That you ended up at Custer County Sheriff's Office with me rather than at Weatherford with Chief Big Mac Bum Knee."

Kimberley lightly pushed his shoulder. "Yeah, I'm so lucky," she said sarcastically. But deep down, she did feel lucky to have found a sort of work partner like Sam. "I wouldn't have lasted a full shift working for that guy."

"I'm surprised you kept your cool the hour we were there," Sam teased.

"Almost lost it with his last comment, 'we'll keep in touch… I'd love that.' Nearly decked him." Kimberley perked up the corner of her lip.

"How about the rap sheet being as long as his you know what?" Sam laughed. "What a jackass." He shook his head. "Sorry about him. Should have warned ya ahead of time."

"No worries. I've dealt with men like that more times than I can count."

Kimberley looked out her passenger side window. A sliver of the sun peeked above the horizon. She found sunsets beautiful every other day of the year, but not this day. The setting sun signaled it would be dark in a few hours and nearly impossible to find Piper.

Kimberley looked over at Sam. His face had turned serious as he focused on the road, driving twenty miles over the speed limit. The light they had found in the darkness was gone, and reality had set back in. It had been nearly twenty-four hours since Piper had last been seen. They were in the red zone, where a happy ending was becoming more and more unlikely.

"Whatcha thinking?" Kimberley asked, trying to bring Sam back to her.

He glanced over at her for a moment and then back at the road. "I'm thinking we're losing light, and we've got too much ground to cover before nightfall."

They were on the same bleak page.

"We don't have much of anything, other than perhaps the potential route Piper took to Miley's, if that's where she was even heading. So, we either have nothing or jackshit," he said, biting at his lower lip. Kimberley knew this was hitting him especially hard. A wound that never healed torn further open. The loss of a child wasn't the type of grief you got over or through. It stayed with you like a thick fog that wouldn't let up.

"You doing okay?" Kimberley asked. They had grown close over the past year, more than colleagues, they were friends. And sometimes, Kimberley thought they could be more than that, but she always kept it professional, as did Sam. There had been a couple of times that something almost happened. A touch of the hand, a few lingering looks. But they were friends, and they'd always be friends.

Sam glanced over at Kimberley again. She gave him a concerned look. He softened his face and let his bottom lip slide out from his teeth. Sam repositioned himself in his seat, letting one hand fall from the steering wheel, and propping his elbow on the center console.

"Yeah, you know me, I'm fine. I'm always fine."

"Sam." Kimberley adjusted her body, so she was nearly turned toward him. "I know this is hard for you. A case like this is hard for everyone, but I think it's hitting you a little harder. You don't have to act tough around me." She slid her hand on top of his and gave it a squeeze.

Sam brushed his thumb against hers. "I'm not acting tough. I am tough." He grinned.

Kimberley rolled her eyes playfully. "You know you can talk to me, right?" She tilted her head. "Right?"

"Yes, yes, I know." He nodded.

She gave his hand another squeeze. "Good." Kimberley patted him on the shoulder and resituated herself in her seat. "And don't you forget it."

CHAPTER ELEVEN

Kimberley trudged through the tall wheat beside Sam. There was a row of ten officers on one side of them and a row of ten on the other. They were covering as much ground as possible, walking on both sides of Nerge Road, the road that led to Black Heart Lane. A group of volunteers continued up the road where Arthur and Edna lived, just in case Piper had taken that route. They had three canine units, one from Dead Woman Crossing and two from Weatherford. Kimberley's phone rang. She had finally had the sense to charge it and make sure it stayed charged on their drive back and forth to Weatherford earlier. She quickly brought it to her ear.

"Chief Deputy King," she said.

"Kimberley, this is Margaret from Happy Trails Daycare. I've been sitting here with Jessica for—"

"Oh shit. I'm on my way. I'm so sorry," Kimberley interrupted. "I'll be right there." She ended the call.

"Sam," she said.

"It's fine. Go."

"Are you sure?"

"Yes, of course. I'll call you right away if we find anything."

"Thanks, Sam," she said with a small smile. She took off running through the wheat field and down the road back to her vehicle.

Just as Kimberley pushed open the door to the daycare center, she felt the door pulling in from the other side. The extra force brought her crashing through the doorframe and falling into a man she did not recognize. Kimberley tumbled on top of him, just as he pushed a little boy around Jessica's age aside, out of harm's way. She quickly slid herself off of him, but not before taking in his appearance. With her face being mere inches from his, it was hard not to notice the stubble that covered his strong jaw, the peppering of gray that sprinkled his jet-black hair, and the faded scar that ran along his right cheek, a couple inches in length. Most of all, she noticed his scent, a mix of cinnamon and sawdust. Before she pushed herself off of him, she inhaled it. Her hands touched the ridges of his chiseled core as she slid off of him. Kimberley's cheeks flushed.

"I'm so sorry," she stammered. She was never at a loss for words, but right now, she was. And she didn't know if it was because of the strange man she had tackled to the ground or everything else she had going on in her life.

The man sat up and got to his feet first. He gave Kimberley a small smile and helped her up.

"It seems we're both not winning parent of the year," he joked, picking up the boy and hoisting him on his hip. The little boy had golden blond hair and dark blue eyes in complete contrast to the man standing in front of her. The mother's genes must be strong, Kimberley thought. "I'm running late to pick up my kiddo too," he said, tousling the boy's hair. "I assume you're here to pick up your kid," he added.

"Oh yes, yes. Jessica, my daughter." Kimberley nodded. "I'm late. Sorry. I'm not usually this scatterbrained," she added.

"I'm Caleb by the way," he said, extending his hand.

Kimberley shook it. "I'm Kimberley."

"King," he added.

She gave him a peculiar look, furrowing her brow. How did he know her name? She didn't recognize this man. Had never seen him around before. The man picked up on Kimberley's confusion, and quickly cleared it up by pointing to the gold name tag pinned to her shirt. "Chief Deputy King," he added.

Kimberley looked down at her shirt and let out an awkward laugh. "Oh yeah. Forgot about that." She looked back at him with a silly smile. It wasn't like her. "Yes, Kimberley King."

"Sounds like royalty," he said, returning the grin. "Like I said, I'm Caleb and this here is my boy, Flynn. We're new to the area. I just started working at a construction company."

Kimberley smiled at the little boy. "Nice to meet you both," she said, taking them both in again. Caleb was attractive in an immediate sense, not the type of guy you had to decide whether he was good looking or not. Having a kid on his hip made him a hundred times more attractive to Kimberley. She was aware that it was because of her own father issues and the fact that Jessica's father didn't want anything to do with her. Realizing she was staring, she spoke up. "Welcome to Dead Woman Crossing. I haven't been here long myself, but it's a nice place to raise kids." Kimberley immediately regretted the words that left her mouth. With Piper Chase missing, she was no longer certain if it was in fact a nice place to raise a child.

"So far, we like it just fine. Only been here a few weeks."

"There you are," a stern voice called from behind her. Kimberley turned around finding Margaret, a plump woman with curly red hair walking toward her holding Jessica's hand.

"I'm so sorry, Margaret. Work's been crazy today, and I lost track of time."

Jessica ran to Kimberley saying Mommy over and over again. Although she hated being away from her, seeing the excitement in her daughter was the sweetest and best moment of motherhood. Kimberley swooped her up with Jessica's legs wrapping around her waist. She planted several kisses on her.

"I missed my smart girl so much!" Kimberley exclaimed.

"Missed you more, Mommy," Jessica squealed. She snuggled her head in the crook of her mother's neck, settling down immediately.

Margaret pursed her lips together and threw her hands on her hips. But her irritation only lasted a few seconds before she softened her face and dropped her hands. "It's okay, Kimberley. I got the alert earlier today. I hope you find her."

The daycare teacher gave Kimberley a sympathetic look. It was clear she understood the pressure she was under not only in her personal life, but also in her professional life. Kimberley mouthed thank you to Margaret as she ran her hand down the back of Jessica's head through her soft, rich dark brown hair. She was nearly asleep already after an extra-long day at daycare, thanks to her losing track of time.

"Alert? Is it something I should be worried about?" Caleb asked, looking at Margaret and then at Kimberley.

Kimberley turned to him. He held his son a little tighter, clearly concerned for the well-being of his child. She understood that feeling more than anyone, for she herself was holding Jessica a light tighter. "As of now, there's no danger to the public. We're looking for a missing girl, so nothing personally for you to worry about," she assured him.

"Wow. Poor thing. I hope you find her," he said. His mouth turned into a slight frown as he rubbed his boy's back.

"Well, I've got to lock up," Margaret said, pulling a set of keys from her pocket and putting an end to the conversation.

"Of course," Kimberley said, walking through the door with a sleeping Jessica. "Thanks, Margaret, and I'm sorry again."

"Yeah, my apologies, too. Won't happen again," Caleb said, following behind Kimberley with his own child in tow.

Margaret peeked her head out waving them off. "It's fine. I understand how difficult it is for single parents. Have a good night! Bye, Jessica. Bye, Flynn," she called out, before pulling the door closed and locking it.

Single parent. The words registered in her mind for a moment. She looked back at Caleb and his boy again. Caleb smiled as his boy's head slumped onto his shoulder, falling asleep almost immediately.

"Sorry again for tackling you," Kimberley said, walking to her vehicle.

"No need to apologize. I didn't mind it." Caleb grinned. Kimberley couldn't help but smile either.

"Maybe I'll see you around, or we could get the kids together for a playdate sometime," he offered, walking to the pickup truck parked directly in front of hers on the side of the street. He opened the back door, leaning in and buckling his son into a car seat.

"I'd like that… I mean, I think Jessica would like that," Kimberley said, correcting herself. She pulled open the back door of her SUV.

"Good. It's a date then." He nodded, closing the door of his truck and opening up the driver's side. "Have a good one, King." Caleb flashed a toothy smile and hopped into his truck.

"Have a good night," Kimberley said with a wave of her hand as he headed off. "Caleb…" she said aloud, realizing she hadn't caught his last name.

Kimberley glanced back in the rearview mirror, checking on Jessica. She was fast asleep, her little head craned to the side, her pouty bottom lip pushed out and her hands crumpled up in little fists in her lap. Since her daughter was sleeping peacefully, she decided to take the long route home. She had an hour before she was set to be at her stepsister Emily's house for her divorce dinner, although it was the last thing Kimberley wanted to do. She'd prefer to lie in her bed, staring up at the ceiling, letting the facts of the case flip through her brain like a Rolodex. But first, she wanted to drive down Black Heart Lane. There was something that was still calling her to it, intuition, gut feeling, she didn't know, but it was something. Driving past Edna and Arthur's house, she noticed all the lights were on… every last one of them, as if they could light the path home for Piper. There were cars up and down the street and a couple of squad cars parked in the driveway. Despite it being nearly dark out, the search was still on. Kimberley drove slowly past the house, all the way down to Nerge Road, where she took a left.

Out in the fields she could see a dozen flashlights and the silhouettes of people. She should be out there with them, searching. Kimberley instantly felt a surge of guilt. She kept her eyes open, watching for people and animals, and, deep down, Piper. There was a sliver of hope that maybe, just maybe, the little girl would run right across the road in front of Kimberley's headlights. Kimberley would slam on the brakes, hop out of the car, and scoop the little girl up, declaring her safe and calling off the search and rescue. As she drove, nothing crossed the road in front of her, not even little Piper Chase. She came to a street sign that read 'Black Heart Lane' and turned her car slowly onto the road. She was unfamiliar with it, but immediately recognized why the children played here. The woods came right up to the road, thick and twisting, full of wonder. When Sam and Kimberley had driven over to the Bakers' house, they had taken a different route to their home, not this one. It was naturally beautiful even in the dark. The road ahead twisted and sloped, as though it was carved around the trees and not the other way around. It was just the kind of place children would love riding their bikes, going fast down the hills, the curvy turns, and very little traffic. She could see why Arthur and Edna would have thought it was a safe place for Piper to be. Kimberley looked back in the rearview mirror, checking on her sleeping daughter once again. She hoped the Chases' instincts were right.

*

Kimberley walked in the kitchen carrying a couple of dirty dishes she had gathered from the living room. Her mom was tidying up, ensuring everything was wiped down and spotless.

"Jessica's down for the night, so I think it'll be a quiet one for you," Kimberley said, placing the dishes in the sink.

"Just leave them. I got them." Nicole shooed her away from the sink and began washing-up the dishes. "You should have told me you were running late. I could have gone and picked up Jessica," her mother said, pursing her lips together.

"I know. I didn't even realize I was running late until I got the call." She grabbed the half-drunk bottle of Bud Light from the counter and took a swig. It was room temperature now, but she didn't mind it as she didn't think she deserved more than a warm beer… not with a missing child somewhere out there.

"You still heading over to Emily's? I know you've got a lot on your mind with that case and all, but she'd appreciate the company." Nicole finished washing and rinsing the dishes, wiping down the sink and counters once more.

"Yeah." It was all Kimberley managed to get out. She looked out the kitchen window but could see nothing but black. The darkness had descended upon Dead Woman Crossing, and all she could think about was the little girl that could be out there trapped in it, like a pit of tar. Life just wasn't fair.

"Try to enjoy yourself and be present for Emily tonight. You've done all you can today." Nicole patted her hand on Kimberley's, giving it a small squeeze.

"All I can wasn't enough today."

"It could be enough tomorrow." Nicole delivered the words the way only a mother could, warm and encouraging, wrapped in love.

Kimberley took a deep breath and finished off her beer. She considered bringing up the divorce her mother should be filing for but didn't want to ruin this moment. It could wait for another day. Nicole picked up the empty bottle and dropped it into a recycling bin underneath the kitchen window. Kimberley smiled at her mom, but it quickly faltered when she thought of David. How could she still be married to him? A cold-blooded killer?

She closed her eyes for just a moment and, in that moment, David was there again, standing in front of her, bloody and bruised just as she was. She lay on the ground reaching for her Glock, while he raised the 38-caliber pistol to the side of his head. Click. Snap. The Glock was out of her holster, pointed up at David. He was about to take the easy way out, but she wasn't going to let him have that satisfaction. She fired first. The bullet hit his arm, kicking his gun and turning it from a fatal shot to a flesh wound. He'd live with what he did for the rest of his life. At the time, she didn't realize her mother would be in tow. Perhaps, she should have let him kill himself. It seemed the only way for her mother to free herself from the toxic men in her life was through death. At least, that's what it had taken for her mom to be free of her dad.

"Well, I'm going to head over to Emily's," Kimberley said, before she said something that would turn into an argument. She pushed herself off the stool at the counter and left the kitchen without another word.

Kimberley walked up the steps to the large white farmhouse, each one creaking beneath her weight. With Wyatt, Emily's ex-husband, not around, the maintenance outside hadn't been kept up with, aside from the garden Emily managed. They would have lost the house if it weren't for the money David had stowed away over the years. Forgoing using it on a pricey defense team, and instead giving it to his daughter, Emily, and his wife, Nicole, was the only good thing he had done. In Kimberley's mind, he did it for himself, though, as the family farm was his source of pride. Before she could knock, the door was thrown open. Emily stood there with a cracked smile. Her dirty blonde hair had been cut extending just past her ears. Having your heart broken always came with a haircut. Instead of her usual muted appearance, she had applied cherry red lipstick, rosy blush, and mascara that made her lashes thick and long. The effort she had put into her hair and makeup didn't carry out to her attire as she was dressed in a summer dress that extended past her knees. Modest and practical.

"Come in. Come in," she squealed, wrapping her arms around Kimberley not because she greeted people that way, but because she was the one that needed the hug, so Kimberley hugged her back.

When she released from Kimberley, her eyes glistened and she sniffled. She quickly turned away beckoning her guest down the hall into the dining room.

"How was work?" Emily asked.

Before Kimberley could answer, Emily slapped a hand over her mouth, turning back. "I'm sorry. I know how it was. I got the Amber Alert earlier today."

Kimberley shook her head. "It's fine, and I don't really want to talk about work. I'm here for you tonight. We've got a divorce to celebrate."

Emily nodded. She folded her lips and exhaled deeply through her nose. "You're right. It is a celebration… to be free from that asshole."

It took Kimberley by surprise as she rarely heard Emily cuss, but she liked it. She followed Emily into the dining room. A bottle of champagne was already opened and half drunk, as well as a bottle of red wine.

"Help yourself," Emily said as she grabbed her glass and moseyed over to the counter unpacking takeout Chinese food. It also wasn't like Emily to order out as homecooked meals were her specialty. Kimberley poured herself a glass of red wine and took a seat at the table.

"How have you been holding up?" Kimberley asked, taking a sip. She planned to have no more than two glasses. She wanted to be up at the crack of dawn, so she could be out searching for Piper right when the sun rose.

Emily looked back over her shoulder. "Perfectly."

That was a lie. Kimberley could see it in the way she talked and walked and moved around the kitchen. She didn't float like she used to, she lumbered like she was dragging around a weight behind her. She still loved Wyatt despite all he had done to her.

"Where are Tom and Jack? I thought my mom was going to watch them tonight." Kimberley took another sip of wine, bringing her foot up to rest on her knee and slouching in the chair.

"I thought so, too, but Wyatt showed up asking to take them tonight." She shrugged her shoulders.

"So, the co-parenting has been going well?"

Emily nodded not saying a word. She turned on her foot bringing a plate of rice with beef and broccoli to Kimberley and set it down in front of her. "Did you know he's seeing another woman?" she asked.

Kimberley took another sip. "I did. I saw them together at The Trophy Room a couple of times. Seems a bit fast to me."

Emily slammed the rest of her wine and refilled it with a mix of champagne and wine. Kimberley shuddered thinking of the killer hangover she was going to endure in the morning with that type of mixture.

"Yeah, her name is Ginger. That's not even a name. It's a root." Emily seethed. She rolled her eyes and took a drink of her champ-wine concoction.

Kimberley stabbed her fork through a piece of broccoli and a chunk of steak and took a bite, chewing it slowly to give Emily all the time in the world to get out what she needed to get out. She could tell this was deeper than losing a husband, Emily had lost a part of her identity. She had played the role as a dutiful housewife for nearly a decade. But what was she now that she was no longer a wife?

"I could have eventually forgiven him for the moonshine and the lying and sneaking around. He just had to be patient.

Instead, he went and got himself a girlfriend." She stamped her feet, punctuating her hatred. "And now, he thinks he's done nothing wrong because we were separated. What are we, Ross and Rachel?" She crossed one arm over her chest and brought her glass to her mouth with her other hand, taking a long sip. "There was a chance I would have gotten back with him. We have kids together, for God's sake… but now, not a chance in hell. He can have the skanky root vegetable."

Kimberley nodded, taking another sip of her wine and another bite of her food. She knew Emily needed to vent. She had been putting on a happy face the past year, but now that the divorce papers were finalized, her façade had shattered. And she had to pick up the pieces and build herself back up, to be a different version of herself, one she never dreamed she could ever be.

"Ginger…" she said again, twisting up her lips and crinkling her nose. She prepared herself a plate of food and brought it to the table along with her glass, taking a seat across from Kimberley. She poked her fork around the plate never bringing it to her mouth. The only thing she brought to her mouth was her wine/champagne.

"My mom tells me you have a couple of side gigs," Kimberley said, looking at Emily, hoping she could convince her divorce wasn't the end, it was just a new beginning.

Emily nodded. "Yeah. Well, I have the garden, the chickens, which have been producing a good amount of eggs, and I've taken up knitting. Selling pieces at the farmers' market. Anything to keep me busy and bring in a little extra money."

"That's good. Did your dad leave you enough?" Kimberley asked. She knew he had left a good chunk to her mom and the rest to Emily, but she wasn't sure how much he had actually squirreled away and how long they could both live off of it.

"Yeah, oh yeah. We're fine. Is it bad…" she paused, looking at Kimberley "… that I still love him?"

"No, you were married to him for nearly a decade and you have kids together," Kimberley said, popping another piece of broccoli in her mouth.

"No, not Wyatt. My dad."

Kimberley pulled her brows together.

"I know what he did was horrendous, and I'll never forgive him for that. But he's my dad, and I still love him. Like I check in on him with a monthly call and write to him. I've even sent some of the pictures the boys drew to him to brighten up his room... well, cell." Emily looked down at her lap, fidgeting with her fingers.

"I don't think it's bad that you still love him. I think it's normal. After everything my father put me through growing up, I still sought his approval and praise. No matter how many times he abused me, I loved that asshole. But at the same time, I hated him. I really fucking hated him, too," Kimberley said, taking a sip of her wine, trying to wash away the bad taste in her mouth that arose when she thought of her father.

"Yeah..." Emily pushed her food around some more and looked up at Kimberley. "I think that's exactly how I feel."

"It gets easier."

"It does?" Emily's eyes lit up.

"Yeah, after they die." Kimberley smiled to show she was kidding, but really, she was only half kidding.

CHAPTER TWELVE

I knew when they stopped looking for you, because I was out there 'looking' for you too. A volunteer. A concerned neighbor. An upstanding citizen of Dead Woman Crossing. I was all of those things, but I was so much more. I trudged through the woods, the wheat, shoulder to shoulder with other volunteers. Branches snapped beneath our shoes and our eyes were peeled, hoping we'd find you. I knew we wouldn't. A burly officer with a long ponytail and a deep voice had called it off, telling all the volunteers and officers that we'd start again in the morning. It was too dark and dangerous to be out searching now. But not for you and I. Our search was just beginning. I left with the other volunteers, and then I waited, waited until I knew everyone would be gone and that I could return with you this time. I considered driving you to another town and burying you where no one would find you. But deep down, I wanted them to find you. I knew where they had searched and where they hadn't yet, and in the middle of the night, I made my way to your final resting place.

It wasn't far back from a clearing on Black Heart Lane, an area unsearched, that I trudged in. You were wrapped tightly in a blanket I would burn when I returned home. I found the softest patch of moss and placed you on top of it. I had a shovel in the car, but like I said, I wanted them to find you. Plus, I didn't have the energy after pretending to look for you. I pried open your eyelids, revealing those big, blue eyes. I figured you'd want to look up at the full moon, the smattering of stars, and the thick branches that looked like hands and fingers reaching up at the night sky. I placed your hands on your stomach, folded on top of one another and coiled your golden blonde hair around the side of your head. You looked like an angel. You hadn't been in life, but you would be in death.

CHAPTER THIRTEEN

Kimberley jumped from her bed at the sound of a ringing phone. It was her own. She scrambled to grab it in the dark before it woke up Jessica who was sleeping in her toddler bed on the other side of the room. She clicked the side button to silence it and then answer before even looking at the screen.

"Chief Deputy King," she said into the phone, but it came out weak and raspy.

"King, it's Sam. We found her, we found Piper Chase."

Kimberley breathed a sigh of relief, rubbing her forehead and pushing her hair back as she sat up in her bed. "Oh, thank God," she whispered.

"No, we found her body. She's dead," Sam immediately corrected.

Kimberley squeezed her eyes tightly closed and opened them again. She hoped she was dreaming, but she was still sitting in her bedroom and rays of the sun were seeping in from behind the blinds.

"You still there?" Sam asked.

"Yeah."

"Get here as soon as you can. We're at Black Heart Lane."

Kimberley ended the call feeling as though she had just taken a punch to the gut. Her heart ached for the little girl, the little girl that believed in magic.

*

Sam had met Kimberley by the side of the road, waving her down to pull her vehicle off. There were police and emergency vehicles parked up and down it, probably the most traffic the area had ever seen. She shut the engine off and closed her eyes for a moment before exiting her SUV. No matter how many crime scenes she had worked, bodies she had seen, they never got easier. Most things you can get used to; death wasn't one of them. A light fog enveloped the wooded area of Black Heart Lane, wrapping through the thick trees, swirling just above the ground. The towering arbors were a vanguard for the lost life within them, black and foreboding up to blooming verdant peaks, capable of blocking all light. This was an environment of struggle and dominance for life. Everything competing for the resources available and the losers eventually collapsing back into the earth, the decomposers returning their life back into the soil to start all over. This place was full cycle, life and death, ugly and beautiful, a place to frolic and play, and a place to…

The morning birds sang, the crows cawed like they were playing a sad song for the life lost. She looked at Sam and as much as he tried to hide what he had seen; she could see the horror and the sadness on his face. The terrible scene of a dead child, something that had hit too close to home, was something he now had to relive in another. His eyes were bloodshot with deep circles beneath them. His teeth slightly chattering as an internal cold swept through him. The type of cold from a body running out of steam: no food, no sleep, no joy for life. Pale and frozen in anguish. She didn't blame him.

"Megan and her team just arrived," he said. His lips immediately pursed together as if he was trying to keep something contained, grief. Megan Grey was their designated pathologist from Oklahoma City. She only came around for cases like this… murder, that is.

Kimberley considered telling him that she'd like to take the lead on the case, knowing what Sam had been through in his personal life. She looked at him closely, taking in his sad appearance, and decided not to say anything... at least for now.

"Good." Kimberley nodded walking alongside Sam. They left the road entering the woods, carefully bypassing the twisting trees and thick weeds. It's not so much the trees were actually twisted, it just felt that way to Kimberley. Branches like arms reaching out at her, slithering against her skin, entangling her limbs. The ground was a little damp, covered in moss, pine needles and fallen leaves. Sam's footsteps were heavy, snapping sticks beneath them. He attempted to pull branches aside and hold them high or step on them to make it easier for Kimberley, but they still managed to touch her. The smell of dirt and soggy leaves invaded her nose. Any other day, it might have been refreshing, but today it reminded her of death. As they walked deeper into the woods, she could start to hear voices up ahead... they were getting close.

Kimberley prepared herself with a couple of deep breaths and thinking of nothing but the color white. It was how she cleared her mind, made it a blank slate. She'd need it for the crime scene, need it to find the smallest of clues that could lead them to the person responsible for the death of Piper Chase.

"Right up here," Sam finally said. He hadn't spoken a word since the road, focusing only on keeping the path safe and clear for Kimberley to traverse.

"When was she found?"

"About fifteen minutes before I called you. So, about an hour ago."

"Have Edna and Arthur been notified?"

Sam shook his head. "No, I figured you and I would go and tell them after. It's only our team and Megan's team here. Volunteers and Weatherford won't get here for another few hours. By then, we'll have called off the search."

Kimberley could now see it... the crime scene. A small clearing within the woods, covered in dirt, fallen leaves, moss... and now Piper Chase. Several officers stood around the perimeter, including Bearfield, guarding the resting place for the little girl. She could see others out in the woods, searching, but she didn't know what for yet. Deputy Hill walked Winston deep into the woods. Kimberley and Sam ducked under the police tape, greeted with nods and solemn faces from those that were already there.

Megan Grey crouched down near the body, her hands covered by white gloves. She was dressed in all black. If Kimberley hadn't known her, she would have assumed she had dressed that way for the crime scene. But Megan being from Oklahoma City, a little over an hour away, rather than a small town, always dressed a little more sophisticated. Her scarlet-red hair fell just below her chin, never shorter, never longer. Her sharp features played in her favor as they matched her bulldozer attitude. Megan was always polished from head to toe.

"Detective King," Megan announced as soon as she saw Kimberley approaching. She stood and nodded at her.

"Megan." Kimberley nodded back. Under any other circumstances, she would have smiled at Megan, because she liked and respected her, but she couldn't bring herself to... not with the body of a ten-year-old little girl lying between them. "What have we got?"

Megan pursed her lips together looking at Kimberley, then Sam, and then down at the little girl. Kimberley's eyes followed. She hadn't looked at Piper yet. She expected it to be worse, but the little girl looked as though she was peering up at the sky, peaceful almost, lying in a soft mossy grave. For a moment, Kimberley thought she could snap her out of her daze, tell her to go back home, that her grandparents were waiting for her. But reality kicked in as she stared at the little girl. Her chest didn't rise and fall. She didn't move. She just lay there, frozen. Her body was dressed in dirty jeans and a graphic pink tee adorned with a princess and a sword. Above the tough princess were the words '*I can slay my own dragons.*' Kimberley let out a silent sigh as the ache in her heart went from dull to a sharp pain.

Piper's skin was pale, purple in some areas, like the blood was settling just beneath it. Her blonde hair was swept up and gathered around the top of the head. Her eyes were big and blue with the sheen of glass. Just looking at her, Kimberley still couldn't see what had caused her to stop living. Aside from some bruising and scrapes on her legs and arms, which most kids that played outside sported, there was nothing.

"It's too early to say exactly how Piper died, but I think she was murdered." Megan crouched down again, pushing the soft, blonde hair out of the way, revealing dried blood and skin split five inches in length. The skull of the little girl was partially exposed. "Given the state of the body, it feels cold and stiff, the death occurred between thirty to thirty-six hours ago. As of now, I'd say this head trauma was the cause." Megan pointed to the gaping wound.

"Was she moved here?" Sam asked.

Kimberley searched the ground for rocks or anything that could have caused that type of trauma. A piece of wood, maybe.

Megan stood up. "I'd say yes. There's no blood around the body and, so far, we haven't found any in a fifteen-foot radius. We'll continue sweeping the area. But if the murder did take place here, there'd be a lot more blood. Head injuries bleed a lot because of the amount of blood vessels. And twenty percent of the blood flowing from the heart goes to the brain. There's just not enough here," Megan explained.

Megan wasn't one to overexplain nor go into details about science or the human body. Kimberley presumed she was trying to fill the silence, stop herself from thinking of the life cut way too short just in front of them.

"What do you have them looking for?" Kimberley asked Sam as she scanned the woods. Deputies were spread out; their heads tilted down at the ground. They were searching.

"Her pink bicycle. We haven't been able to locate it," Sam said. His eyes got tight for a second as if he were holding back tears.

"There's no tracks to this spot either. Too many fallen leaves for footprints," Megan said.

"And the scrapes and bruises?" Kimberley pointed to the little girl's legs.

"A couple of them, the darker ones, had to have happened recently, perhaps around the time the head trauma occurred. The yellowish one, maybe days ago, probably from playing or bumping into something. The scrapes on the knees are scabbed over, so they also had to have opened premortem as well." Megan pulled her eyes from Piper, looking back at Kimberley.

"Anything else you can tell us?" Sam asked.

"Anything else would be speculation. My team will finish sweeping the area and get everything collected. I'll start the pathology report today, expedite everything, and will have my results and findings to you both tomorrow," Megan said matter-of-factly.

They all took another glance at the little girl lying in the moss, a mental photo snapped of who they were fighting for. It was an image, Kimberley was confident, would be etched in her brain until the day she herself passed. There were some things the mind would never let go of, and Kimberley was sure this was one of them. All she could do now was make certain she found the person responsible.

CHAPTER FOURTEEN

"You can follow me back to the Chases' house," Sam said, standing beside his vehicle with his hand on the door handle. Kimberley could see the pain in his eyes and the hurt on his face. His shoulders weren't pinned high like they usually were, they hung like he could barely hold himself up. His skin was pale as if the blood had drained from it and his heart was no longer pumping the twenty percent his brain needed.

Kimberley stopped just beside him. "Sam, are you sure you want to do this? I can deliver the news to Edna and Arthur," she said, keeping her voice calm and low.

Sam looked down at his muddy boots, attempting to scrape some of the mud off by rubbing one foot against the other. He jolted his head up. "I'm fine," he snapped.

Kimberley tilted her head and bit at her lower lip, her dark blue eyes staring right into Sam's clouded ones. "Okay, Sam." She gave a small nod. There was no point in arguing with him, even though she could see Sam was anything but fine. "I'll follow behind. We'll tell them together." Kimberley placed a hand on his shoulder and gave it a small squeeze before turning on her foot and walking back to her vehicle.

Kimberley drove behind Sam... the facts spinning in her head like a Rolodex once again. Last seen at 5:15 p.m. the day before yesterday. No one knew where Piper was off to. Her bicycle was still missing. She was murdered sometime between 5:15 p.m. and 11:15 p.m. based on the thirty to thirty-six-hour preliminary window Megan had given. Kimberley hoped with the pathology report the window would be significantly reduced. She looked down at her speedometer noticing Sam was driving nine miles under the speed limit, which was unlike him. But she understood. She herself wasn't in a rush to tell Arthur and Edna. Kimberley made sure to keep her vehicle back, not to push him to go any faster. She knew Sam needed this time.

Kimberley got out of her vehicle first, despite the fact that Sam had parked first. She walked up to the driver's side and opened the door for him. He sat there for a moment, almost in a daze... like he was experiencing more than everyone else, and Kimberley was sure he was. He stared at the little gray ranch home.

"You okay?" she asked.

He immediately snapped out of it, clearing his throat, opening his eyes a little bit wider and stepping out of the vehicle. "Yeah, just got lost in thought for a second there," he said.

Kimberley looked up at him.

"King, I'm fine, really. I'm not the one you should be worried about," he said, looking at the house again.

She couldn't help it, though; she was always worried about Sam. But he was right. Her eyes followed his looking at the home. They walked side by side up to the front door and knocked. Inside, voices and footsteps.

"It could be Piper," Edna said from behind the door.

A pain settled in the pit of Kimberley's stomach.

Arthur swung open the door. His face immediately dimmed when he saw Sheriff Walker and Chief Deputy King. Edna stood beside him still clutching both the home phone and the cell phone.

"Did you find her? Did you find Piper?" Edna asked. Her voice full of hope.

Arthur scratched his wrinkled forehead. His mouth became a narrow line and his eyes followed suit as if he already knew the bad news that was about to be delivered.

"Can we come in?" Sam asked.

Kimberley's and Sam's faces were like stone, hard with no emotion. They needed both Edna and Arthur seated and calm before they told them what had happened to their granddaughter.

"Yes, of course. Of course. Come in. Come in," Edna said, beckoning with her phone-clutched hands. She was repeating herself again. "Sit. Sit." She motioned to the living room area.

"Why don't you two have a seat," Sam said. It wasn't a question nor a recommendation, it was a command. It was the stern tone that made that clear.

Arthur and Edna nodded, while Arthur guided Edna to the seat beside him on the couch, wrapping one arm around her. Sam and Kimberley took seats in the wingback chairs on either side of the couch. They turned their bodies toward Piper's grandparents, leaning forward slightly.

"Did you find Piper?" Edna asked again. Her voice cracking at the end.

Kimberley glanced down at Edna's hands. Her fingers were completely white as she clenched the phones even tighter now.

"Yes," Sam said.

Before he could continue, Edna and Arthur were sighing with relief.

"Where is she? Can we see her?" Arthur stammered.

He took a small audible breath. "I'm so sorry. We found Piper's body."

Edna erupted, a howl of a scream exiting her body. The phones fell to the ground with a clatter as she finally released them from her hands. She threw herself into Arthur's chest as he wrapped his arms around her, allowing her to bury her face. Edna's shoulders shook. Her body convulsed. Arthur tried to stop her body from shaking, but it was no use. The grief was more powerful than him. His lips quivered, and tears ran down his face in a stream, dripping from the tip of his nose and the edge of his jaw. Kimberley and

Sam just sat there. This was the hardest part of the job, trying to be strong and pretend that the loss of a life didn't affect them. It did. It always did. Kimberley bit at the inside of her mouth to keep her own lips from quivering. She blinked rapidly to keep her eyes from tearing. She looked over at Sam and watched him do the same. Kimberley could see a vein in the side of his neck appear… throbbing almost. His jaw tightened. His sadness had turned to anger. She felt the same. What kind of monster could have done this to a child?

It was nearly five minutes before Arthur could speak, get out all the questions that were building up in his jumbled brain. Who? Why? Where? When? How?

"Where did you find her? Where was Piper?" His voice shook. Edna continued to cry into his chest, more like a soft whimper now.

"In the woods over by Black Heart Lane," Kimberley spoke up, noticing that Sam was still clenching his jaw.

"When… when did she pass?" Arthur wiped his eyes knocking his glasses off in the process. He didn't put them back on, instead opting to set them down on the coffee table.

"We don't have an exact time, but we know it was between the hours of five fifteen p.m. and eleven fifteen p.m. on Sunday, August second, the night she left here." She tried to deliver that news with her calmest and most soothing voice. She knew how they would feel… guilty. It was now Tuesday morning, and they finally knew where their granddaughter was. If they had told Piper no, she'd still be alive. If they had driven her, she'd still be alive. Kimberley was sure those thoughts were running through their minds.

Arthur nodded his head slightly, lowering his chin as if he were hanging it in shame. He ran a hand through Edna's hair.

"How?" That was the only word he was able to say, but Kimberley knew what he was asking. How did she die? How was she killed? Did she suffer? Who did it? Did she know she was going to die before it happened? Was it an accident? All those questions were stuffed into how.

"We'll know more tomorrow when the pathology results are in. But as of now, blunt force trauma to the side of the head is the preliminary cause of death," Kimberley said as if she were reading it from a teleprompter. It was the only way she could deliver this type of news. She looked back over at Sam. He appeared to be a statue in the room, still as a rock, unmoving. But inside, she was sure his heart and thoughts were racing.

Arthur and Edna gasped. Edna finally pulled her head from her husband's chest leaving a damp shirt behind.

"Was Piper murdered? Was my baby girl murdered?" Edna's face crumbled as she pushed out the questions.

"I'm sorry to say, but we believe she was."

"Why?" Edna screamed a raspy scream. "Why would someone want to hurt her? She was just a little girl."

"We don't know that yet, but rest assured we will find out," Sam said through gritted teeth.

"We have a few more questions that may help us find the person responsible," Kimberley said, pulling out her pad of paper and a pen.

Edna wiped her face and nodded. Arthur put his glasses back on.

"You mentioned Piper attended a summer camp last time we spoke. Which camp was that?"

"Camp Beaverbrook," Arthur said. "It's just a weeklong sleepover camp. Do you think someone there had something to do with this?" His eyes darted to Sam and then back to Kimberley.

"We don't know that," Sam said, repositioning himself. He no longer looked like stone. "But we have to cover all of our bases, anyone that might have been in contact with Piper."

Kimberley made a note to follow-up with the camp on her pad of paper. She wrote 'Camp Beaverbrook' and circled it twice.

"Where is Camp Beaverbrook located?" Kimberley looked to Arthur.

"Just about an hour north of here on Canton Lake."

Kimberley made a note.

"And you mentioned previously, Miley was the only friend you knew of Piper's?" Kimberley asked, tilting her head.

Edna looked to Arthur. "Yeah, right. She never mentioned anyone else?" she said almost as though she wasn't so sure herself.

"Not that I can recall," Arthur reiterated. His voice cracked again or maybe it was broken and it would always be broken. They say parents aren't supposed to outlive their children. Kimberley was sure they said the same thing about grandparents and grandchildren.

"What about from school? Any teachers she was close with? Classmates?"

Arthur shook his head. "Piper was shy. Kept to herself. That's why we put her in the camp this summer, so she could make some friends and bring her out of her shell." He wiped his brow.

"I'm sorry," Edna cried. "This is my fault. I should have been more attentive. Got Piper a cell phone. Not let her ride around on her bicycle by herself. If I would have maybe…"

"That's enough, Edna. I won't have you go down that road again. You did the same thing with Shana." Arthur's voice was stern causing Edna to cry harder.

"Your husband is right," Sam spoke up. "The what ifs don't help. Trust me. They'll do you no good. Just be there for one another and let us know if you think of anything else. We'll be in touch," Sam said, standing from his seat.

Kimberley followed suit, putting away her notepad and pen, and standing up. She couldn't tell if Sam was done with the conversation because he knew Arthur and Edna had nothing to tell them that would help or if he just couldn't sit there any longer.

Outside, Kimberley turned to Sam, looking him up and down, taking him in for a moment. His hard exterior had returned accompanied with the clenched jaw he was sporting inside the Chases' house.

"What now?" Kimberley asked.

"Not much we can do until the pathology results come in. I've got officers combing the woods and surrounding area looking for that pink bicycle. Hoping for a break, maybe fingerprints on the body or we just stumble upon the bicycle on someone's property." Sam folded his arms in front of his chest. "It's never that easy."

"It never is," Kimberley said, shaking her head. "Well, I'm going to head over to that Camp Beaverbrook and see if I can talk to someone there. Wanna join?"

Sam looked out at the black road surrounded by still wheat. There was no wind today making it eerily silent. Perhaps a day of silence for the little girl that was forever asleep on a bed of moss.

"No, you go ahead. I've got to notify Weatherford, volunteers, and the local media. Make sure this town stays intact while we find this sick bastard." Sam uncrossed his arms and walked to his vehicle. "Let me know if you find anything."

Kimberley, although surprised by Sam's decision, also understood. It wasn't like him to say no to any aspect of an investigation. He was always involved every step of the way, doing whatever he needed to do to get the job done. Sam was the type of man that would never ask anyone else to do something he wouldn't do himself. But today was different.

"I will," Kimberley said, giving him a tight smile.

CHAPTER FIFTEEN

It was an hour later that Kimberley pulled her SUV into a long gravel driveway. The wooden sign just off to the side of it read 'Camp Beaverbrook.' The gravel driveway wound around before taking her to a nearly empty parking lot. Only one car, an old, red Chevy Impala was parked nearest to a building with a Camp Counselors' Office sign right out in front. Kimberley pushed her aviators on top of her head, scanning the area around the office. It looked like a typical summer camp with a couple rows of cabins, a dining hall, a campfire pit, and a few sheds. She knocked on the office door once before pulling open the screen door. Inside were a few desks in an open space, a door to a restroom and another door that appeared to go to an office.

"Hello," Kimberley called out. "Sheriff's Office."

Kimberley slowly walked past the desks toward the closed office door. Someone had to have been here. She knew summer camp had ended, or at least that's what the website had said. But with the car outside and the place unlocked, someone was here. She took another few steps. There was no sound coming from the closed door. A restroom was just up off to the left. Just as she was about to pass it, the door of the restroom swung open, startling Kimberley and the woman. The woman screamed.

"Sorry," Kimberley said. "I'm Chief Deputy King from the Custer County Sheriff's Office," she explained even though her uniform told the woman that quicker than Kimberley did.

"No, I'm sorry. I didn't hear you come in." She rubbed her face and came all the way out of the restroom. The woman was young, maybe eighteen, with hazel eyes and long, golden blonde hair that was tied up in a high ponytail. She was fit and tanned, wearing jean shorts and a green top that read 'Camp Beaverbrook: Your best summer yet.' "I'm Chloe," she added. "I'm a camp counselor here. We're closed, but I'm just here taking care of the rest of the seasonal shutdown."

"Have you worked here all summer?" Kimberley asked.

"Every one since I was fifteen," Chloe said proudly.

"I wanted to ask you about one of your camp attendees. She would have stayed here earlier in the summer at one of your one-week camps. Piper Chase."

Chloe furrowed her brow. "Yes, I think I remember her. Hold on." She walked back out to the open area with the three desks and pulled open a filing cabinet. Kimberley followed standing behind her. Thumbing through the files, she slid one out. "Let me see." She opened it up revealing several filled-out forms and a picture paperclipped to the top. It was a picture of Piper, taken outside, smiling widely at the camera wearing a Camp Beaverbrook T-shirt just like the one Chloe had on. Her cheeks and nose were rosy from the sun.

"Yes, I do remember her. We get a lot of kids, and she was just a one-weeker, but I remember." Chloe closed up the folder and looked at Kimberley.

"What's all in there?" Kimberley motioned to the folder.

"We have one for every camper. Medical forms. Emergency contacts. Any food or allergy information. If they misbehave or break any of the rules, we document it. Any reports or incidents. And then, of course, we take their picture when they arrive, in case, God forbid, they go missing." Chloe smiled awkwardly. "It's only happened once under my watch, and we found her quickly."

"Can I take a look at that?" Kimberley asked.

"Oh yes, of course." Chloe handed the folder over.

Kimberley scanned the contents of it. No reports or incidents. No documentation on any sort of bad behavior. Just a photo and the necessary paperwork to attend the camp.

"Did Piper have any friends at camp?" Kimberley closed up the folder and looked at Chloe.

Chloe tilted her head, giving a puzzled look. "You said did… Did something happen to Piper?"

Kimberley kicked herself for making that mistake. She didn't want to deliver this sort of news twice today. But the town would find out soon and since Arthur and Edna were notified, she could tell Chloe.

"Yes. Unfortunately… we found her body this morning."

Chloe gasped throwing her hands over her mouth. She shook her head as a couple of small tears fell from the corners of her eyes. "That's awful. What happened?" She could barely get the words out.

"She was murdered, so I'm going to need you to focus and think back to the week Piper was here at summer camp. Can you tell me about any friends she made? I don't see any incidents in this folder, so I assume she didn't make any trouble."

Chloe took a few steps back sitting into a desk chair, her legs practically giving out beneath her. "Yes, yes, of course. Anything I can do to help." She nodded several times. "No, Piper was very well behaved. I'm the main girls' counselor, and I didn't have any issues with her. Oh, she loved smores. She'd always ask for an extra one, and I gave it to her. She loved kayaking out on the pond and even though we have the cabins, she was always up for spending a night in a tent. It's one of the activities we do here, have the girls set up their own tents and sleep in them one night." Chloe smiled fondly.

"What about friends? Did Piper have any?" Kimberley tilted her head trying to get Chloe to focus.

She blinked a few times and looked up at Kimberley. "Oh yes. Miley Baker. They shared a bunk together. They were two peas in a pod, attached at the hip as soon as they met that week. They were very different from one another, though. Miley was much more outgoing than Piper. Piper was shy. Seemed a bit sheltered, like she wasn't sure of herself. But regardless they were very close."

Kimberley nodded. "Anyone else Piper was close to?"

Chloe shook her head. "Not that I can remember. It was just Piper and Miley."

"Is that odd? How many camp attendees do you usually get?" Kimberley tilted her head.

"Not really. Kids clique up quick, especially since a lot of our activities require a partner. Like kayaking and the tent set-up and sleepover. We're capped at twenty-four attendees for the one-week summer camps."

Kimberley nodded, accepting that answer. It made sense. It was only a one-week camp, and the partnered activities almost required Piper to make a friend. And from what she heard from Arthur and Edna, Piper didn't have an easy time opening up and making friends.

Realizing Chloe didn't have any valuable information, Kimberley handed back the folder. She pulled a card from her utility belt and handed it over as well.

"Thank you for your time, Chloe. If you think of anything else, please let me know."

Chloe looked at the card and stood from her seat. "Of course, I will."

Kimberley left the camp with nothing more than what she had already known. It was after four and she had an hour drive home. Her mom was picking up Jessica today so she didn't have to worry about being late for that. She pulled out her phone and dialed Sam. He answered on the third ring.

"King," he said.

She could hear music in the background. The slamming of balls on a pool table. The sound of loud voices and gambling machines. She knew where Sam was. The Trophy Room.

"Find anything?" he asked.

"No. It was a dead end."

"Damn," he huffed.

"Where are you?" Kimberley asked.

"My office," he lied.

Kimberley rolled her eyes. "Since when did we get a pool table and a jukebox at the station?"

"You really are a detective," he said sarcastically.

"I'll be there in an hour." Kimberley said, ending the call.

CHAPTER SIXTEEN

Kimberley walked across the gravel parking lot of The Trophy Room. The sun was falling once again, signaling the end of another day, and she felt like she had nothing to show for it. She hoped the pathology results tomorrow would give them more to go on. She had heard on her way over from her mother that the town had come together and put up a reward of ten thousand dollars for information that would lead to the arrest of the person responsible for Piper Chase's death. Kimberley hoped that would help too. But she knew rewards a lot of times lead to a bunch of bullshit tips. People treating it like the lottery. She nodded at the men smoking cigars sitting on the picnic tables off to the side of the entrance. They all nodded back, giving tight smiles. A year ago, when she arrived in Dead Woman Crossing, they would have just stared, not acknowledging her in the slightest, but now she was practically one of them, an Oklahoman. Kimberley wasn't sure if she was proud of that or not. Their solemn glances made it clear that they had heard of Piper Chase. In a small town, news traveled fast, bad news even faster.

Pulling open the door, a hundred eyes greeted her, most of them black and lifeless. The heads of deer, hogs, antelopes, and bobcats adorned the walls spread out all over, no rhyme or reason to their placement. The same went for the taxidermy birds perched up on branches. Hawks, pheasants, and quail frozen forever, looking down at the patrons. The bar was busy with several men playing pool at the tables off to the right and older men bellied up to the bar and slot machines. Thick cigarette smoke created a fog over the bar. Kimberley coughed. She'd never get used to it. Kimberley scanned the room finding Sam sitting at a booth by himself, sipping on a glass of scotch. She didn't think it was a good look for the sheriff of the town to be kicking back drinks at the local watering hole with a killer out on the loose. Even if he had already worked the past twenty-four hours. Kimberley knew he hadn't slept the night before, probably spent the night mulling over the case files, and then was up and searching before the sun even rose. The townies didn't seem to mind his presence. She watched several walk over and pat him on the back, bending down whispering something to him. Another brought him a refill of his drink. They understood what Sam had been through. But still, Kimberley decided she'd have one drink with him and then get him home.

Before walking over to Sam, she ordered a scotch on the rocks from Ryan. Last year, when she arrived, she found the greasy bartender to be a sleazeball, but now she found him to be pathetic. He didn't give her shit this time, simply told her it was on the house, shooting her a look of understanding. His father, Jerry, the owner of The Trophy Room, sat at a stool just behind him, giving Kimberley a nod. He looked like Ryan would look in thirty years, potbellied and bald. Kimberley threw down five dollars and made her way to Sam.

She slid into the booth across from him, taking a sip of her scotch, her eyes peering over the glass, taking in Sheriff Walker. His eyes gave an inward gaze with lips pressed slightly and eyebrows pulled close together.

"Hey," Kimberley said, but he responded with a slow nod rather than speaking. She assumed he was too tired, too somber, too broken.

His mood was bleak, and Kimberley didn't expect anything else. She sat in silence with him. Perhaps just the presence of another person was what he needed right now or dozens, she thought, scanning the bar. You could be surrounded by people and still feel so alone in this world. She knew it better than anyone else.

"Tell me about the camp," Sam finally said, clearing the silence between them.

"Run-of-the-mill summer camp. Talked to Chloe the camp counselor. She remembered Piper and reiterated that Miley was her only friend. Two peas in a pod. I can't imagine how she's feeling right now, losing her best friend." Kimberley took a sip of her scotch. She enjoyed the burn of it, but today she didn't feel it at all. It went down like a glass of lukewarm water.

Sam let out a deep sigh before taking another drink. "Tip line is up and running. I've got Burns and Hill fielding any calls that come in."

Kimberley nodded. "Anything on the pink bicycle?"

Sam shook his head. "I've got night shift scanning front yards, open garages, parks, anything within five miles of where we found her. We had Weatherford and part of our team search the rest of the woods and didn't find anything."

"Shit. We've really got nothing." Kimberley shook her head, bringing the glass up to her lips again.

"Jackshit."

"What's the plan then?"

"Wait on Megan's pathology report. Hopefully, we get something to go on there. Pray someone calls in with a tip, that someone saw something." Sam shrugged his shoulders.

"Think this could have been random?"

"It usually never is, but it's not out of the realm of possibilities."

"I'm thinking we should pull missing children reports in a one-hundred-mile radius. See if there's a pattern. And criminal records in the area," Kimberley said. It might be nothing, just busy work, but it was better to have something to do in these types of cases, rather than just sit around and wait.

"Yeah. Good thinking. I'll put Bearfield and Lodge on it in the morning. See what they can find. Maybe you're right. Maybe whoever did this didn't know Piper. Perhaps she was just in the wrong place at the wrong time." Sam drained the rest of his drink and just as he was putting his hand up to signal to the bartender that he wanted another, Kimberley grabbed it.

"Let's get you home," she said.

"Is that an order?" Sam raised an eyebrow. He was on the verge of teasing playfully and anger, the line between buzzed and drunk.

"It's a request, sir," Kimberley said with a soft smile. "I'll take you home."

Sam gave a challenging look back, hesitating for a moment. His face relaxed and the corners of his lips turned upward. "Alright, King. I accept your request," he said, standing from the booth. Kimberley left her half empty drink on the table and followed Sam through the bar.

CHAPTER SEVENTEEN

Kimberley had gotten the call from Sam bright and early that the preliminary autopsy results were in. She pulled her SUV in front of Sam's home and honked once. Immediately, the front door opened and out walked Sam. He looked different from the day before, well rested, bright eyed, like he was ready to take on the world. Sam carried two Thermos, one in each hand. He gave Kimberley a smile as he walked in front of the vehicle. Kimberley leaned over the middle console to push open the door for him.

"Made you a coffee," he said, handing the Thermos over.

Kimberley took it from him. "Thanks, you didn't have to do that."

"Didn't have to. Wanted to," Sam said, hopping onto the seat and closing the door.

"Well, thanks," Kimberley said, taking a sip and then putting the car in reverse.

"I hope Megan's got something for us. Bearfield and Lodge are working on pulling those reports we talked about last night, and, so far, we've got nothing valuable from the tip line," he said as Kimberley put the car in drive and headed toward the medical examiner's office.

The inside of the medical examiner's office was just how Kimberley remembered it. It had been a year since she had been there, the last time there had been a murder in Custer County. It was nearly all white, sterile, and unwelcoming. A place created for the dead. They were greeted at the front by Megan dressed in a white doctor's coat.

"Hope you got something for us," Sam said.

Megan gave a slight nod. "Follow me."

That wasn't a good sign, Kimberley thought. They followed her down the long, brightly lit corridor. Megan took a sharp left into the medical examining room at the end of the hallway. Inside, Piper Chase's body lay on the embalming table. A white sheet covered her from the chest down, leaving just her arms and shoulders exposed. She looked so small on the table that was big enough to hold a full-grown man. Part of her head had been shaved, so the wound on her head was fully exposed. They could finally see the damage that had been done, what had caused her to take her final breath. The flesh had been pulled back even further and a portion of her skull had been removed. Kimberley wanted so badly to put the little girl back together. Sam sighed deeply, rubbing the back of his neck. This wasn't easy for any of them, Megan included. Kimberley could see it on her face. As professional as she was trying to be, she could see that this one got to her. Her eyes were red-rimmed, her skin not as vibrant. Megan too had lost sleep over this little girl's death.

"I performed a sexual assault forensic exam. Piper Chase was not sexually abused," Megan said.

There was a collective sigh of relief.

"Good," Sam said, running a hand over his face.

"I removed a portion of the skull," Megan pointed to the head, "to determine cause of death. The head trauma caused swelling in her brain."

"Was she hit with something?" Kimberley asked.

"Based on the injury, that's a possibility. She could have fallen or been pushed and hit her head as well."

Megan grabbed a clipboard from the table beside the body and flipped through her report quickly. "I've narrowed the window of time of death down to sometime between seven p.m. and nine p.m. Unfortunately, I wasn't able to pick up any fingerprints or foreign fibers. I've taken swabs of her hands and the top of her head to see if we can pull different strands of DNA. If we find any, we'll have them sent out for further testing."

"Did your team find anything else at the crime scene?" Sam took a step closer toward the body. He looked down at her, closing his eyes tight for a moment.

"No, because that was definitely just the dumping area, not the scene of the crime. After doing another sweep yesterday, we found nothing."

"Shit," Kimberley said. "So, no fingerprints, no witnesses, no foreign fibers, no suspects, and no crime scene."

"We might get DNA. But I wouldn't hold my breath. Since the body was clearly moved and the killer ensured they left nothing behind, I'd assume they wore gloves when they were handling the body, and the body was freshly cleaned." Megan gave a solemn look. It appeared she was disappointed in her findings too.

Kimberley furrowed her brow. "Like bleach?"

"No, like with soap and water."

"How can you tell that?" Sam gave a quizzical look.

"I found some dried soap suds around the right knee," Megan explained.

"Odd," Kimberley said.

"Very odd."

"What about sweat? From carrying the body?" Sam looked over at Megan.

"Maybe, but I doubt it. Piper weighed sixty-five pounds, on the smaller side for a ten-year-old girl. It wouldn't take much effort for a full-grown man to carry her," Megan said. "There was a lot of care in regard to the handling of the body."

"What do you mean?" Sam raised an eyebrow.

The image of Piper Chase lying in the soft moss flashed before Kimberley's eyes. "Megan's right. She wasn't dumped. The killer laid her down on her back in a clearing of the woods on a patch of moss. Her hair was positioned to cover the wound, almost as if they couldn't stand to see it. She looked peaceful, like she had just lain down for a nap in the forest," Kimberley said.

"Exactly." Megan nodded.

"So, you're saying the killer knew Piper since they cared how she was presented?" Sam folded his lips.

"Maybe, or maybe it tells us more about the killer's M.O."

"Think we're dealing with some sort of serial killer here?" Sam looked to Kimberley and Megan.

Kimberley didn't want to go down that road. They had one body, and nothing here said the killer would kill again. "I wouldn't go that far. But the way the body was preserved and presented is something we should keep in mind. Maybe they knew Piper. Maybe not."

Sam nodded. "Anything else?"

"I'll have the final report to you within forty-eight hours," Megan said.

"Alright, let us know as soon as you know more on potential DNA evidence." Kimberley turned toward the door.

"You got it. I'll be in touch." Megan walked back over to the body, looking down on it.

"Thanks, Megan," Sam and Kimberley called over their shoulder as they exited the medical examining room.

Back at the Custer County's Sheriff Office, Sam and Kimberley were greeted by Barb sitting at the front desk knitting what looked to be the start of a pink blanket.

"There you two are," she said, standing from her seat. "I've got the burn room set up." Barb smiled.

Kimberley smiled back. The last time they investigated a murder, Kimberley had taught the team what a burn room was, something back from her NYPD days. It was the mission control center for the investigation; everything you got on a case was in that room, which right now wasn't much. You set up the burn room to ensure a case didn't run cold. It was more wishful thinking than anything else, but it brought the team working on a case together in close proximity.

"You remembered?" Kimberley arched an eyebrow.

"Of course. This baby…" Barb pointed to her head. "Is a steel trap. Lodge and Bearfield are in there. Burns and Hill are out patrolling as well as looking for the missing pink bicycle. I've got a carafe of coffee and homemade apple pie set up in the burn room. I figured we could all use a piece of pie today," she said with a frown.

"Whatcha knitting over there?" Sam asked.

"Oh, a blanket for the Chases. Thought it would go nicely with some of the homemade baked goods I'm dropping off after work. Poor Edna and Arthur." Barb shook her head. "I can't imagine what they must be feeling."

"You know Arthur and Edna, Barb?" Kimberley tilted her head.

"Not well. We've been going to the same church for years and years, but they kept to themselves."

"What about Piper?" Kimberley asked.

"She was a sweet girl, real quiet. She usually sat between them at Sunday church service." Barb's voice cracked. "Can't imagine what they're going through right now."

Kimberley patted Barb on the back to comfort her. She composed herself and wiped at her eye.

"Well, you two get in there. I know where to find you," Barb said, shooing them away.

Sam and Kimberley nodded.

Lodge sat at the far end of the conference room table eating a piece of apple pie as if he were on break. A corded telephone was on the table in front of him. Bearfield was on the other corded phone taking a call and jotting down notes.

Kimberley and Sam sat at the other end of the table where their laptops had already been set up, most likely by Barb. They were quiet until Bearfield put the phone down on the receiver. He looked up at them flipping through a pad of notes.

"Anything?" Sam asked.

"Nothing useful. Had a couple of people call in and say they found the bicycle. But Hill and Burns went and checked them out and it wasn't the one we're looking for," Bearfield said. His eyes were dark with anger and sadness and his long black hair wasn't shiny and kempt like usual. It was dry and knotted as if he hadn't taken care of himself in a couple of days.

Lodge on the other hand appeared unphased, stuffing forks full of Barb's apple pie in his mouth. His nose was still crooked and his face still smug.

"What about you, Lodge?" Kimberley narrowed her eyes.

"Same as Bearfield. A bunch of dead ends." He shrugged his shoulders, stuffing another chunk in his mouth.

"And the reports?" Sam clenched his jaw.

"Still working on them."

Sam slammed his fist against the table. "I need you working on them now, not stuffing your face with goddamn apple pie."

Lodge jumped, leaning forward in his seat. He set the plate aside and pulled his computer in front of him, burying his head behind it. "I'm on it," he said meekly behind the screen.

Sam took a deep breath, shaking out his hand. It wasn't like him to jump to anger so quickly. Kimberley stood from her seat and walked to the whiteboard. She picked up a dry erase marker and wrote Piper in all caps in the center of the board. She wrote 'Miley and Linda' and extended a line to it. She wrote 'Chloe' and extended a line to it. Before she could write another name, her cell phone rang. Kimberley quickly capped the marker and answered.

"Chief Deputy King."

"Hi, my name is Mary, and I have some information on the Piper Chase case," a woman's voice said on the other end of the line.

Kimberley's eyes widened and she looked at Sam, motioning for pen and paper. He quickly handed them over as she took a seat in the chair beside him. "Go on."

"I'm Arthur and Edna's neighbor. I live right across the street from them." The woman's accent was deeply southern.

Kimberley instantly remembered the two-story yellow house. She recalled looking at it and wondering what they had seen or if they had seen anything. She also remembered telling Lodge to go and interview whoever lived there. Kimberley narrowed her eyes at him, while listening to Mary.

"I didn't think anything of it until I heard the news of Piper's passing. But on the day she disappeared, there was a strange car in the Chases' driveway. They don't get much company, which is why I say it's strange."

"What kind of car was it?" Kimberley asked, jotting down notes.

Sam gave Kimberley a strained look like he couldn't wait to hear what was being said on the other end of the line. Lodge typed away at his computer attempting to finish the reports that should have been completed already, and Bearfield leaned forward in his seat, trying to listen.

"I'm not too good with types of cars."

Kimberley sighed, thinking this was a real quick dead end.

"But I did write down the plate number. I'm much better with those."

Kimberley gave a sly smile. Thank God for nosy neighbors. It might be nothing, but it also might be something. Especially since Arthur and Edna failed to mention there was anyone else at the house that day.

"License plate was 236-LMN. It was a Texas plate too." Mary had a tinge of pride in her voice.

"Thank you, Mary. Anything else?"

"Oh yes, that wasn't the strangest part. I saw a man come out of the house. He was an older gentleman. Never saw him before… but he come out of the house and Arthur did too. And they were arguing with each other, yelling and screaming. Real ruckus," Mary said.

Kimberley could almost see her wagging her finger in shame.

"Did you hear what they were arguing about?"

"No, by the time I came out to my porch to try to hear what they were saying, the man got into his car in a fury and sped off like a bat out of hell. My hearing's not too good anyway. Thank goodness my eyesight's still sharp though," Mary said. "But I figured I'd better call and tell ya in case it was important. Piper was a good girl. She always waved at me when I was on the porch. She was a quiet one, but she waved and smiled whenever she saw me."

"Do you know what time this man was at the Chases' house?"

"It was sometime in the afternoon. Had to have been there for at least an hour," Mary said.

"Anything else you can remember?"

"Not off the top of my head, but if I do, I'll call. I hope you catch that son of a bitch."

"Thanks for calling, Mary. You've been very helpful. And we will," Kimberley said, ending the call.

She immediately pulled her laptop in front of her going into the police database.

"What is it?" Sam asked.

Kimberley typed the license plate number in and waited for a record to populate. Bingo. There it was. The car belonged to Benjamin Fry.

"Well?" Sam asked again.

"Mary the neighbor called." Kimberley glanced over at Lodge. "Lodge, you were supposed to go and talk to whoever lived there." Her voice was firm.

Lodge rubbed his forehead. "Oh yeah. I did, but no one was home."

Sam's face turned red. "First the reports and then not following up with a potential witness. You're on thin fucking ice, Lodge."

"Sorry, sir. It won't happen again." He practically hid behind his computer.

Kimberley shook her head. To her, he wasn't even on ice. He was useless and unfit to even call himself a member of the Custer County Sheriff's Office.

Sam took a deep breath and redirected his attention back to Kimberley. "So, what did Mary have to say?"

"Apparently, the Chases' had a guest the day Piper went missing. Benjamin Fry was there earlier in the day and she witnessed him and Arthur arguing before he sped off," Kimberley explained.

"Who is Benjamin Fry?" Bearfield asked.

"Edna's brother."

"Bearfield, expedite a background check on him," Sam commanded.

"On it." He hopped from his seat and left the office.

"I think we should go have a talk with Edna and Arthur," Kimberley said, looking over at Sam.

"I think so too. This is something they should have mentioned to us." Sam rose from his chair. "Lodge, I want that report before lunch. Otherwise, I'm putting you on suspension."

Lodge grumbled but continued plugging away. Sam was clearly done tiptoeing around Lodge and his behavior.

CHAPTER EIGHTEEN

"Hello, Sheriff Walker. Chief Deputy King," Arthur greeted, holding the door partially open. He was dressed in the same clothes from the day before and didn't look as though he had slept a wink. He glanced at Sam and then Kimberley. "Did you find them? The person who murdered our granddaughter?"

Kimberley hesitated, looking at the old man. Why hadn't he told them about Edna's brother? Why didn't he mention they had had a visitor the afternoon Piper went missing? It wasn't something that should have just slipped his mind… especially with what Mary, their neighbor had said. Arthur and Benjamin had had a disagreement. They had fought. Benjamin had stormed off. That wasn't something you just forgot.

"No, we're here to have a look around, and we have a few more questions to ask," Kimberley said, cutting it right back to business.

Arthur gave a slight nod, but didn't move out of the way nor invite them in. "But we've told you everything we know, and your men ransacked this place just the other day." He scratched at the back of his head.

"We know. But we do have some follow-up questions, and we'd like to take a second look around." Sam raised his chin.

Arthur hesitated, but finally opened the door up for them to come in. "Alright, Edna is in the kitchen with Miley. Come on in."

Kimberley shot Sam a peculiar look, which he returned. Why would Miley be here? Especially on her own? From Kimberley's understanding, the Chases didn't know Miley all that well.

Sam and Kimberley followed Arthur's lead through the living room and into the kitchen. It was outdated with wood-colored cabinets and a lime green backsplash. In the far corner was a round table big enough for four people. Edna and Miley were seated there, with Edna drinking tea and Miley having milk and cookies. Her color had come back from the last time Kimberley had seen her. Her long black hair was clean, not greasy like it had been before.

"Edna," Arthur said, getting their attention. "Company."

Edna looked up to find Sam and Kimberley walking in behind Arthur. Miley sat with her back toward them eating a cookie.

"I really miss Piper," Miley said. "We had so much fun together."

"I know, sweetheart. I miss her too. She was lucky to have you as a friend."

"Edna," Sam said.

Miley turned back. Her hazel eyes were wide. She set her half-eaten cookie down on the paper towel and stood up from her chair.

"I actually have to get going," she said just about a whisper.

Edna nodded and stood up, hugging the little girl. Sam and Kimberley exchanged another look. They were on the same page. This was odd behavior. Then again, she just lost her best friend, and she's just a little girl. Kimberley tried to put herself in Miley's shoes, but couldn't seem to. Was this normal? Miley took a step back and smiled at Edna. She gave a brief glance at Sam and Kimberley just as she was leaving the kitchen. Kimberley smiled at her, but it wasn't returned.

"Any news?" Edna picked up the half-eaten cookie, paper and empty glass, bringing it to the garbage and then the sink.

"Yes, the pathology results are in," Kimberley said. She thought it was important for the Chases to know that from what they could tell, Piper did not suffer. Somehow, that helped the living to know their loved ones didn't suffer in death.

"And?" Arthur asked.

"Piper was not sexually abused. The cause of death was blunt force trauma to the head."

"With what?"

"We're not sure," Kimberley said.

"Where did this happen?" Arthur cut in.

Kimberley looked to Sam. They didn't have any answers.

"We're not sure. We do know it didn't happen where we found her in the woods as her body was moved."

"Who would do this?" Edna shook her head.

Before Kimberley could answer, Arthur interjected. "Did she suffer?" His voice shook.

Finally, Kimberley had an answer to one of their questions. "No, her death was quick and painless." Kimberley could see the relief on each of their faces. She had felt the same way when Megan told her and Sam.

Edna walked to the kitchen table and sat down again. She wiped her eyes with her pointer fingers and took a sip of her tea, washing down the information she had just received. Arthur sat down next to her and held her hand in his.

"That's good. That's good," she said.

"We do have a few questions for you both that should help in the investigation." Sam readjusted his stance.

"Whatever we can do to help," Arthur said with a nod.

Edna set her cup of tea down. There was a stack of photos in front of her, each of them of Piper. She flipped through them slowly, running her fingers down each picture. Her eyes were glossy, but no tears fell. Perhaps, she had cried them all out already. Edna seemed to be in a sort of daze.

"From my understanding, you two didn't know Miley all that well. Is that true?" Kimberley asked glancing between Arthur and Edna. Edna snapped out of her daze, setting the photos down in front of her. She pulled her eyes from them to look at Kimberley.

"Well, yes. I found a letter and some drawings in the mailbox yesterday and saw they were hand delivered from Miley. It was very sweet of her. So, I called her up and invited her over today for cookies and milk. I think she just needs a friend, now that Piper…" Edna frowned and didn't finish her sentence.

"What did you two talk about?" Kimberley asked.

"Piper, of course. She told me about their time at camp. The two of them were the fastest to set up their tent out of everyone. But Miley said it was because of Piper. She was a whiz at reading the instructions and putting it together." Edna smiled proudly. "Piper was whip smart. And Miley said they were the fastest kayakers too. And then she told me about all the fun they had this summer. Riding bikes. Playing hide and seek in the woods. They also loved watching old Disney shows during their sleepovers. We don't have cable, so I didn't even know that Piper loved *Lizzie McGuire*. Didn't even know what that was." Edna frowned. "She brought over some more of her little stories and drawings too. It's so nice to have more memories and reminders of Piper." She wiped her eyes.

"Can we have a look at the letters and drawings?" Kimberley asked.

"Yes, of course." Edna rose slowly from her seat, disappearing out of the kitchen.

Perhaps the letters and drawings contained a clue as to what happened to Piper. Maybe she had drawn pictures of her and Piper and a third person. At camp? At Black Heart Lane? Kimberley wasn't sure, but it could be something. When it came to police investigations, the littlest things could turn out to be what solved the whole damn case.

Edna emerged back into the kitchen carrying several envelopes. She handed them to Kimberley and immediately took her seat again. Kimberley quickly thumbed through them. The drawings were of Miley and Piper riding their bikes, swimming at summer camp, playing in the woods, and kayaking. She unfolded the letters that were more like little stories, detailing Miley and Piper's friendship. There was a story about the fun times two little girls had riding their bikes over on Black Heart Lane, building forts and playing hide and seek in the woods. Piper was a very good hider, Miley noted. Even in death, she was too, Kimberley thought. The rest of the stories were about their week at camp. There were many mentions of Chloe, of how nice and fun and pretty she was, like a cool, big sister for Piper and Miley. Miley described Piper as her sister, too, calling her her long-lost twin. Kimberley felt a strong pang for the little girl that lost her friend. The last story described a man named Will. He used to talk to Miley and Piper at camp. He was friendly and kind, another one of their camp counselors.

Will was the nicest camp counselor of them all at Camp Beaverbrook. He was friendly and kind and would always talk to us, well mostly me. Piper was quiet, so sometimes I talked for the both of us. The day Piper and I put together our tent in the fastest time, we got to sleep overnight in it, just the two of us. We stayed up nearly all night talking, and I told Piper I had a crush on Will and that I was going to marry him. She stuck her tongue out and said boys were gross. I told her one day she would feel different about boys because I used to think they were gross too. She said she would always think boys were gross, even her husband. It was so funny. We laughed so loud, we got in trouble because it was lights out.

Kimberley bit at her lip and handed the papers over to Sam, so he could have a look. Chloe never mentioned there was another camp counselor the girls had contact with. She had described herself as the main counselor. Kimberley made a mental note to re-interview Chloe and find out more about Will.

"They're sweet, aren't they?" Edna asked. Her eyes were a little misty, and she quickly wiped them.

"They are," Kimberley said with a nod.

Sam finished looking through them and handed them back to Edna.

"We received information that you had a visitor the day of Piper's disappearance. Do you want to tell us about that?" Sam crossed his arms in front of his chest.

Arthur and Edna exchanged a worried glance. Edna dropped her head in her hands, stricken with guilt. "I'm so sorry. It completely slipped my mind," she said. "Yes, my brother Benjamin dropped by unexpectedly." She picked her head back up, looking at Kimberley and then at Sam like she was waiting for a 'we forgive you' but their faces were impassive.

"From what we've heard, there was an argument of some sorts. Benjamin peeled off in his vehicle. Doesn't sound like something that would just slip your mind." Sam raised an eyebrow.

"I honestly just didn't think it was relevant that Edna's brother was here." Arthur's voice was rattled as if he wasn't confident in what he was saying either.

"That's for us to decide," Sam challenged.

"Okay. Well, yes. You're correct, Benjamin did show up here. Unexpectedly. He came here asking for money," Arthur explained.

"Is that normal behavior for him?" Kimberley asked.

"No, not at all. We hadn't seen him in years. Caught us by surprise." Edna was on the verge of another breakdown. Her voice cracked, and she spoke too quickly.

"What did he need the money for?" Sam unfolded his arms.

Edna glanced over at Arthur and then back at Kimberley and Sam, almost as though she was ashamed. "He told us he lost his job as a senior council official. He had no money. His landlord threw him out. He was just miserable."

"Did he tell you why he lost his job?" Sam asked.

Edna shook her head.

"But you gave him money?" Kimberley tilted her head.

Edna looked down at her hands for a moment. "Yes. I gave him some. He is my brother. Of course, I wanted to help him."

"I've never liked the guy." Arthur turned up his nose.

The comment took Kimberley and Sam by surprise. "Why's that?" they asked in unison.

"Don't trust him. Always seemed a bit shady to me. It's why he's not in our life. I shooed him off the property, told him to never come back again." Arthur shot Edna a glance of irritation. They clearly had not agreed on giving Benjamin money.

"Shady?" Kimberley questioned. "What do you mean by that?"

"Never been married. Never had kids. Kind of a loner. He only turns up when he needs money. Seems shady to me, or at the very least odd. You think he had something to do with Piper's death?" Arthur scowled.

"No, Arthur. He would never," Edna cried. "He's my brother. He wouldn't hurt Piper."

"Never say never," he said, biting his lip and folding his arms in front of his chest.

Kimberley found the timing of Benjamin's visit and Piper's death to be too much of a coincidence not to look into it further. She glanced over at Sam. He gave her a slow nod. He was thinking the same thing. Benjamin Fry was a person of interest.

CHAPTER NINETEEN

I missed you when you were gone, more so than I thought I would. But you were never mine to begin with, were you, Piper? I hoped now that you were found and your family had closure, it would all go away. How naïve of me. They wanted more. Everyone always wants more. They wanted to know what happened to you. They wanted to know who could have done this. They wanted the person responsible… and I guess, in a way, I was that person. But you were the one that didn't listen. You were the one that was difficult. So, they already found the person responsible. It was you. You did this to yourself. I thought if I cleaned you, placed you thoughtfully in the woods where they'd find you right away, and burned everything else connecting you to me, that I would be free of it. Life just isn't that easy. You wouldn't know that though, Piper. If anything, I saved you from enduring a long and difficult life. No need to thank me. As I was saying, I thought I would be free of it all, but I had another problem to worry about…

CHAPTER TWENTY

Kimberley parked her car in front of Happy Trails Daycare. She was finally on time to pick up Jessica, which made her feel somewhat accomplished. At work, she felt like she was failing. The person responsible for killing Piper was still out there, and the case would consume her until it was solved, like a snake slowly digesting its prey, a bulge of guilt lodging in her throat. Her mind kept going back to Benjamin Fry. It was too convenient that he had been in town the day Piper was murdered. And he had had a disagreement with Arthur hours before the little girl was last seen. Bearfield was running a thorough background check on Benjamin, and she hoped they'd have something to go on in the morning. She also hoped the night shift would miraculously stumble upon the pink bicycle sitting in the murderer's open garage. But that was just wishful thinking.

Kimberley got out of the vehicle and made her way to the front door. She was excited to see her little girl, to hold her, to plant dozens of kisses on her, and to tell her 'no' over and over again all night as she inevitably tried to get into anything and everything. Pushing open the door, a man on the other side of it was immediately in front of her and she was startled before she recognized who it was. Caleb. The man from the other day. He held the hand of his little boy. Flynn, Kimberley remembered.

"Sorry," Kimberley said with a smile.

Caleb held the door. "They really need to put a window on this thing. It's a hazard for us." He delivered a smile back.

Kimberley noticed he had shaved, the salt and peppered hair gone from his face, revealing smooth, tan skin. She hadn't noticed his eyes before, but today she did. They were a forest-green, the type of green that draws you in. Earthy and familiar. An open invitation that she was strongly considering accepting. She glanced down at Flynn. He rubbed his sleepy, blue eyes with one hand. His blond hair stood up in all different directions. He had clearly had a long day at daycare.

"You're right. I'm always running into people because of this thing," Kimberley said. As soon as she said it, she felt a pang in her stomach, remembering the first person she had run into just the year before. Hannah Brown. Who was now dead.

Kimberley swallowed hard, looking at Flynn and then Caleb, hoping this door wasn't cursed. Would Caleb and Flynn face a similar fate? Stop, she told herself. Her work was getting to her.

"Maybe next time, we should run into each other on purpose," Caleb said with a half-smile.

Kimberley closed her parted mouth and inhaled through her nose. There it was again… that scent. Cinnamon and sawdust. It was familiar, familiar before she smelt it on him. Was he flirting with her? She couldn't tell. Couldn't really remember what it was like to flirt with or be flirted with by another man. She hadn't dated in years, not since Aaron walked out of her and Jessica's life when Jessica was just a week old. Was this flirting?

"Like a date?" She raised an eyebrow. Was she flirting back? Or was she interrogating him? Kimberley wasn't sure.

Caleb stammered, looking down at his son and then at Kimberley.

"Umm…"

That solidified it. She was interrogating him, hazard of the job. She tried to soften her face and eyes and turn the corners of her mouth upward.

"Or a playdate for the kiddos," he added.

"Oh, yeah. That'd be nice," Kimberley said. "I think Jessica would love that."

Suddenly, it hit her. Oh, Jessica. She needed to pick her up. "Well, I better go get her before I get reprimanded by Margaret again."

Caleb let out a small chuckle. "Yeah, don't want that happening." He reached into the back pocket of his jeans and pulled out his cell phone. "Here," he said, handing it to her. "Can I get your number then? So, we can set up a playdate sometime?"

Kimberley hesitated for a moment, immediately feeling uneasy. She hadn't handed her number out to a man she wasn't co-workers with in over four years. She looked at the flip phone and then back at Caleb. A flip phone. How odd, she thought. But Caleb seemed like a simple man. Perhaps the flip phone was a way for him to hold onto a simpler time before apps and social media consumed every waking moment. Should she give him her number? Or just say, if it's meant to be, we'll run into each other again. No, that would be weird and rude. Her hand reached for the phone and her fingers tapped on the keys before her mind knew what she was doing. She was giving her number to a man, a good-looking man at that. She reminded herself, he was nothing like Aaron, her ex. Aaron had left her and Jessica, while this man was raising his son alone. She wondered where Flynn's mom was. Had she run out on him too?

"Here," she said, handing the cell phone back, the faintest smile on her face.

He nodded and slid the phone in his back pocket. Bending down, he picked up Flynn and held him. Flynn's head immediately rested on his father's shoulder and his eyes shut as if on cue.

"I'll give you a call sometime then, King," Caleb said. He gave her another small smile and sidestepped around Kimberley. "Have a good night."

"You too," she said. As Kimberley walked toward the daycare room where Jessica was waiting for her, she thought perhaps it was time to focus less on her work and more on living her life. Maybe a date wasn't such a bad idea. The thought quickly faded and guilt took its place. The murder of Piper Chase was still unsolved. Life would have to wait.

Pulling into the long gravel driveway, Kimberley parked her vehicle in front of the large, white farmhouse. Several lights were on inside and she could see silhouettes of her nephews bouncing around in the windows. Emily sure had her hands full raising those boys practically on her own. She noticed her mother's car wasn't parked in the driveway or on the side of the house as she walked around the side toward the cottage with Jessica held against her chest fast asleep. It was after six, and she wondered where her mother could be. Typically, she was fixing dinner at this time. Kimberley got her keys from her utility belt and opened the door. The cottage was still and dark. She flicked on the living room light. Pillows were strewn about and there were a couple of dishes on the coffee table. It was unusual that the place wasn't tidy. That was her mother's specialty. Kimberley walked to her bedroom and gently placed Jessica in her bed, opting to let her sleep for a bit longer while she prepared dinner. It was easier to do everything when Jessica was asleep. She closed the bedroom door behind her and made her way to the kitchen. There were dishes in the sink, a coffee cup left out on the counter, and the coffee pot was partially full. Where was her mother? Kimberley pulled out her phone and sent a quick text to her mom, asking where she was. She left the phone on the counter as she tidied up and pulled out the supplies needed to make a box of Kraft mac and cheese with some cut up hotdogs. It was Jessica's favorite. She filled a pot with water and a dash of salt and placed it on the stove, turning the burner up to high. Kimberley slid out a couple of drawers, looking for a wooden spoon that she'd use to stir the noodles. She worked a lot, so her mother did the majority of the cooking and she wasn't familiar with where all the kitchen stuff was located, even after a year of living in the house. Sliding open one of the drawers, a stack of torn open envelopes caught her eye. She figured they were unpaid bills or junk mail, but the return address made her look twice.

Written in black ink were the words Oklahoma State Penitentiary.

Her fingers thumbed through them for a moment before snatching the stack. She set them on the counter, looking down at them. Kimberley knew who they were from. A queasy feeling settled in the pit of her stomach. David. David was writing her mother letters. What was he saying? What could he even say?

Kimberley grabbed the letter on the top of the stack, postdated for the week before. She slid the yellow paper from it and unfolded it. The writing was sloppy at best. Her eyes scanned over the first paragraph, taking in the words that were written by her stepfather, a cold-blooded murderer.

My Darling Nicole,

There isn't a day that goes by that I don't think of you, that I don't regret the things that I have done and the way that I have treated you. I will spend my life trying to make it up to you. Thank you for continuing to write back. It's the only thing I have to look forward to.

Kimberley immediately crumpled the piece of paper and stuffed it back into its envelope. Her mother was writing to David. How could she? Kimberley took a couple of deep breaths. The sizzling of boiling water spilling onto the stove got her attention. She immediately slid the pot onto another burner and turned off the stove.

"I'm home," Nicole's voice bellowed from the front of the house.

A second later, Jessica's cry spilled from the back bedroom. Kimberley rushed out of the kitchen, through the living room, past her mother. She couldn't even look at her.

"Sorry, I'm late. I picked up dinner on the way home. Dakota BBQ." Nicole held out a large brown paper bag.

Kimberley scooped up Jessica and held her against her chest, trying to quiet her. Her face was flushed and her cries sounded more like a banshee than a toddler waking up confused. Perhaps Jessica had had a nightmare. Right now, Kimberley felt like she was in one. Her mother had been lying to her. She had been in contact with David.

It took a few minutes to quiet her. Kimberley paced the room holding her daughter. She didn't want to speak to her mother, but Jessica had to eat. After Jessica was composed, Kimberley composed herself. Retying her long dark hair and taking a couple of small, deep breaths, she left the bedroom, walking quietly down the hall with Jessica in tow. The living room had been picked up. The pillows were fluffed and lined the couch. The coffee table had been cleared off. Her mother had gotten to work quickly. Where had she been all day? The small dining room table already had the food set out. BBQ chicken, mac and cheese, mashed potatoes, French fries, and gravy. Kimberley placed Jessica in her high chair.

"I hungee," Jessica said, bouncing her hands against the tray table, while Kimberley fastened her in.

"I know. Hold on a second," Kimberley said. She broke up some French fries into tiny pieces and set them on the tray table. That would tide her over for a few minutes.

Kimberley made her way into the kitchen, finding her mother shoving the envelopes back into the drawer.

"Do you have anything you want to tell me?" Kimberley asked, folding her arms in front of her chest.

Nicole slightly jumped and turned around to face her daughter. Her face was pale as though she had just seen a ghost and maybe that's what Kimberley would be to her now... someone from her past. She couldn't understand why her mother would want to have any interaction with David. He was a murderer. He had threatened Jessica. He had assaulted Kimberley. He could have killed her. Maybe he would have if he had had the chance.

"Why were you going through my things?" Nicole slightly raised her chin as if she had a leg to stand on.

"It's the kitchen, Mom. I wasn't going through anything. Answer the question." Kimberley was in full detective mode.

"He's my husband," Nicole said, tightening her eyes. Kimberley couldn't tell if she was tightening them in anger or sadness, but she didn't care.

"He's a *murderer*."

"You wouldn't understand." Nicole turned away from Kimberley, pulling a couple of glasses from the cupboard.

"I wouldn't understand what... because I think you're the one that's not understanding. How the hell are you still married to him? Why the hell are you still talking to him?" Kimberley took a step into the kitchen.

"You don't just stop loving people."

"Yes, you fucking do. If they threaten your granddaughter, attack your daughter, cheat on you, and murder their mistress. What is there to love?"

"Enough, Kimberley." Nicole turned back around facing her daughter. "You don't get to tell me how to live my life."

"How is that living? How is standing by a murderous piece of shit living? You're better than that." Kimberley pressed her lips firmly together.

Nicole exhaled a deep breath.

"Where were you today?" Kimberley tilted her head and narrowed her eyes. "Did you go to visit him? Did you?"

"That's none of your business."

"It is my business."

"So, what if I did?" Nicole threw her hands on her hips.

"Then I would take Jessica and I would leave." Kimberley jutted out her chin. She was serious… dead serious. She stood by her mom all throughout her childhood, while she chose her abusive, drunk of a father over her. She wouldn't do it again, not now, now that she had Jessica.

Nicole's eyes became glossy and her lip quivered. "He's still my husband." Her voice cracked.

"And I'm your daughter… and Jessica is your granddaughter." Kimberley shook her head and turned on her foot.

"Where are you going?" Nicole called out after her.

Kimberley quickly wiped off Jessica's hands and mouth and picked her up from her high chair.

"Grandma," Jessica said, reaching her hands out.

"Where are you going?" Nicole asked again, following behind.

"We're leaving. You want your husband, then you can have him. But you won't have me or Jessica."

An hour later, Kimberley found herself sitting in a booth across from Jessica at Andrea's Café. It was different now. There weren't many people dining, but the ones that were there were quiet, almost solemn, keeping to themselves. Their voices just above a whisper. A heavy-set woman clutched her child a little tighter, while sitting in a booth. The death of Piper Chase had affected everyone. A life cut short was a reminder that any moment could be their last. It had struck too close to home for the people of Custer County. So close, they could actually feel it. Kimberley had ordered herself a cheeseburger and fries, and chicken nuggets and fries for Jessica. Jessica sipped at a sippy cup full of chocolate milk. Kimberley took a bite out of her cheeseburger. It didn't taste good, not because of the food, but because of the bad taste she had in her mouth. She couldn't seem to get rid of it.

"Is it yummy?" Kimberley forced a smile. But just looking at her blue-eyed girl, it immediately widened.

Jessica nodded her head. "I love chickies," she said, dipping her chicken in a mound of ranch and taking a small bite.

Kimberley tapped her nails against the table, deciding what she should do. She didn't know where to stay. Perhaps a hotel. But the nicest ones were over in Weatherford. There were a couple of motels in Dead Woman Crossing, seedy at best. And with Piper's murderer out there, Kimberley didn't feel comfortable staying in a motel with Jessica. Kimberley pulled out her phone and brought up her contacts. She clicked call and the phone rang a few times.

"Hello," Barb said.

"Hi, Barb. It's Kimberley."

"Oh heavens. Is everything alright?"

"Yes, well no. Jessica and I need a place to stay tonight, and I wouldn't—"

"Come on over. I'll get the guest bedroom made up. Plus, I've got some cookies in the oven that I was going to bring into work tomorrow. But you and Jessica can have some early."

"Thanks, Barb. We'll be over in an hour."

"No need to thank me. See you soon, my dear."

Kimberley let out a sigh of relief as she ended the call. She looked over at Jessica who was smiling happily, completely content with her nuggets and fries. They were going to be okay. She took another bite of her cheeseburger. This time, it tasted a little better.

"Hey," a voice said, pulling her from her thoughts.

There stood Caleb dressed in jeans and a T-shirt. They just kept running into one another. Flynn was standing behind him with his arms wrapped around his dad's leg. He peeked his little head around to look at Kimberley, but then disappeared behind Caleb again, clamming up.

"Hey there," Kimberley said, looking up at Caleb.

"You two having a dinner out?" he asked with a smile. "I see you went with the toddler special, nuggets and fries. Excellent choice," he teased.

Jessica giggled and stuffed a French fry in her mouth.

"It's Flynn's favorite as well. Actually, I can't get him to eat anything else." He tousled Flynn's golden locks. "Isn't that right?"

Flynn giggled and stayed hiding behind his dad.

"Yeah, just having a little dinner out," Kimberley said. She wasn't about to tell a stranger about her twisted family drama.

"Same here." He bent down scooping up Flynn. "I like to mix it up. Home cooked nuggets versus restaurant cooked nuggets. Right, Flynn?" Caleb tickled the boy's sides, making him laugh and squirm.

There was something familiar about the little boy's laugh, more like a snicker, than an outright laugh. Jessica giggled too and held out one of her chicken nuggets to Flynn.

"Here," she said, but it sounded more like 'ear'.

Caleb dipped Flynn close enough to take the nugget.

"What do you say?" he said.

"Thank... you," Flynn said with a shy smile.

"Well, we'll leave you two alone before Flynn here eats all Jessica's nuggets. Y'all have a goodnight." Caleb smiled as he turned to walk away.

"Tomorrow," Kimberley said. The word came out of her mouth before she knew what she was even saying.

Caleb turned back. His eyebrows pinched together.

"Tomorrow... do you want to do a playdate with the kids tomorrow at Rader Park after daycare?"

Caleb gave her a big smile. "I'd love that... I mean we'd love that."

"Good." Kimberley allowed the corners of her mouth to curve up. "We'll see you then."

He gave a nod and a wave of his hand. "See you tomorrow, King."

Kimberley glanced over at her daughter. She couldn't believe it herself. She had agreed to a date of some sort. Was it a date? No. But maybe. At the very least, they could be friends. She wasn't sure. But maybe this is what she and Jessica needed. A real fresh start.

CHAPTER TWENTY-ONE

Barb pulled open the oven, sliding out a dozen fresh blueberry muffins. She was already dressed for work but had a pink apron on over her chino pants and loose-fitting blouse. Kimberley stood in the doorway and waited until the muffins were safely placed on the counter before she said anything. Barb lived alone as her husband had passed years before, and she didn't want to startle her. Kimberley was dressed in her uniform. She had opted for half a can of dry shampoo rather than showering.

"Good morning," Kimberley said as Barb removed her oven mitts.

Barb turned back and smiled. "How'd you sleep?"

"Wonderful. Thanks for letting us stay the night."

"You're more than welcome anytime. Here, have some coffee," Barb said, pouring a mug and handing it over.

Kimberley took it from her and thanked her.

"The muffins will be ready to eat in just a few minutes. Where's Jessica?"

"I'm letting her sleep a little bit longer. She was tossing and turning all night." Kimberley took a sip of her coffee.

"Poor thing. Probably not used to the bed." Barb poured herself a mug of coffee and took a sip. "How ya feeling today?"

Kimberley shrugged her shoulders. "I don't know if I'm doing the right thing?"

"I don't think there's a right thing or a wrong thing, Kimberley. I'm all for loyalty, but your mother standing by David... well, only a few words come to mind, and none of them are good." Barb shook her head.

"Is it wrong of me to keep Jessica away from her?" Kimberley tilted her head. The night before she was sure of her decision, but now she felt guilty.

"Your mother isn't thinking clearly. So, no, I don't think it's wrong of you. If she really wants to be in yours and Jessica's lives, then that's her decision to make not yours. She needs to stand by you two, not that murderer." Barb twisted her lips.

Kimberley's phone buzzed. She pulled it from her utility belt. On the screen read, *We got the report back on Benjamin Fry. Get here as soon as you can.*

"It's Sheriff Walker. He needs me in the office." Kimberley looked up at Barb.

"You go ahead. I'll get Jessica ready and take her to daycare."

"Are you sure?" Kimberley placed her mug on the counter.

"Absolutely. Now go. I've got everything taken care of here." Barb shooed Kimberley away with a flick of her hands and a big smile.

Kimberley smiled back and took off out of the house.

Bearfield and Hill were seated at the conference table in the makeshift burn room. Hill was flipping through pages of reports, while Bearfield typed vigorously at his computer. It was obvious they were run down as they were silent while they worked, not delivering the typical banter.

"Hey," Kimberley said in the doorway. She entered dropping her bag on an empty seat. "Where's Sam?"

Bearfield looked up first. His eyes were dark and his skin dull. "He stepped out to take a call. Should be back any moment."

"Any news?" Kimberley walked to the whiteboard where she had started writing the names of the people that were connected to Piper. Chloe and Miley and Linda. She picked up the dry erase marker and filled in the rest of her web. Every person had a circle of people connected to them. Seventy-nine percent of victims knew their murderers. Kimberley always began her murder investigations looking into those that knew the victim. She wrote Benjamin Fry and connected it to Piper. She wrote 'Mary' the neighbor down too. She had to have known Piper. She wrote Shana but crossed her name out. She had a solid alibi. She wrote Edna and Arthur Chase. Hovering her marker over the names, she considered striking them out, but decided against it. The fact that they hadn't mentioned Benjamin Fry's visit rubbed Kimberley the wrong way. How could they have forgotten to mention him? Especially since he and Arthur had gotten into an argument and the fact that he had showed up demanding money. Her mind started going down different tunnels, outcomes, things that could have happened. Perhaps it was an accident and the Chases covered it up. Or Benjamin used Piper as some sort of ransom. She wrote down the name Will from Miley's letters. She wasn't sure who he was or how he was connected, so she just circled his name as a reminder to follow up.

"Who's Will?" Bearfield asked.

Kimberley turned around. She reached inside her bag and pulled out the stack of stories and drawings Miley had given to Edna, and handed them to Bearfield.

"What's this?" Bearfield asked, flipping through the papers.

"Miley gave them to Edna. They're drawings of her and Piper and stories about their time together. She mentions a camp counselor named Will, which is odd because I spoke to a Chloe that worked at Camp Beaverbrook, and she didn't mention him at all... actually."

"Good, you're here," Sam said, interrupting their conversation.

Kimberley redirected her attention to Sam, losing her train of thought, and placed the cap back on the marker. Sheriff Walker strolled into the conference room holding an open file folder.

"Is Barb in?" he asked, more so to the room than anyone in particular.

"Haven't seen her," Hill said.

"She'll be in soon. She took Jessica to daycare for me."

Sam looked up from his file folder and gave Kimberley a quizzical look. "Everything alright?"

She bit at her lower lip and nodded. "Yeah, just was in a pinch," she said, not going into further detail. "Whatcha got on Fry?"

Sam tilted his head but gave a slight nod. Kimberley could tell he wanted to ask her about everything, make sure she was alright, offer to help. That was just the type of man he was. He was one of the good ones.

"Background check came in. He was fired from his job." Sam closed up the folder and looked at Hill, Bearfield, and then Kimberley.

"That's not so bad," Hill said, shrugging a shoulder.

"For downloading child pornography." Sam raised an eyebrow.

"I stand corrected." Hill lowered his head.

Sam pulled out a photo of Benjamin Fry and held it up. It appeared to be an employee ID photo, taken of just the chest up. He looked to be in his fifties with dark hair and darker eyes. His nose was long and crooked, and he had an avian look to him.

"So, we bring him in… now." Kimberley folded her arms in front of her chest. "Fucking slimy bastard."

"We put out an APB on him a half hour ago as soon as the report came in. The problem is, he might have left town. No one's seen him since he left the Chases' house on Sunday, the afternoon Piper went missing. He could be long gone or lying low. I had Burns notify all the police departments in the surrounding area, from here all the way to Texas. Hopefully, we'll hear something." Sam slipped the photo back into the folder and dropped it on the table.

"What about Edna and Arthur? Shouldn't we talk to them? See what they know about Benjamin?" Kimberley asked. She turned looking back at the whiteboard.

"Yes, we will today."

"Does Benjamin have a criminal record?" Kimberley's eyes bounced between the names on the board, but they kept going back to Arthur and Edna.

"Aside from a couple of traffic violations, it's clean," Sam said.

"So, there's a chance Edna didn't know about her brother?" Kimberley turned back, facing Sam. She noticed the dark circles under his eyes and his unkempt facial hair. It typically always looked like a five o'clock shadow like he kept it trimmed that way, but it was a little more grown out. He appeared to have aged a year in the past few days, and Kimberley was sure she looked the same way.

"There's also a chance she did."

"I thought we ruled out Edna and Arthur," Hill spoke up. He looked to Bearfield and then Sam and Kimberley.

"We determined Piper left that house," Bearfield said. He ran his fingers under his chin as though he were thinking deeply. "But maybe they took her out of that house."

"Or Benjamin did. Maybe he did something to Piper, and they helped cover it up." Hill pursed his lips together.

"Let's not get ahead of ourselves," Sam said. He picked up the coffee cup from the table and took a sip of it. "Ugh, who made this?"

"Burns did." Hill cracked the faintest of smiles.

"It tastes like brown water. King, let's head over to the Chases. We'll stop for something drinkable on the way."

Kimberley nodded. "Yeah, I'd like to see their reactions when we tell them why Benjamin was fired." She prided herself on being able to read others. Liars had tells... even the best of them. And in her experience the eyes could rarely lie. They always found themselves revealing the truths the mouth refused to utter. A glance to the left. A flicker of uncertainty. Regardless of what Edna and Arthur told them, Kimberley was positive she'd know the truth whether they said it or not.

"What do you want us working on?" Hill asked.

"How's the tip line coming along?" Sam began gathering his things.

"It's slowed down." Bearfield rubbed the back of his head and retied his ponytail.

"And the bicycle?"

"Lodge and Burns are out patrolling. Nothing yet, and the night shift as you know didn't spot it."

Sam let out a groan. Kimberley knew what that groan was… it was the same one she felt and let out dozens of times a day since Piper went missing. It meant they didn't have anything to go on, but maybe something would turn up. She was hoping Benjamin Fry was that something. Sam rubbed his forehead.

"Bearfield, I want you back out on the road. The more eyes we have out there, the better. Hill, man the tip line. You and Lodge can switch at noon. And I want to know the second we know where Benjamin is." Sam nodded.

"You got it, boss," Hill said.

"What about Will?" Bearfield glanced at the colorful pages in front of him and then at the whiteboard where Will's name was circled twice.

"Who's Will?" Sam asked.

"He's mentioned in Miley's stories. The ones she gave to Edna. Apparently, he worked at the camp," Kimberley said, quickly filling him in. "But Chloe, the counselor I spoke with, never mentioned him."

"Bearfield, see if you can find out about this Will character. See if anyone named Will actually worked there or get ahold of Linda, so we can talk to Miley again," Sam rattled off.

Kimberley could see he was itching to talk to Edna and Arthur. His vision was tunneled.

"I'm on it," Bearfield said with a nod.

Sam backed his vehicle out of the Custer County Sheriff's Office and headed toward Dead Woman Crossing, while Kimberley sat quietly in the passenger seat, looking out the window. The world around her passed by in a blur. In the past few days, her world had begun crumbling around her. Not like a building coming down. It was never that sudden. It was like a cookie crumbling… parts of it breaking off in bigger chunks than other parts. First, the case of Piper's murder. No leads. Nowhere to look. Just little crumbs to follow. Then her home life. Her mother lying to her. Sneaking around behind her back. Pretending as though money had anything to do with the fact that she hadn't yet divorced David. She had chosen a murderer over her and Jessica. Some would argue that the heart wants what the heart wants. But Kimberley had learned, the heart was a hell of a dumb thing. She had moved here because Oklahoma was supposed to be simpler, calmer. But as it turned out, life was complicated no matter where your location was, no matter where you called home. Life was fucking hard.

"Want to tell me what's going on with you and Jessica?" Sam asked, pulling her from her crumbling cookie of a world. He looked over at her briefly with concerned eyes. The big heavy ones with eyebrows knitted together.

Kimberley let out a deep breath. It wasn't one she had been holding in. It was one she had to exhale before she exhaled everything that was swirling around her mind.

"It's my mom," she said, not meeting his eyes. She just stared forward as if she were looking at something. But really, she was looking through everything.

"I thought we were closer than that, King," he said. There was a sadness in his voice. Kimberley looked over at him to be sure she was hearing his tone right. When she saw his face, she knew she was.

"What do you mean?" She raised an eyebrow.

"If something's bothering you. If something's wrong. I'd hope, as your friend, you'd be able to tell me. And if you didn't think you could. Then, as your boss, I'd make you." Sam grinned.

Kimberley slapped a hand against his shoulder playfully. "You know I'm not one to talk about myself or my problems."

"I know, King. But I'm here to listen… as your friend." He nodded.

Kimberley sighed heavily. "She's seeing David. Writing to him. Visiting him."

Sam glanced over at her again. "So, you took Jessica and left?"

Kimberley nodded. "Yeah."

"And you're questioning if you did the right thing or not?"

"Yeah."

"Well, my opinion might not count for anything, but I would have done the same."

"Thanks, Sam."

Sam gave a nod, placing his hand on hers for a second, he squeezed it. He pulled his vehicle up next to a local coffee shop and put the car in park, shutting off the engine.

Before he stepped out of the vehicle, Kimberley spoke up. "Sam. It might not count for anything, but your opinion means more than you know."

The coffee shop was quaint with just a couple of tables and chairs. Nothing inside matched as if the owner decided randomly one day to open a coffee shop and brought all the odds and ends they had lying around to run it. The chalkboard on the back wall behind the old cash register had their daily offerings, which consisted of black coffee, tea, and their fanciest drink, espresso. There was a dessert case half filled with homemade cookies and brownies. A middle-aged woman named Candy with box dye red hair and heavy eyeliner took Sam's order of two large black coffees. She was the kind of woman that looked older because she hadn't learned that less was more. Kimberley leaned against the wall staring at the back of Sam, from his head down to his broad shoulders all the way to his feet. When she realized she was staring, she looked away, down at her scuffed boots. She tried to rub the scuffs off with either foot. It wasn't like her to wear scuffed boots. She took pride in her appearance when it came to her work attire. Rubbing one boot against the other just made it worse.

"King," a voice called out beside her. For a moment she thought it was Sam. He was one of the only people that called her King, but it wasn't. And her cheeks immediately flushed when she saw Caleb walking into the coffee shop. He was dressed in dirty jeans, a white T-shirt, steel-toed boots, and a construction worker's vest. His skin was sweaty and partially coated in gray dust. Concrete, she assumed.

"Hey," Kimberley said, standing up straight just as Sam turned around handing her a coffee.

"Ready to head out?" Sam asked, not noticing Caleb.

Kimberley nodded, hoping she could bypass this introduction… she didn't understand why she didn't want Sam and Caleb to meet, but she didn't.

"Yep," she said, taking a sip of her coffee. It burned, and she winced slightly.

"We still on for tonight?" Caleb took a step closer. His eyes lit up, and he gave a small smile.

Sam looked at him and then at Kimberley and then back at him.

"And you are?" Sam cocked his head.

"Oh sorry. I'm Caleb," he said, holding out a hand.

Sam looked down at his hand for a moment before reaching out his own. Kimberley could tell that both of them were shaking forcefully as if they were sizing one another up.

"I'm Sheriff Sam Walker." It looked as though Sam puffed out his chest, but she couldn't be sure. "How do you know Kimberley here?" Sam asked.

Caleb signaled to Candy, holding out a finger. "My usual," he said with a grin. He was fitting in this town faster than Kimberley had.

"Just met a couple days ago over at Happy Trails. My boy and her girl are in daycare together."

Sam slightly raised his chin. "Ahh… and you two are getting together?"

"For a playdate," Kimberley quickly cut in. She didn't know why she didn't want Sam to think she was dating or having a regular date with Caleb, but she didn't. She also wasn't sure it was a regular date.

"Yeah, a playdate…" Caleb said, but his smile faltered.

Was it a regular date? Kimberley thought. His reaction told her it was. Did she want it to be?

"You new in town? Because I haven't seen you around." Sam widened his stance.

"We should head out," Kimberley said, looking over at Sam, but his focus was on Caleb.

"Yeah just a few weeks now. Moved here for a construction job as you can see." He looked down at himself and chuckled at his dirty appearance.

"Well, welcome to Dead Woman Crossing. And yeah, we gotta head out but it was nice meeting ya. The bad guys aren't going to catch themselves," Sam said with a laugh.

Kimberley raised an eyebrow. Did Sam make a joke? That wasn't like him… well at least not with strangers.

"Thanks, and hopefully, I'll see you later." Caleb nodded.

"Caleb, coffee's up," Candy said.

He stepped around Kimberley and Sam and exchanged a small smile. "Good luck catching those bad guys."

Outside, Sam gave Kimberley a sly glance as he got into the vehicle. A half grin met with narrowed eyes.

"What?" Kimberley cocked her head.

"Oh nothing."

"Say it," she said, taking a sip of her coffee.

Sam pulled out of the parking spot and headed toward the Chases' house. He glanced over at Kimberley again.

"Well, say it," she repeated.

"Didn't realize you were dating."

"I'm not. And even if I was, I didn't realize I had to tell you." Sam shrugged his shoulders.

"You jealous or something?" Kimberley raised her chin and smirked.

He glanced over at her again. "No… just worried about you. That guy seemed a bit off."

Kimberley rolled her eyes. Sam had barely interacted with him.

"Are you sure that's the reason you're worried?"

Sam let out a small laugh. "Of course, King."

Kimberley wasn't so sure about that, though. Was Sam interested in her? She had always felt there was a little bit of a thing between them, but they had both always kept it professional. Did she like Sam? Of course she did. He was one of her closet friends. But was there more there?

"He's a nice guy, though. You don't really know him." She couldn't help but to push him to see what he was really getting at.

"There's a lot of nice guys out there." Sam pulled his SUV into the Chases' driveway and put it in park. He shut the engine off and looked over at Kimberley. "Heck, I'm a nice guy," he said with a smile as he hopped out of the vehicle. She couldn't help but smile back, but looking through the windshield at the Chases' ranch style house, her smile faded. They had a job to do.

CHAPTER TWENTY-TWO

"Did you find Piper's murderer?" Edna asked. She sat at the kitchen table beside Arthur sipping at a cup of lukewarm tea. Arthur leaned his elbows on the table, his eyes pleading for Kimberley and Sam to say yes. They wanted their nightmare to end. But Kimberley knew finding the murderer never ended the nightmare. It would stay with them forever like a shadow hanging over their entire existence. Sam and Kimberley exchanged a glance. They both knew why they were there… to get the truth.

"No, but we have a lead, and that's why we're here," Kimberley said. She carefully looked at Edna, studying her eyes, the lines on her face, the coloring of her skin. Save for some dark undereye circles, she was pale. Her eyes locked with Kimberley's, not looking away, begging to know more.

"Who? Who is it?" Arthur asked. His eyebrows knitted together, and he leaned further forward in his chair.

"Do you know why Benjamin was fired from his job?" Sam asked.

Arthur and Edna looked at one another and then back at Kimberley and Sam, shaking their heads.

"No, he didn't tell us." Edna's eyes began to water. Was it because she was lying or because she knew she was about to hear something that would turn her world upside down? Kimberley wasn't sure.

"He was fired for downloading child pornography." Kimberley kept her eyes on Edna's.

Edna's hand immediately slapped against her mouth. The water that had been pooling in her eyes escaped, running down her cheeks. She shook her head back and forth as if she couldn't believe what she was hearing.

"I damn well knew it. I told you I didn't like him. That's why I never wanted him around." Arthur raised his voice as he stood from his chair. "I told you, Edna." Arthur paced the kitchen shaking his head.

"Wait, you don't think he had something to do with Piper's murder...?" Edna looked up at Kimberley.

"Of fucking course they do. That's why they're asking about him. And he showed up on the day Piper went missing. We should have never let him in this house, and you shouldn't have given him money," Arthur seethed. He pointed at Edna and shook his finger.

Edna's shoulders shook as she cried. She dropped her head into her hands. "I didn't know. I didn't know he was like that."

Arthur let out a deep breath and walked to his wife, taking a seat beside her. He put a hand on Edna's back and rubbed it. "I'm sorry, sweetheart. I shouldn't have said that. Regardless, it's not your fault," he whispered.

Kimberley looked over at Sam, and they gave each other a slight nod. There was no way Edna and Arthur knew about Benjamin. Their reactions were too raw to be faked, Kimberley thought. She knew Sam was on the same page.

"How did Benjamin act around Piper?" Kimberley cut in.

Edna looked up at her, taking a moment to compose herself before she spoke. "Honestly, he acted as though she wasn't there. Barely looked at her."

"Makes sense now." Arthur shook his head. "Piper must have been like heroin to that sicko."

"Did they ever spend time alone together?" Kimberley asked.

"Hell no," Arthur snapped. "I told ya, I never liked him. I didn't realize he was that type of a monster, but I knew there was something wrong with him." He was clearly confident in his ability to read others.

"Do you know where Benjamin is?" Sam asked.

Edna looked up at him with bloodshot eyes and a wet face. "No. We haven't heard from him since he stormed out of here on Sunday afternoon."

"Can you try to get a hold of him?"

Edna nodded. "Yes. Yes. I can call him."

Arthur rose from his seat and grabbed the cordless phone from the kitchen counter and handed it to his wife. She looked down at it and squeezed her eyes shut for a moment.

"We need to find him," Sam added.

"We've put out an APB on him but haven't had luck locating him yet. Just pretend that nothing's wrong, and you just want to check on him. Can you do that?" Kimberley asked in her calmest voice.

Edna opened her eyes and looked up at Kimberley and Sam. "Yes." She nodded.

"Maybe try to lure him back. Say we'll give him more money," Arthur suggested. He looked over to Sam for approval.

"If you can get him to come here, that'd be great. Just try to find out where he's at." Sam gave a quick nod.

"Okay." Edna slowly pressed the buttons on the phone, trying to make sure she didn't misdial.

She put the phone to her ear. Sam and Kimberley took a step closer, so they could hear it ring over and over and over again. When it went to voicemail, Edna ended the call.

"Should I try again?" she asked, looking up at them.

Sam nodded. "Yeah. Go ahead and leave a voicemail expressing concern if he doesn't pick up."

Edna dialed again and held the phone to her ear. It rang over and over and over again, until his voicemail picked up. She waited for the beep. "Benjamin." Her voice cracked. "It's your sister, Edna. I'm sorry about the way things ended the other day." She glanced at Sam and Kimberley. They nodded at her to keep going. "I was just calling to make sure you were okay. And I talked to Arthur.

We can spare a little more if you need it." Arthur rubbed Edna's back. "Just give me a call, so I know you're okay. Love you. Bye."

Edna hit the end call button and set the phone face down on the table.

"That was good, sweetheart," Arthur said. Holding Edna's hand, he gave it a squeeze.

"Now what?" Edna asked.

"Now, we wait," Kimberley said just as Sam's phone rang. He picked it up immediately.

"Sheriff Walker."

The color drained from his face as he listened. Kimberley had seen that look before. It was the look he had the day they got the news of Hannah Brown's murder the year before. He let out a deep breath as he clicked the phone off.

"What is it?" Kimberley asked.

Sam looked over at her. "We've gotta go… now."

"Wait, what should we do?" Arthur asked.

"If you hear back from Benjamin, call the station immediately," Sam said over his shoulder as he ran out of the house with Kimberley following behind.

Outside, Kimberley grabbed Sam's arm. "Tell me."

He looked back at her and then at the house. Lowering his voice, he tightened his eyes and forced out the words. "That was Bearfield. Miley is missing."

CHAPTER TWENTY-THREE

I thought I was done when I laid Piper to rest, but I couldn't help myself.

CHAPTER TWENTY-FOUR

Kimberley rapped her knuckles on the door to the gray ranch house, the same one they had visited just a few days before. This time would be different, because Miley wouldn't be lying on the couch engrossed in colorful images flashing across the television screen. Sam and Kimberley exchanged a look while they waited. They didn't need to say anything to know what the other was thinking. They were worried. More than worried, they were scared. What if there was someone out there taking little girls? What if Miley was already gone for good? Would they find her in a mossy grave like Piper? Would they ever find her? The questions swirled in Kimberley's head, crashing into one another, the answers just out of reach. It took nearly a minute before Linda appeared in the doorway. Her long black hair was pulled back into a low ponytail. Her face was flushed and her heavy makeup was smeared as if she had been crying or sweating.

"Thank God, you're here," she said. Her voice was panicked as she beckoned Sam and Kimberley into her home.

The house was still messy as Linda clearly hadn't picked up or cleaned since they were there the other day. "Come in, sit," she added.

"Why don't you have a seat, Linda," Kimberley suggested.

She needed Linda calm before they started asking questions. Linda nodded a couple of times and made her way to the couch, plopping down on it. She grabbed a crumpled-up tissue from the coffee table and wiped her eyes. Linda took a couple of deep breaths. Kimberley looked around the living room, careful to take it all in. She couldn't tell if anything was truly out of place since the home was so messy to begin with. Kimberley and Sam made their way around the couch and took a seat in the chairs on either side.

Sam pulled a fresh tissue from a box and handed it to Linda. She nodded and mouthed thank you as she wiped her eyes with it, further smearing her mascara and dark eyeliner.

"Tell us what happened."

"I came home early from work because I wasn't feeling well. I probably caught what Miley had, and she wasn't here. I phoned the station right away… because of what happened to Piper, ya know." Linda's voice shook.

Kimberley noted that Linda's skin was pale and her under eyes were dark and heavy. She looked ill.

"When did Miley go missing?" Sam asked, diving right into detective work. Kimberley wanted to wait a few more moments for Linda to calm down, but she knew they had no time to waste. Piper had gone missing around five thirty at night and within eight hours, she was dead according to the autopsy. If Miley had the same fate, they had hours, maybe less.

"I don't know. Sometime this morning between six when I left for work and eleven when I got home. She wasn't here. She was supposed to be here," Linda sniveled.

Kimberley pulled out her pad of paper and jotted down '6 a.m. and 11 a.m.'

"And where do you work again?"

"The Walmart Supercenter over in Weatherford," Linda said.

"She was supposed to be here, you say. Is that normal?" Kimberley tilted her head.

Linda nodded. "Usually, unless she was out playing. But she wouldn't be now. Piper was her only friend. And school's out. And she knows not to go out now. Not until y'all find out who murdered Piper. She knows it's not safe. There's nowhere else she'd be."

"You said you left work early."

"Yes. I was supposed to work until two thirty, but like I said, I wasn't feeling well."

"Is that your normal shift time?" Kimberley asked.

Whoever took Miley clearly knew she'd be home alone. They had to know of Linda's schedule. Unless Miley left the house.

"For now, it is. When school starts up again, I'll work the hours that Miley is in school," Linda explained.

"Did she say anything to you this morning?" Sam asked.

Linda looked to him. "Not this morning. I was gone before she woke up. But last night she said she was going to run over to visit Edna and Arthur today. She was over there yesterday, too. I tried calling them, but the line was busy. So, then I called the station. You have to find her." Her face crumpled as she blotted the tissue against her eyes.

"We were just over at the Chases' house. They didn't mention seeing Miley today," Kimberley said as she jotted down 'Edna and Arthur.'

Linda's shoulders shook.

"Did you see your daughter this morning? Check on her before you left for work? Are you sure she was in bed?" Kimberley asked. She wanted to be clear on this, especially since the Chases hadn't known Piper was missing for sixteen hours.

"Yes. I went in her room and kissed her on the forehead before I left for work. She was fast asleep. Her bed is made too, so I know she got up. She makes her bed every morning. Unlike me, she's very organized," Linda said while tears swam in her eyes.

Sheriff Walker grabbed the radio from his shirt and clicked it. "Officer Burns."

Static followed for a moment before Burns clicked on. "Sir."

"Get on over to the Chases' house. I want you to ask them about the last time they saw Miley Baker."

"You got it, sir," Burns said over the radio.

Sam cleared his throat and swallowed hard. He clicked the radio again. "Officer Bearfield."

"Yeah, boss."

"I want you to arrange a search party for Miley Baker. Cover the same ground we did for Piper Chase. I need all available units on this."

There was a pause before Bearfield's voice came over the radio. This time, it was laced in sadness. "Right away, sir."

Linda's eyes were wide and bloodshot, a mix of disbelief and shock. "Do you think she's dead?" she asked.

Kimberley tilted her head.

Sam pulled his hand from his radio. "No, but with what happened to Piper, we don't have any time to lose. We're going to find her."

Linda didn't nod. She just sat there frozen.

"Can we take a look around?" Kimberley stood from her chair and pocketed her notepad and pen.

Linda gave a slight nod and slowly rose. "Yeah. Her bedroom is down the hall on the right."

Kimberley walked through the living room, toward the hall, but stopped before passing by the kitchen. It was outdated with oak-colored cabinets, yellow tile backsplash, and peeling linoleum flooring. Her eyes scanned the room. The sink was full of dirty dishes. The stovetop had pans caked in grease. It was clear Linda was struggling. As a single mother, she could understand. Sam stood behind her, taking in the kitchen too.

"What about Miley's father?" Kimberley whispered over her shoulder. She looked back, locking eyes with Sam. He pursed his lips together for a moment and gave her a slight nod.

"I'll ask about it," he whispered back.

Kimberley was just about to continue toward Miley's room when her eyes landed on a cell phone on the table. It wasn't a smartphone. No fancy apps, nothing like that. Just a small black flip phone.

"Linda!" she called out. "Whose cell phone is this?"

Footsteps pounded behind them, and Linda slipped by Sam and Kimberley into the kitchen. She walked to the table and picked it up. "It's Miley's."

"Is it normal for her to leave the house without it?" Sam scratched at his chin.

Linda nodded a couple of times. "Yeah. I just got her a basic one for phone calls to let me know where she's at." Her bottom lip trembled, and she bit at it. "She was always leaving it behind. Maybe if I would have gotten her one of those iPhones like she wanted…"

Sam pulled a bag from his utility belt. "We're going to need to take that, just in case there's anything on there that can help us find her." He held out the open bag.

Linda lowered her head, dropped the phone into it, and folded her arms against her chest. "I understand," she added.

"You said her bedroom is down the hall?" Kimberley asked, trying to keep Linda engaged.

She raised her head. "Yeah. On the right."

"Why don't you have a seat at the table, Linda," Kimberley suggested.

Without saying a word, Linda took a seat. She was in shock, Kimberley thought. She quickly grabbed a mug from beside the half-full coffee pot and filled it. It was lukewarm, but it would have to do. Kimberley set it in front of Linda. "Here."

Linda looked up at her and let out a deep breath.

Kimberley put a hand on her shoulder and squeezed it for a brief moment. "Don't worry. We're going to find Miley."

Linda gave the faintest of smiles. It was more like a straight line, but Kimberley could understand. It was hard to believe everything was going to be alright when they had just experienced loss so close to them. Linda brought the mug to her mouth and took a long drink. Sam beckoned Kimberley with his hand and they made their way down the hall to Miley's room.

Immediately, Kimberley noticed a stark difference between Miley and Piper's rooms. Where Piper's was childlike with stuffed animals and Harry Potter books, Miley's was more grown-up. Posters of teen heartthrobs covered the walls from Tom Holland to Timothée Chalamet. The bed was covered in a plain dark purple bedspread with matching pillowcases, and, unlike the rest of the house, it was made and tidy. A long dresser contained just a mirror and a wooden jewelry box. Above it, hung several summer camp certificates. Kimberley couldn't recall there being any in Piper's room.

"It's quite tidy," Sam noted.

Kimberley nodded as she walked around the bed to the closet. "Almost as though it doesn't belong in this house."

She opened the closet, secretly hoping she'd find Miley sitting inside of it, playing a cruel joke on everyone or just a really good game of hide and seek. But all that was inside was an empty clothes hamper and a bunch of hanging clothes. Plain shirts, blue jeans, and even blouses. Unlike Piper, Miley's clothes were more grown-up. From what Kimberley and Sam had been told, the two girls had been inseparable ever since meeting at summer camp, but just looking at their rooms made Kimberley realize how different they were. And she had heard the same from Chloe, the camp counselor. The two were opposites in every way. Her mind immediately went back to summer camp. It was the one thing they both had in common. She slid the hangers, looking at each of the shirts, not a graphic tee in sight. For Piper, it had been nearly her entire wardrobe.

"Anything seem odd to you?" Sam pulled up a corner of the bedding and the pillows. He lifted the mattress slightly, looking underneath, but there was nothing.

Kimberley glanced over at Sam as he was pulling back up the covers and resituating the pillows. "Just how different Piper and Miley are."

Sam tilted his head. "What do you mean?"

"Well, Piper's room was almost childlike and Miley's is so much more grown-up. They're the same age. It's just a little odd, isn't it?" Kimberley closed the closet door.

"Not really. Kids mature at different ages. And, unlike adults, they don't need to have so many things in common to get along." Sam bent down and pulled up the bed skirt, looking under the bed.

"Yeah, maybe," Kimberley said, not fully convinced. "My mind keeps going back to that summer camp."

Sam popped his head up and got to his feet. "Nothing under there but a couple of dust bunnies. Thought you looked into that?" He dusted off his pants and looked over at Kimberley.

"Briefly. I think there's more there. It's the only thing these two girls have in common. They both attended that summer camp." Kimberley walked to the bedside table.

"That's not necessarily true, King. They both rode their bikes, played over at Black Heart Lane. They were friends. Both had fathers that weren't in the picture. They lived in the same town. They were the same age."

"Okay, okay. You're right," Kimberley said, looking over at him and then at the framed photo on the bedside table. She picked it up and brought it up to her line of sight. The picture was of two little girls. One was clearly Miley at a much younger age, just a few years old. The other was a little girl, around the age of five. They're sitting side by side, smiling up at the camera, the spitting image of one another.

"What is it?" Sam asked.

Kimberley held up the photo. "This one is obviously Miley, but who's the other little girl," she asked, pointing to the picture.

Sam walked around the bed and stood next to Kimberley, looking down at the photo. "They look like sisters."

"Linda made it seem like it was just her and Miley."

Sam nodded. "Sounds like we've got more questions for her."

They made their way back to the kitchen, finding Linda still sitting at the table.

"Find anything?" she asked, looking up at them.

Kimberley held up the photo. "Can you tell us who the other little girl in the photo is?"

Linda squeezed her eyes tight and nodded. "That's my daughter, Sophie. She passed several years ago from cancer." She opened her eyes and tears streamed from the corners.

Kimberley lowered the photo, immediately regretting asking about the little girl. Her stomach dropped, hearing the words come out of Linda's mouth. She looked over at Sam, seeing the strain in his eyes that had begun to shine. He blinked it away. Kimberley couldn't imagine losing Jessica, so to be in a room with two people that had lost a child of their own broke her heart. She felt an urge to wrap her arms around Sam and hold him. For some reason, she wanted to comfort him right then and there.

Sam cleared his throat. "And Miley's father. Where is he?"

Linda took a sip of her coffee. "A year after Sophie's death, he left. It's just been Miley and me ever since."

Sam bit at his lower lip and nodded. Kimberley knew exactly what he was thinking. How could that man walk out on his wife and daughter? How could any man do that?

"Do you have a phone number where we can reach him?" Sam asked. He clenched his fist, but then quickly relaxed it.

Linda stood up from her chair and lumbered over to the kitchen counter, pulling open a junk drawer. She grabbed a piece of paper and a pen, and quickly jotted down a name and number. Linda tossed the pen back in the drawer and slammed it closed. She walked over to Sam and handed it to him. "His name's Oliver and that's his phone number."

"Where does he live?" Sam asked.

"Over in Oklahoma City."

Kimberley found it odd. Oliver lived about an hour away and hadn't seen his own daughter in years. What was keeping him away? How could he be so close, yet abandon his own daughter?

Sam nodded and folded up the piece of paper and slid it into his front pocket.

"Linda," Kimberley said, hesitating for a moment. The summer camp was still bothering her. "Do you know who Will is? Did Miley ever mention him to you?"

Linda glanced off in the distance as though she was conjuring up every conversation she had had with her daughter. Finally, she shook her head. "No. Who is he?"

"We're not sure yet. But Miley had mentioned him in a story she wrote for Edna about Piper."

Linda's eyes went wide, then filled with tears. She quickly brought the Kleenex to them. "She never mentioned a boy to me. I guess she didn't feel comfortable telling me about boys yet." Linda's shoulders shook. "I didn't even realize she was interested in boys."

Kimberley immediately regretted asking Linda about Will. She should have waited until she knew more. Now it had opened up new wounds for Linda. Kimberley cleared her throat and glanced over at Sam.

"Linda, I promise you this. We'll do everything we can to find Miley," he said.

"Isn't that what you said about Piper?" Linda narrowed her eyes. She picked up her mug and brought it to the sink and began to busy herself by washing up dishes.

She was moving quickly through the stages of grief, Kimberley thought. Sadness to anger. Kimberley understood. With what happened to Piper, she'd feel the same way if her child was missing.

"Please give me a call if you think of anything else or need anything. We'll be in touch," Sam said. He waited a moment for Linda to say something, but she kept her back facing them and her hands busy washing.

CHAPTER TWENTY-FIVE

Kimberley pulled the ringing phone from her utility belt. "Chief Deputy King."

She looked over at Sam for a moment as he drove through the small town of Dead Woman Crossing.

"Search team is up and running. We're starting on Black Heart Lane," Bearfield said into the phone. If the same person that murdered Piper also took Miley, they would have a pattern. And since Piper was found in the woods off of Black Heart Lane, it was a good place to start the search. Especially since Miley had told her mother she was going to visit Arthur and Edna. Plus, Miley would have taken the same route which included Black Heart Lane.

Kimberley nodded. "Good. We're on our way." She ended the call, sliding her phone back into her utility belt.

"Search team is a go. They have a team of volunteers already out there as well."

Sam clenched his jaw. She could see how tightly his hand was squeezing the steering wheel as his knuckles had turned white.

"You alright?" Kimberley tilted her head. She wanted to put her hand on his but resisted.

"How in the hell is this happening in my town?" He slammed his fist against the steering wheel. There were a few moments of silence. Kimberley didn't know what to say. She knew he was hurting, that these two cases were bringing up grief he thought he had long digested. Grief from losing his wife and young son a few years back. That's the thing about grief, it was always there.

Even when you thought you'd finally gotten rid of it, it reared its ugly head.

"Sorry," he said.

"No need to apologize, Sam. I know you're having a hard time. I get it. But just know, we're going to find Miley. We're going to find the person responsible for Piper's death. You and I are going to do that," Kimberley said, placing her hand on Sam's.

He looked over at her, but he didn't need to say anything. 'I know we are,' is what Kimberley gathered from the intensity in his eyes.

Sam refocused his attention back on the road ahead. He gave her hand a squeeze just as Kimberley pulled it away.

"Are you sure the same person is responsible for Piper's death and Miley's disappearance?" Sam asked. His head was back in it.

"Yes. It has to be. Too much of a coincidence." Kimberley's eyes followed the blue horizon. They had to be connected, she thought. She believed in facts, numbers, patterns… but she also believed in gut instincts, and her gut told her it was connected.

"Who would do this, though? And for what reason?" Sam asked. He was good at forcing Kimberley to think aloud. She was so used to keeping everything inside, but she appreciated that Sam made her exhale her thoughts.

"Benjamin Fry. Being fired for child pornography and showing up in this town the day Piper went missing is odd. The summer camp. I'd like to look into that more." Kimberley's eyes bounced from the black winding road to the gold wheat to the blue horizon and back again.

"Linda knew nothing about Will. Think he's even a real person if that camp counselor hadn't mentioned him either?" Sam asked.

Kimberley hadn't thought of that. Kids had imaginary friends. And Miley had written her letters as little stories. Maybe Will wasn't even real.

"If he is, I've got a load of questions for him."

Sam nodded, pulling his vehicle onto Black Heart Lane. They were met with the same environment from just a few days before. The woods came right up to the road, thick and twisting. It had lost the beauty Kimberley had witnessed her first time driving down the road. Now, it held a deep, dark secret. The final resting ground for a life cut too short. Perhaps, more than one final resting ground, Kimberley considered, but quickly pushed the thought aside. They would find Miley, and they would find her alive and well. The road ahead twisted and sloped, a snake slithering its way through wooded land. Cars lined the road on either side. The search team was already out looking. Sam parked his SUV and just as Kimberley reached for the handle, he asked her to wait.

Sam pulled his cell phone and the piece of paper from his pocket and utility belt and dialed. Kimberley knew he needed her here with him when he made the call to the asshole that abandoned his family.

"Hello, this is Sheriff Sam Walker of Custer County. Is this Oliver Baker?"

Kimberley could hear mumblings on the other end of the phone but couldn't make it out. She glanced up ahead, noticing a group of people in yellow vests entering the woods. They were volunteers. She could tell by the way they walked, apprehensive, careful, scared. Officers carried themselves a different way in these situations. They were trained to. Careful, yes. But also, hopeful, a sense of fearlessness radiated off of them, whether it was real or fake, it didn't matter. Courage was just like confidence, you faked it 'til you made it. Within a matter of moments, she could no longer see the yellow vests. The woods had swallowed them up, and she hoped it would spit them back out with Miley. Kimberley looked up at the sky. Once again, the sun set the countdown as it started to slide down the horizon. They had a few hours of solid daylight left.

Sam ended the call and slid the phone back into his pocket. He exhaled a deep breath and dragged his hands down his face.

"What is it?" Kimberley asked.

Sam shook his head and looked over at her. His face was flushed red with anger. "He hasn't seen Miley in years, not since he left. And when I told him she was missing he didn't even react. I could practically hear that asshole shrug his shoulders."

Kimberley shook her head.

"He agreed to come into town for an interview. We should expect him tomorrow."

Kimberley didn't say anything. She could see Sam was trying to get out more as his body was tense and he had yet to reach for the door handle. He just sat there like a fractured stone statue, ready to fall apart at any moment.

"How can a father just abandon his child? How can he not care that she's missing?" he finally said.

"We care, Sam. We care enough for that piece of shit. We're going to find her." Kimberley gathered his face in her hands and stared into his eyes. He blinked a few times, but this time they didn't lose their glossiness. He didn't push the grief down. He let it sit there on his face for Kimberley to see. She, however, knew how easy it was for some parents to walk out on their children. Jessica's father had done the same. Once in a while, she'd get a text. A fucking text. And now her mother had turned her back on Jessica and Kimberley. She hadn't even attempted to get in contact with Kimberley yet. And then there was her own father who had only shown her the back of his hand. She knew what it was like to not be loved.

"I never even got to say goodbye," Sam said. A tear rolled down his cheek. Kimberley wiped it away, turning more of her body toward him.

"I was working a late shift when I got called to report to the scene of a car accident. I didn't know it was my wife and son until I arrived, until I saw their battered and bloodied bodies, until the drunk driver that had caused it stumbled out of his car, unphased by the lives he had destroyed. I could have killed him right then and there. I nearly did. Right over there, actually." Sam pointed off to the side of Black Heart Lane. Kimberley nearly gasped, realizing why these cases had been so hard on him. He had been forced to revisit the place his family was taken from him multiple times. Sam's shoulders shook. It was the first time he had opened up to Kimberley about the night of the accident. She pulled him in for a hug, wrapping her arms around him tightly. She wanted to hug away his pain, but she knew she couldn't. Like a scar, it'd always be a part of him.

A knock on the driver's side window interrupted them. Startled, they pulled away from one another. Sam immediately composed himself. His eyes dried up. His face turned serious. He quickly stepped out of the vehicle, and Kimberley did the same.

"Sorry to interrupt," Bearfield said. His face was full of concern as he glanced at Kimberley and then at Sheriff Walker. Kimberley was sure he was going to tease them for what he just witnessed, Kimberley and Sam hugging each other, but he didn't.

"No worries, Bearfield. Catch me up," Sam said as the three of them started off on foot up the winding road, passed the parked vehicles, and toward the only part of the woods with enough of a clearing to safely enter.

"We've got multiple teams on both sides of the road, scouring the woods. I called in another canine unit from Weatherford Police Department, so we've got two, one on each side of Black Heart Lane. The first group of volunteers just headed in with Lodge leading the way." Bearfield didn't pause as he spoke, almost as though he was manic, but Kimberley understood. He knew just like the rest of them, there wasn't time to spare.

"Burns is getting an Amber Alert sent out," Bearfield added.

"Good." Sam nodded.

"We talked to Miley's mother, Linda Baker. Said Miley went missing sometime between six a.m. when she left for work and eleven a.m. when she arrived home, but we don't have an exact time. She was supposed to be heading over to Arthur and Edna's house for a visit," Kimberley said. Loose gravel crunched beneath their boots as they walked up the road.

"We spoke to the Chases. They said they didn't have any contact with Miley today and weren't aware she was intending to visit, but then again, they mentioned the last time she dropped by was unannounced anyway," Bearfield said.

Sam scratched at the back of his neck. "And still nothing on Benjamin Fry's whereabouts?"

"Zilch."

"Can you verify the times Linda was at work? Speak with her supervisor to confirm she arrived at six a.m. and left early at eleven a.m. as she said?" Kimberley asked.

"Where does she work?"

"At the Walmart Supercenter over in Weatherford," Kimberley recalled.

Bearfield, spoke into his radio, relaying the request from Kimberley to Burns.

"I'm on it," Burns replied. "Over," he added.

They stopped in front of the clearing in the woods. Despite the daylight, it was dark and ominous. Twisting trunks, weaving branches, all competing with one another for nutrients in the soil and glow from the sun. Save for the shouts for 'Miley' from people far off in the distance, the woods were eerily quiet.

"Is Benjamin Fry our only lead then?" Bearfield looked to Kimberley and then to Sam. He slightly raised his chin.

"It's looking that way," Sam confessed.

"There's Camp Beaverbrook too. Did you get a chance to find out if there's a Will working there?" Kimberley asked Bearfield. There was something there. She could feel it.

"Shit." Bearfield rubbed at his forehead. "Sorry. I was working on that when I got the call from Linda about Miley missing. I'll follow up."

"It's fine." Kimberley pulled her ponytail tight, readying herself to charge into the woods. "I'll look into it."

"First thing tomorrow, King. We're losing daylight here, so let's get on with the search," Sam said with a nod. He entered the clearing with Bearfield and Kimberley in step behind him.

CHAPTER TWENTY-SIX

Another day, another Amber Alert. They're all out there again searching, looking for you, Miley. Aren't you so special? Too bad you couldn't be special for me. You should have listened. If you had, things would be different. But you didn't and, unlike Piper, they won't find you. Because as long as they're looking for you, they won't look for me.

CHAPTER TWENTY-SEVEN

Kimberley was running late to pick up Jessica from daycare again. She stayed as long as she could helping with the search and rescue. Too long, actually, until she received an irritated phone call from Margaret at Happy Trails. Just as she got out of her vehicle, Kimberley watched the front door of the daycare center open. Her mother, dressed in a floral top and blue jeans, emerged from inside with Jessica on her hip. This was the last thing Kimberley wanted to deal with… this being her mother.

"What are you doing?" Her voice was loud.

"Picking up my granddaughter. Margaret called and told me you hadn't shown," Nicole said.

Kimberley's footsteps were heavy as she marched toward her mom. What gave her the right? She had chosen David over her daughter and granddaughter, and now she was trying to act as though she was some sort of savior.

"I'll take her," Kimberley said. It was less of a suggestion and more of a demand.

"You can't keep her away from me. I'm her grandma." Nicole lifted her chin, while she rubbed Jessica's back.

"Momma," Jessica squealed.

"You made your choice." Kimberley had had enough. She closed the distance and reached for her daughter. "Hi, my smart girl," she said. Jessica reached out her hands toward Kimberley.

Rather than fighting, Nicole released her, allowing Kimberley to take Jessica. She held her against her chest and gently swayed. Tears sprung from Nicole's eyes.

"You're really going to keep her away from the only family she has?" Nicole's voice shook.

"I'm her family, and I won't let you do to her what you did to me." Kimberley planted a couple of kisses on the top of Jessica's head.

"What did I do to you?"

"You stayed with Dad. He abused the both of us, and yet you loved him and stood by him until his very last breath."

"You think I didn't want to leave? You think I didn't try to leave?" Nicole's eyes narrowed.

"No, I don't think you did, Mom. I think you stayed because you didn't have the strength to leave. And even now, your cheating, murdering husband is sitting behind bars, and you still don't have the strength to leave." Kimberley gritted her teeth. She felt like a mother bear with her cub. Why couldn't her mother ever be like that with her?

"You don't understand, Kimberley." Nicole's face crumbled.

"No, you don't, Mom. Just stay away from me and my daughter."

"Is everything okay?" a deep voice called out from behind her. Kimberley turned back to find Caleb walking around his truck dressed in dirty jeans, steel toe boots and a flannel button-up. Several of the top buttons were undone, revealing a patch of chest hair.

"Yeah, everything's fine," Kimberley said. Her cheeks flushed as she was embarrassed that he had heard their conversation.

Caleb walked up to Kimberley standing beside her. His stature towered over her.

"You sure?" he asked again as he gave Nicole a once over.

"Who's this?" Nicole asked, folding her arms across her chest.

Before Kimberley could speak, he was already introducing himself.

"I'm Caleb." He reached out a hand and briefly shook Nicole's.

She was apprehensive. "I'm Jessica's grandmother, Nicole."

Kimberley took her greeting as a small dig. Why hadn't she introduced herself as Kimberley's mother? And why was she making nice with a stranger, but she couldn't do the same with her own daughter?

"Jessica and my boy, Flynn, attend daycare together," Caleb explained, folding his arms into his chest. "Oh, shoot. Gotta go get him. Margaret tore me a new one for being late again. But glad to see I'm not the only one." He gave a small smile.

"We still on for a playdate tonight?" Caleb called over his shoulder as he started off toward the front door of Happy Trails.

"Rain check?" Kimberley said. "I had a crazy day at work."

Caleb stopped dead in his tracks and turned back. "Ahh, yeah. I got the Amber Alert. It's been a tough week for you. Well, when you wrap up the case, let me know. Perhaps, I can take you out to dinner or something."

Kimberley swallowed hard, but the words left her mouth before she knew what she was saying. "Yeah, I'd like that."

Caleb grinned and gave a small wave. "Alright then. Nice to meet you, Nicole," he said, turning back and jogging into the daycare center.

"Well, you'll need a babysitter for your date," Nicole said, tilting her head as if she had just called checkmate in a game of chess.

"If that happens, I'll ask Barb." Kimberley turned on her foot and headed toward her vehicle. She could hear her mother let out a soft cry, but she didn't turn around. It was her time to turn her back on her mom.

Kimberley walked sluggishly into the Custer County Sheriff's Office the next morning. She hadn't really slept the night before. Between the tiff with her mother, Piper's death, and Miley's disappearance, she couldn't get her mind to shut off. The thoughts swirling around just above her, just out of reach for hours and hours and hours. None of it resulted in anything, except for lost sleep. Barb was seated at the front desk on a phone call. Just as Kimberley approached, she set the phone down.

"How ya doing, Kimberley?" she asked. "You look exhausted."

"Didn't sleep well." Kimberley shrugged her shoulders.

"I completely understand. It's been a rough week for all of us. Maybe this will brighten your day." Barb placed a to-go cup of coffee on the top of her desk. She bent down and grabbed a vase full of fresh flowers and set them down beside the coffee.

"Oh, thank you, Barb. You didn't have to do that." Kimberley smiled.

"I didn't."

The door behind them opened.

"Who are those from?" Sheriff Walker asked. Kimberley turned back to find him walking toward her. His chin was raised slightly and his chest puffed out.

"A man named Caleb dropped them off for Kimberley." Barb gave a small smile.

Kimberley's cheeks began to warm. Was she blushing? Was she embarrassed? She couldn't tell the difference. She had never received flowers from a man before. Did she even like flowers? She wasn't sure of that either. But these were beautiful, pink and vibrant. Although Kimberley didn't know what type of flower they were, she liked the sweet scent they gave off.

"You two dating or something?" Sam tilted his head. His expression was unreadable.

"No," Kimberley said almost too quickly.

"He's trying to woo her." Barb winked. "You gotta woo before you do."

"Barb," Kimberley groaned.

"What? I've been around the block. I know how this goes." Barb smiled.

Kimberley grabbed the coffee and tried to gather the vase too, but the base was too thick for her to get her hand around it. She wanted to retreat to her office to get back to work on the case. She also wanted out of this conversation, especially with Sam standing beside her.

"Let me help you." Barb stood from her desk.

"I've got it," Sam said. He picked up the vase and looked at it with disdain. "Shall we?" He glanced at Kimberley with a small smile.

She nodded as she took a sip of her coffee. "I'll bring you some coffee, Sam," Barb called out.

The two of them walked through both sets of doors, Sam holding the door open for Kimberley at each of them. The main office area was empty as the deputies were all out getting the search parties ready to resume.

"He's sending you flowers, huh?" Sam finally said.

"I guess." Kimberley shrugged her shoulders.

"Is it getting serious?"

"It's nothing, Sam."

Kimberley entered her office and walked around to the other side of the desk, setting down her bag and coffee. She picked up a stack of mail and started flipping through it quickly.

"Where do you want these?"

"Right there is fine." Kimberley pointed to the corner of her desk.

Sam hesitated for a moment, but then set the vase down. "Well, I'm glad you're getting some work/life balance. I know that was one of the reasons you originally came to Oklahoma."

Kimberley set the stack of mail down and looked over at Sam. He was still staring at the vase of flowers. "I'm going to head out for an interview. I set one up with the summer camp director, Joy, at her house," Kimberley said, changing the subject.

Sam snapped out of his trance and nodded. "Good. Let me know what you find," he said. He took a few steps back and left the office without another word. Kimberley could tell he was upset, and she assumed it was from the case and having to revisit the place that took his family away. It was all hitting too close to home for him. She wanted to be there for him, but first, she had to be there for Piper and Miley, and that started with following her gut instinct on Camp Beaverbrook.

"Hey, Chief Deputy King," Burns said with a knock on her office door.

Kimberley looked up as she was gathering her things to leave. Deputy Burns stood in the doorway. He pulled a pad of paper out and flipped through it quickly. His eyes were red-rimmed and his skin pale. His goatee that he usually kept trim was unkempt and his blond hair went in all different directions. She remembered how difficult a time he had had on his first murder case the year before. She remembered having to send him away from the scene of the crime because Kimberley was sure he was going to throw up. But he wasn't a rookie anymore. He had grown into his role as a deputy.

"I spoke with Linda's supervisor. Supervisor verified her clock-in and clock-out times. She punched in at six a.m. on the dot and out a few minutes after eleven a.m. Her supervisor said she asked to leave early because she wasn't feeling well. Her story and timeline checks out." He closed up his notepad and slid it into his front shirt pocket.

"Okay. Thanks, Burns. Good work," Kimberley said, walking toward him.

He backed up and nodded.

That was one thing checked off the list. Now, it was time to figure out what had happened at Camp Beaverbrook.

CHAPTER TWENTY-EIGHT

Kimberley knocked once on the two-story house that sat just outside of Weatherford. It belonged to a woman named Joy. She immediately opened the door as she was expecting Kimberley. The woman was average sized with curly brown hair, streaked with gray. From what Kimberley could pull on her at the station, she was fifty-five, a widow of a few years, and had lived outside of Weatherford nearly all of her life. Her record was clean, not even a traffic violation, and she had worked at Camp Beaverbrook for over twenty years, starting out as a camp counselor and now she was the director.

"Hi, I'm Chief Deputy King. We spoke on the phone," Kimberley greeted.

Kimberley had called her the night before, unable to focus on anything else. She tried to play with Jessica, help Barb with dinner, but finally she gave in to her vices, her vice being her work and sequestered herself in her room, laboring over the case. Barb was understanding and took care of Jessica until it was time to put her to bed. After all those hours mulling over files and interviews, the only thing she had accomplished was setting up this time to speak with Joy.

"Yes. Come in." She beckoned. "I'm Joy."

She escorted Kimberley to the kitchen where she offered her a cup of coffee. Kimberley took a seat at the kitchen table while Joy poured two cups. She placed one in front of Kimberley and took a seat across from her.

"I heard about Piper and now Miley." Joy shook her head. "Such a shame. Any way I can help, I will."

Kimberley took a sip of her coffee and pulled out her notepad and pen. "Did you know the girls?"

"My job is a bit more high level, so, unfortunately, I didn't know them personally. But my heart aches for them and their families," Joy said convincingly. She seemed like a no-nonsense woman, honest and straight to the point.

"Understandable. Can you tell me about a camp counselor named Will?"

Joy exhaled and took a sip of her coffee. "Oh, Will. He was one of our camp counselors. Good-looking boy. Very popular with the campers."

"You said was?" Kimberley arched an eyebrow.

"Yes, I had to let him go mid-summer. We received some anonymous reports that Will had been inappropriate with some of the younger, female campers. Apparently, he was spotted at the bunkhouses after hours and had become overly familiar with the girls." Joy shook her head.

"Was there an investigation done?"

"I talked to him about it. He swore up and down that the reports weren't true. I had to let him go. I can't have allegations like that getting out. It would destroy Camp Beaverbrook. What parent would send their children to a place with those types of rumors swirling around? So, I just nipped it in the bud." Joy took another sip, swallowing hard this time.

It was obvious to Kimberley she had not wanted to fire Will. Maybe because they were close or because she believed him.

"And you say the reports were anonymous. How did you receive them?"

"Email. They came right to my inbox. Several of them all in a row from different addresses."

Kimberley jotted down a few notes.

"Did you believe the reports?"

"Goodness, no. Will had always been so professional, and he'd worked at the camp since he was fifteen. Like I said, I couldn't take the risk though. It doesn't matter what I thought. It mattered what people would believe. Will's a good-looking boy. Over the years, lots of the female campers developed crushes on him, but he would never act on them."

Kimberley gave a slight nod. Joy was right. Public perception declared what was valid or not. The truth had nothing to do with it. Perhaps, the reports had been true, though, and Will had been inappropriate. Regardless of how Joy felt about Will, people weren't always who they appeared to be. Could he be responsible for Piper's death and Miley's disappearance? Maybe he blamed the girls for getting fired. That was motive, and it was enough to look into Will.

"Do you have Will's contact information?" Kimberley folded up her notepad and placed it in her pocket.

"Yes. Let me get it for you." Joy rose slowly from her chair and left the kitchen. A few moments later, she returned with a piece of paper in hand. "There's his address and phone number."

Kimberley glanced at it, noticing Will lived in an apartment in Weatherford. She pocketed it and thanked Joy.

"And those emails. Can you forward them to me?" Kimberley stood from her seat.

"Of course. I'll forward them over today. Is that everything?"

"For now. Thank you for your time. I can see myself out." Kimberley pushed in her chair and turned on her foot.

"I really hope you find the person responsible. Good luck to you," Joy said as Kimberley left the room and made her way out of the house. Outside, her phone rang.

"Chief Deputy King," she answered.

"We located Benjamin Fry," Sam said.

"Where?"

"Over in Fort Worth, Texas. State troopers picked him up about thirty minutes ago. They're going to meet us halfway in Wichita Falls." The phone call was starting to cut out.

"Was Miley with him?"

"Negative."

"Do you want me to come with?" Kimberley asked. It was hard to hear Sam. He sounded like he was in a wind tunnel.

"I'm already on my way. I'll be back at the station in a few hours."

The call disconnected before she could say anything else. Kimberley pulled out the piece of paper that contained Will's address and phone number. His apartment was only a fifteen-minute drive away. She considered heading back to the station or over to Black Heart Lane, but her mind was already made up. She was going to pay Will a visit.

Kimberley pulled into the parking lot of a two-story apartment building in Weatherford. The outside was brick and there were at least twenty apartments in the building. She parked her vehicle and glanced at the piece of paper again. Apartment 4A, she noted. Making her way across the parking lot, Kimberley stopped when she spotted Chloe getting out of the passenger side of a red Subaru. It was parked right in front of 4A. Her long golden blonde hair was tied back in a high ponytail, and she was dressed in a jean skirt and a crop top. A young man with a strong jawline and golden tan skin got out of the driver's side. His hair was brown and cut short, and he was dressed in a T-shirt and cargo shorts. They met in front of the vehicle and held hands, walking toward the apartment.

"Chloe!" Kimberley called out, placing her hand over her eyes to shield them from the blazing sun.

Chloe turned back and immediately dropped Will's hand when she noticed Chief Deputy King. Kimberley closed the distance.

"Are you Will?" Kimberley stopped right in front of them. They both looked like a deer in headlights, eyes wide with blank faces. She was surprised to see Chloe with Will, especially after what Joy had told her about him. It was clear they were a couple, smitten with one another. Kimberley still found it odd that Chloe had never mentioned Will.

"Yes," he said. His voice was deep and his eyes were like pendulums, swaying everywhere. "What can I help you with?"

Kimberley couldn't tell if he was nervous or guilty of something, or maybe both.

"I'm Chief Deputy King of Custer County. I wanted to ask you a few questions about your time at Camp Beaverbrook," Kimberley said matter-of-factly.

Will hesitated for a moment. "I don't work there anymore."

"I know."

"Whatever you heard, isn't true." There was a tinge of anger in Will's voice. "I never did anything inappropriate."

Kimberley nodded. "Did you know Piper Chase and Miley Baker?"

Will's face slightly crumbled. Was it devastation or guilt? Kimberley still couldn't tell.

"Yes. They were good girls. I'd never do anything to hurt them." His tone was firm.

"So, the accusations that were made were false, you say?"

He nodded vehemently. "I don't know who said those awful things about me or why, but they're not true, I swear it."

Chloe grabbed Will's hand and squeezed it. "They're ridiculous. They should have never fired him over anonymous reports."

"Will, where were you yesterday between the hours of six a.m. and eleven a.m.?" Kimberley asked.

He scratched his chin as if he was thinking. "I was running errands yesterday. Went to the bank, got groceries, gym."

"Approximate time you were at these places?" Kimberley pulled out her notepad and pen.

"Went over to Planet Fitness around six thirty a.m. Came home and showered. First National Bank around eight thirty a.m. when they opened. Walmart for groceries after that, like nine a.m. Dropped those off. I also stopped for gas after Walmart over at Phillips 66 on East Main," he said it all in one breath.

Kimberley noted the times and locations down. She knew she could pull security footage from all of those locations if need be as well as CCTV in the surrounding area. He was very detailed which would make it easy to confirm he was telling the truth or catch him in a lie. Her gut told her it was the former. Will seemed genuinely upset about being let go from Camp Beaverbrook and equally upset over what happened to Piper and Miley.

"What about Sunday, August the second, between the hours of five fifteen p.m. and midnight? Can you confirm your whereabouts then?"

Will paused, using his fingers to count back the few days before.

"I stayed over that night," Chloe said. "I came here after work and stayed until the next morning."

Will nodded. "That's right. Chloe was here with me."

Kimberley raised an eyebrow but jotted down the note. She wasn't sure if she believed that. Chloe was too quick to answer, too quick to tie a neat bow around their alibis.

"And where were you yesterday, Chloe, from the hours of six a.m. and eleven a.m.?"

"I was at my parents' house."

"Alone?"

"Yes. They were at work, and I wasn't feeling great. Had a bit of a headache, so I called in sick to work." Chloe rocked back on her feet for a moment.

Kimberley noted her alibi and pocketed the notepad and pen.

"Thank you both for your time." Kimberley pulled two business cards from her pocket and handed one to Chloe and one to Will. "If you think of anything else, let me know. Otherwise, I'll be in touch." She nodded. Before she walked away, she glanced at each of them, carefully studying their faces. To Kimberley, they both appeared scared, maybe even guilty.

CHAPTER TWENTY-NINE

On her way back to the station, Kimberley got a call from Barb, letting her know Sam was an hour out. He had successfully picked up Benjamin Fry. Her phone rang again just as she ended the call with Barb.

"Chief Deputy King."

"Hey, it's Bearfield. Sam's phone went straight to voicemail, so I'm checking in with you. We're nearly done combing the woods, should be completed before nightfall."

"Find anything?"

"Not a damn thing. I hear we're bringing Benjamin Fry in."

"Yes, Sam's on his way back. Hoping that goes somewhere. Hey, who's the most techie of all the deputies?" Kimberley asked, knowing if Fry didn't pan out, she had a lead with Will and Chloe.

"Definitely, Burns. He's got an associate degree in computer science," Bearfield said.

"Can you send him back to the station?"

"You got it, boss."

"Thanks, Bearfield." Kimberley ended the call.

Before she put her phone away, it buzzed with a notification of a text message. She glanced down at the words briefly.

Hey, it's Caleb. Hope your day is going better today! :)

She dropped the phone into the cupholder and kept her eyes on the road. Kimberley had to put her personal life aside until this case was solved. She couldn't focus on both, and even though the text was from Caleb, she couldn't get Sam off her mind. She pushed them both aside, allowing the facts of the case to swirl around. Piper was dead. Miley was missing. Benjamin Fry had showed up on the day Piper went missing, recently fired from his job for child pornography. Then there was Camp Beaverbrook. Will was fired as well for anonymous reports of inappropriate behavior around the girls. Arthur and Edna had a connection to both Piper and Miley. Perhaps Miley witnessed something they had done. No, Kimberley thought to herself. She was going off the deep end with theories. She cleared her mind, making it blank, like a fresh piece of paper and focused on the world around her. It was all highway from Weatherford to the Custer County Sheriff's Office, just asphalt and wheat that appeared to go on indefinitely. There wasn't much to look at, but she had learned to appreciate that in the year she had lived in Oklahoma. Back in New York, there was so much to focus on that it all became noise. You could feel alone in a city of over eight million. But here, anything and everything stood out. And if that was the case, someone should have seen Piper or Miley. Someone should have noticed two little girls being taken just days apart.

"Hey, Barb," Kimberley greeted.

Barb stood from her desk. "I got you some lunch. Figured you didn't have time to eat with everything going on."

Barb picked up a bag and walked around her desk, handing it over. "It's a cheeseburger and fries."

"Thanks. Is Burns in?"

"Yeah, he's at his desk, working on reports. He told me the search isn't looking too good." She pursed her lips together. The corners of her mouth dipped down.

"That's what Bearfield said too. Sam's on his way with Benjamin Fry. Hopefully, we get something there." Kimberley nodded.

"Alright, well you go and eat. And you'll have to tell me about Caleb when you have a moment. I could always use a little girl talk. I'm an old woman now, so I have to live vicariously through you youngings," Barb said with a smile.

"You got it, Barb." Kimberley let out a small laugh and disappeared through the set of doors.

Through the second set of doors, she entered the deputies' office area, finding Deputy Burns hunched over his desk reading reports.

"Burns," she said, walking to him.

Burns turned around and stood up. "Chief Deputy King. Bearfield said you got something for me."

Kimberley set the bag of food down and noticed he had an empty takeout container with just a few fries in it on the corner of his desk. Barb must have gotten something to eat for everyone. She pulled out her notepad, quickly flipping through the pages. She tore out a piece of paper and handed it to Burns.

"I need you to pull CCTV and security footage in accordance with those times and locations," she said.

Burns looked down at the piece of paper that detailed Will's alibi the day Miley went missing, then glanced back at Kimberley and nodded.

"One more thing." She pulled out her phone, bringing up her email. She scrolled to the email Joy had forwarded her, the one with all the attachments that contained the anonymous reports that had come in about Will. Kimberley typed in Burns' email address and clicked send. "I'm forwarding you a set of emails. They're anonymous reports of misconduct about a camp counselor. I need you to tell me anything you can about the senders of the emails."

"Sure thing, boss. I'll take a look at them."

Kimberley picked up her bag of food, while Burns took a seat at his desk immediately diving into the task at hand. She walked to her office, pausing to look at Sam's before she entered. Papers and file folders were scattered across his desk as well as several half-drunk mugs of coffee. She was sure he had pulled an all-nighter working on the case. He cared more about others than he did himself. That's what she liked about Sam.

Kimberley took a seat at her own desk, unwrapping her burger and fries. She didn't have much of an appetite but figured she should eat something since Barb had gone to the trouble of picking her up lunch. She nibbled at the fries and took a bite out of the burger. Kimberley knew it tasted good, but right now she couldn't taste anything but the sour pit in her stomach. She pulled out her cell phone, rereading Caleb's text, deciding how to proceed. Should she set up a date with him? Or just simply say thank you? Should she continue the conversation? Or keep it short? Caleb was nice and good looking too. He cared about his work and his son. They had a lot in common, actually. Single parents. Relatively new to town. Perhaps she should give him a shot. What was the worst that could happen? Just as she started to text him back, she heard commotion from the deputies' floor. She looked through the window of her office and watched Sheriff Walker enter. He was leading an older man in handcuffs. The man had a pair of glasses lingering at the end of his pointy nose. His hair was dark, falling just above his ears. When he twisted his neck, his hair swished to the side revealing a large bald spot. Next to Sam, the man looked small, around 5'9" with spindle legs and a belly. Kimberley looked down at her phone, her fingers hovering above it for a moment. She quickly texted, *Thank you for the coffee and flowers, Caleb.* Just a short response.

She glanced up, her eyes following Sam again. Kimberley could see him tightening his jaw as he walked the man, she presumed Benjamin Fry, to the interrogation room. For a moment, her focus got lost in Sam, taking him in from his green eyes to his broad shoulders to his… She shook her head and stood from her seat.

"Deputy Burns," Sam called out. Burns immediately stood from his desk. "Put him in interrogation room one and get him something to drink."

Burns walked to Sheriff Walker, taking hold of the cuffs on Benjamin.

"I didn't do anything," Benjamin yelled. His voice was hoarse as if he had just finished smoking a pack of cigarettes.

Burns disappeared down the hall while Benjamin continued to proclaim his innocence. Sam walked to Kimberley who was now standing outside her office, leaned up against the doorway.

"Good work, Walker." Kimberley delivered a small smile with her comment.

"Since when do you call me Walker?" The corner of his lip perked up.

"Since you walked in our main suspect. How was the ride back with him?" Kimberley stood up straight.

"Long. He cried for half of it and the other half he said he was innocent over and over again." Sam shook his head.

"Ready to interview him?" Kimberley raised an eyebrow.

"I'm gonna let him sweat it out for a bit. He's hysterical. Burns will get him something to drink, and then you and I will go in there and get to the bottom of it." Just as he finished speaking, his stomach rumbled loud enough for Kimberley to hear it.

"You hungry?"

"Famished. Barb said she got me a burger and fries but gave it to Burns because he looked pale as a ghost when he came in, and, apparently, she needs to fatten him up. I'm not sure what she's saying about me then," Sam said with a small laugh.

Kimberley disappeared into her office and reappeared a moment later with her takeout container of food. She had only eaten a bite of the burger and a few fries. "Here, have mine."

Sam looked down at the food and then at Kimberley. "You sure? You've barely eaten any of it."

"I had something on the road," Kimberley lied.

He took the container and walked into his office with Kimberley following behind. Sam quickly scooped up all the loose papers that were sprawled out on his desk and stuffed them into folders.

"Did you have a late night here?" Kimberley took a seat in front of him.

"Late night and an early morning." Sam took a seat and dove into the burger taking a large bite.

"Find anything?"

Sam finished chewing before he spoke. "Nothing that we didn't already know. What about Camp Beaverbrook? You said you were interviewing someone today." He stuffed a couple of fries in his mouth.

"Yeah, I interviewed Joy, the camp director. Remember Will, the counselor Miley mentioned in her stories?"

Sam nodded.

Kimberley leaned forward in her chair. "Well, he's real, and he was recently fired from the camp. There were several anonymous emails sent to Joy accusing him of inappropriate behavior with the girls."

Sam wiped his mouth with a napkin. "Jesus. So, we gotta bring him in too."

"I went and talked to him already. He was with Chloe, the other camp counselor. They seem to be in a relationship."

"And?"

"Well, he gave me a list of places he was the day Miley went missing. I have Burns pulling security footage and CCTV to verify his whereabouts." Kimberley plucked a fry from the takeout container and popped it in her mouth.

"Thought you weren't hungry?" Sam tilted his head.

"I can always eat fries, stuffed or not." Kimberley grinned.

Sam smiled. "What about the night Piper was murdered?" The question made his smile quickly falter.

"Chloe chimed in and said they were together at his apartment. He said the same." Kimberley tossed another fry in her mouth.

"We'll see what Burns comes back with and go from there." Sam nodded and put the rest of the burger in his mouth.

"I'm also having him look into the emails." Kimberley raised an eyebrow.

"In what way?"

"It's odd they came in anonymously all within a matter of minutes. Right?"

"Kind of. What do they say?" Sam tilted his head.

Kimberley pulled her phone out and brought up the emails that Joy had forwarded to her. "They all sound the same." Her eyes scanned it as she read aloud. "To whom it may concern: I thought it was important for you to know that camp counselor Will has acted inappropriately with Beaverbrook campers. I have experienced it and witnessed it myself. I do not feel safe with him here. Sincerely, a concerned camper."

Kimberley looked to Sam.

"Seems rather formal for ten-year-old girls to write."

"The camp ranges in ages from seven to thirteen."

"And they all sound like that?" Sam asked.

Kimberley nodded. "All start off with 'to whom it may concern' and end with 'sincerely, a concerned camper.'"

"Well, I have Burns looking into it. I just want to see what we can find out from the email addresses that sent the reports. I've got a couple of theories there." Kimberley leaned back in her chair.

A knock on the door stopped Sam from following up.

"Sheriff Walker. He's demanding to see his lawyer," Burns said.

Sam wiped his mouth and tossed his napkin in the container. He closed it up and slid it in the garbage. Standing from his seat, he clasped his hands together. "Time to interview this son of a bitch. Burns, give his lawyer a call. We've got an hour or so to get what we can out of him."

CHAPTER THIRTY

Kimberley and Sam took a seat across from Benjamin Fry in the small interrogation room. Kimberley placed a folder on the table in front of her. Benjamin Fry picked his head up from the table, which left behind a red mark on his forehead. His face was blotchy and wet. It was obvious he had been crying. Crying because he had been caught? Kimberley wasn't sure. Sam slid a fresh cup of coffee in front of Benjamin. He was apprehensive for a moment, but then took a slow sip.

"Your lawyer is on the way," Sam said matter-of-factly.

Benjamin nodded slightly, then looked up making eye contact with Sam. "I'll talk to you without him because I've got nothing to hide."

Sam and Kimberley exchanged a brief look and then redirected their attention back to Benjamin.

"We recently learned you were let go from your job for possession of child pornography. Is that true?" Kimberley clenched her jaw as she spoke.

He hung his head in shame and nodded. "Yes."

"And you showed up to Edna and Arthur Chase's house on Sunday, August second, the day Piper went missing?" Sam raised his chin.

"Wait, is that what this is about? You think I had something to do with Piper's death?" His brows knitted together and his mouth dropped open. "I would never hurt Piper. She's family."

"So, you'd hurt someone who wasn't family?" Sam gritted his teeth.

Benjamin shook his head. "No, that's not what I'm saying." He ran his hands down his face in frustration. "I wouldn't hurt anyone. But I especially wouldn't hurt Piper."

"The timing is rather coincidental, don't you think? You show up asking for money and hours later Piper disappears…" Sam tilted his head and scratched at his chin. "Were you blackmailing them into giving you money? Did you take Piper?"

"No!" Benjamin slammed his fist on the table. "I'm not a monster."

"Really? Could have fooled us what with the possession of child pornography…"

Kimberley opened the folder in front of her and slid out a couple of crime scene photos. Piper's lifeless body laid on top of a bed of moss. Her long blonde hair was swooped up around her head, covering the bloody wound. Her big, blue eyes were covered in a sort of white glaze, staring frozenly up at the sky. Kimberley pushed them in front of Benjamin.

"Did you do this?" she asked. "Maybe it was an accident. Maybe you didn't mean to kill her. If you cooperate and tell us the truth, a judge will go a bit easier on you. But if we find out you're lying, your life is over." She narrowed her eyes as she spoke.

"My life is already over," Benjamin said just above a whisper. His eyes were closed as he refused to look at the photos. "It was over when I lost my job. Actually, it never really started. I've never had anyone to call my own. No wife, no kids. People just avoided me. My only family, Edna, didn't want anything to do with me. I'm a leper." He kept his eyes closed as he pitied himself.

"Open your fucking eyes," Sam yelled.

Neither of them felt sorry for him. A little girl was dead and another was missing.

Benjamin's head jerked up and his eyes opened. Tears poured out of them as he looked at the photos of Piper. He ran his fingers around her face. "I know you'll never believe me because of what

I've done, but I didn't do this. I could never. I have a problem, yes, but murder isn't it." His shoulders shook, and Benjamin sobbed. His tears falling onto the photos. Kimberley pulled them away, wiped them off, and put them back in their folder.

"You're right. We don't believe you." Sam folded his arms in front of his chest and looked to Kimberley.

She exhaled a deep breath. Sam was right, she didn't believe him either. But there was nothing to prove otherwise. Everything they had on Benjamin was circumstantial. It would never hold up in court. They needed more.

"Where is Miley Baker?" Kimberley asked. Perhaps she could catch him another way.

Benjamin lifted his head and looked at Kimberley. He pulled his glasses from his face and wiped his eyes and nose with the back of his hand.

"Who's Miley Baker?" he asked, sliding the glasses back on his face.

That didn't work, Kimberley thought to herself, but Benjamin wasn't a dumb guy. Prior to being fired, he had a prestigious job. They needed to rule him out or find something concrete. Right now, she felt as though they were wasting time. She pulled out her notepad and pen.

"Where did you go after leaving Edna and Arthur Chase's house?"

He stammered for a moment. "I drove back to Texas."

"Did you stop for gas?"

He thought for a moment. "Yeah, right before I hit Wichita Falls."

"Stop anywhere else?" Kimberley took notes, capturing Benjamin's alibis. They could verify most of this with CCTV or traffic cams. If they could determine where he was the evening Piper was murdered and the morning Miley went missing, they could either eliminate him as a suspect or start to build a solid case around him. Like a set of walls closing in. Sometimes monsters had to be boxed in to be caught.

"Nope, just for gas."

"And where were you yesterday between the hours of six a.m. and eleven a.m.?" Kimberley tilted her head.

He scratched at his chin, tapped his fingers on the table, and looked up at the ceiling as if he'd find the answer hidden there.

"I was in Texas. I met with my lawyer at nine a.m. about the pending case against me. We went over the plea deal the D.A. provided. I also went to a counseling session. My lawyer told me a judge might go easier on me if I show I'm trying to get help." Benjamin looked back at Sam and then Kimberley.

She jotted down the notes, thinking if he was telling the truth, it would easily rule him out.

There was a knock on the door and Barb peeked her head in. "Sheriff Walker. His lawyer is out in the waiting area. Want me to bring him in?"

Sam turned back and shook his head. "No, we've got everything we need. Mr. Fry you're free to go, but we'll be in touch."

Benjamin hesitated but then rose from his seat. "I can go?"

"Yes, you can go," Sam said. "Burns, come escort Mr. Fry to the front," he yelled over his shoulder.

Burns immediately appeared behind Barb. "Right this way," he said to Benjamin Fry.

Benjamin nodded. "Thank you. Thank you," he said as he pushed his chair in and walked around the table toward Deputy Burns. "For what it's worth, I hope you find the person that did this. Piper was my great-niece. I cared about her." A couple of tears rolled down his cheek and he turned to leave, following behind Burns. Kimberley shuddered.

"You two need anything?" Barb asked.

"No, we're okay," Kimberley said.

"Alright, holler if you need anything. I'll leave you two alone," she said, shutting the door behind her.

Sam let out a deep breath and ran his fingers down his face.

"Why'd you let him leave?" Kimberley asked.

"We got nothing to hold him on. All circumstantial. His lawyer was going to get him out anyway."

Kimberley nodded. "His alibis will be easy to prove one way or another. I'll pull Lodge in to look into CCTV from here to Texas the night Piper was murdered. And he can confirm his meeting with his lawyer and his therapy session for the morning Miley went missing."

"Put Burns on it."

"I'd like him to stay on the Camp Beaverbrook until that's sorted out," Kimberley pressed.

Sam looked over at her and raised his brows. "Alright."

"What are we going to do after the woods around Black Heart Lane is finished being searched?" Kimberley asked.

"Widen the search. If we have to, I'll start checking houses. I don't give a damn. We're going to find Miley. Let's focus on Fry and Camp Beaverbrook first though. Too much red tape around searching houses." Sam shook his head.

Kimberley felt the same way. She'd love to go door to door, busting them down and searching every house in Dead Woman Crossing until they found Miley. But she also knew it wasn't a viable nor a legal option. Plus, for all she knew, Miley might not even be in Dead Woman Crossing. She could be anywhere by now. It had been more than twenty-four hours and the chances of finding her alive were dwindling.

Sam clicked on his radio. "Deputy Lodge," he said into it.

It took nearly a minute for Lodge to say anything back. He was always on his own time.

"Lodge here."

"How's the search coming along?"

"Right side of Black Heart Lane is done. They're finishing up the left side. We got nothing," Lodge said out of breath.

Sam let out a sigh. "Alright, I need you to head back to the station. I've got an interview I want you to follow up on. Verifying alibi and capturing CCTV footage."

"I'm on my way," Lodge said. The radio went static.

Sam looked to Kimberley. His mouth parted for a moment, but the door opening interrupted him. Barb popped her head in again.

"Miley's father, Oliver, just called. He's in town staying at the Traveler's Inn. He asked for you all to come meet him there," Barb said.

"When?" Kimberley asked.

"Now. Said he won't be in town long."

Sam rubbed the back of his neck and let out a sigh. "Of course, he did."

CHAPTER THIRTY-ONE

As they drove through the small town of Dead Woman Crossing, Kimberley noticed it seemed almost deserted, more so than usual. There were very few people out and about. Perhaps they were keeping their own children cooped up inside, scared of what their fate may be if they let them out of their sight. Even The Trophy Room had only a couple of Harleys parked out front, most likely out-of-towners passing through.

Sam parked the SUV in the parking lot of the Traveler's Inn. There were only a couple of cars in the lot. Dead Woman Crossing wasn't really a place people visited as it wasn't an ideal travel destination. The Traveler's Inn was a white, two-story building with forest green accents detailed on the doors, shutters, and gutters. It was one of those motels where each room had its own entrance, the creepy kind. There was something comforting about having multiple doors to block out a strange land you were unfamiliar with. The parking lot was a mix of gravel and sand. Walking across the lot, Kimberley and Sam kicked up dust with their boots. They were heading toward the front desk area to find out what room Oliver was staying in when loud shrieks caught their attention.

Kimberley and Sam exchanged a look and followed where the commotion was coming from, all the way at the far end of the building. Linda stood just six feet from a partially open door, bent over sobbing. She jolted into a standing position, her stringy black hair falling behind her shoulders.

"Oliver, you piece of shit!" she yelled. "It's your fault they're gone."

As they got closer, they could see the man. He held the door only partially open, enough for his head and top half of his body to peek out. He sported a crew cut and a clean-shaven face. His hair was a dirty blond, and his eyes were a dark brown. He was tall and built like he worked a strenuous, hands-on job. Dressed in ripped blue jeans that weren't intentionally torn, and a white T-shirt, he kept his distance from Linda who was hysterical. Kimberley could understand why as she had already lost one daughter and her other was missing, and now she was faced with looking at the man that had run out on her.

"Linda, you need to leave." Oliver's tone was firm, but not loud.

"Why did you come back here? You don't give a fuck about Miley or me!" Linda let out a scream and turned on her foot, taking off toward Kimberley and Sam.

"Linda," Kimberley said in a calm tone. "Are you okay?"

She wiped at her face with her forearm, smearing her mascara and red lipstick. "Does it look like I'm okay?" Linda spit. She let out a grunt of frustration and threw her head into her hands.

Kimberley took a couple of slow steps toward her. "Do you want me to take you home?"

Linda let her hands slide from her face through her dark, stringy hair. "No!" she screamed. "I want you to stop wasting your fucking time with my deadbeat ex-husband and get out there and find my little girl. Do your goddamn job!" Linda sidestepped Kimberley and Sam and took off, running toward her car.

Kimberley watched her get into her vehicle and slam on the gas. The tires spit up gravel and sand as she sped off.

"Should we send a deputy over to her house to check on her?"

Sam glanced at Kimberley and then at Oliver who was now standing outside of his motel door with a look of relief on his face. "No, let's let her cool off. She's hurting."

Kimberley nodded, already deciding she'd check on her herself the next day. Sam and Kimberley turned back and walked to Oliver. He had taken a seat at a picnic table that sat off to the side of the motel. Hunched over, he rubbed at his face.

"Oliver Baker," Sam said, taking a seat across from him. Kimberley sat beside Sam.

Oliver picked up his head. "Yep, that's me."

"I'm Sheriff Walker. We spoke on the phone."

Oliver nodded.

"And this here is Chief Deputy King."

Oliver nodded again.

"I drove all the way here and got quite the welcome from my ex. What is it that I can help you with?"

It was obvious to Kimberley he didn't care to be here. His tone was flat, his eyes were dull, and his face was blank as if he had given up on life a long time ago. He was just going through the motions.

"Your daughter is missing. Doesn't that concern you in the slightest?" Kimberley gritted her teeth.

"Of course. It's probably for the best, though." Oliver wiped a few beads of sweat from his forehead.

"What's that supposed to mean?" Sam raised his shoulders a little higher, sitting up straight.

"You saw my ex, Linda." He shook his head and sighed.

"Yes, we have. More so than you have in the past few years. Same with your daughter. Her daughter is missing, and she's hurting, and you don't seem to give a damn." Kimberley pursed her lips.

"Look, I came here as a courtesy. You're right, I haven't been in Miley's life since our oldest, Sophie, passed away. That doesn't mean I don't care about her. I do. And no, I don't know where she is."

"Why did you leave?" Sam's jaw was clenched. His fist followed suit.

Kimberley was scared Sheriff Walker was going to deck Oliver, and as much as she thought he deserved it, she knew it would just muddy the investigation. She cleared her throat and watched his fist unclench ever so slowly.

"After Sophie passed, Linda got loopy. She started drinking heavily and taking painkillers. Think she was trying to numb the pain rather than work through it. I couldn't stand it. She started lashing out at me and Miley. I just couldn't do it anymore, so I left." Oliver slightly shook his head.

"Why not see your daughter?" Sam's tone was stern.

Oliver shrugged his shoulders. "I wanted to. I tried to. Linda didn't want me around. And she was feeding Miley lies. Telling her I was responsible for Sophie's death. So, Miley didn't want me around either. And I just went on with my life. I have a fiancée now. She's got two kids of her own."

Sam's jaw unclenched and his face softened.

"Where were you yesterday between the hours of six a.m. and eleven a.m.?" Kimberley asked.

"Working. I work six a.m. to six p.m., Monday through Friday. I haven't missed a day of work in two years. You can talk to my supervisor. I work over at a cold storage plant in Oklahoma City. Americold Logistics." He looked Kimberley in the eyes as he spoke.

"We'll look into that. How long you in town for?" Kimberley tilted her head.

"Til tomorrow. I just came here to clear my name. Wasn't sure what Linda was saying about me. For all I know, she was telling you guys I did it," Oliver said, shaking his head and rubbing at the sides of his face. It looked as though he was trying to wake himself up from a nightmare.

"Why would you say that?" Sam asked.

"Because she's goddamn crazy, that's why. Like I said, you can follow up with Americold. They'll clear me of any involvement. I'm sure of it."

She didn't like the way he was talking about his ex-wife who was clearly hurting. She also didn't like how blasé he was about his missing daughter. He didn't seem to care about anything other than staying out of it all, which Kimberley found incredibly sad. How could this man turn his back on his daughter? How could any parent do that?

Sam stood up from the picnic table, while Kimberley stared just a little bit longer at the broken man in front of her.

"King. You ready?" She looked up at him and nodded, standing up as well.

"You won't hear from us again, unless your alibi doesn't check out," Kimberley said.

She and Sam started walking back toward their vehicle. Oliver turned around and called out to them. "What if you find her? Or worse? Will you tell me?"

Kimberley turned back. "No, she's already lost to you."

Inside the vehicle, Sam was slow to flip on the engine.

"That was harsh, Detective," he said, giving her a quick glance.

Kimberley stared out the passenger door window at Oliver who was still sitting at the table. His back was hunched over, and she could see his shoulders slightly shake. Or maybe they weren't shaking. Maybe she was seeing what she wanted to see... pain.

"I don't think so. He abandoned his wife and child. And look at the way he talks about Linda and Miley. It's pathetic." Kimberley folded her arms in front of her chest and put one foot on the dashboard.

In her book, there was no excuse for Oliver's behavior or his actions. But she knew Sam saw things differently because he had experienced things differently. He and Oliver had something in common... losing a child, and Sam knew that pain and what it could do to a person better than anyone.

CHAPTER THIRTY-TWO

"It's not looking so good in there." Barb pointed to the double set of doors. Her joyful attitude and contagious smiled had faltered.

Sam rubbed at his temples, while Kimberley stood beside him flipping through her notepad, hoping something would jump out at her. They still had to verify Benjamin Fry's and Will's alibis, so they still had that. They had just finished interviewing Oliver, so she'd have one of the deputies call over to Americold in Oklahoma City to verify his whereabouts. She didn't think Oliver was lying anyway, so she knew that would check out regardless. As she read through the notes, nothing stuck out.

"They all back?" Sam asked.

Barb nodded. "I ordered pizza. Hope that's alright."

"Yeah, that's just fine. I'm sure everyone is famished after spending the last two days searching those woods." Sam shook his head.

"Any new tips or leads come in?"

Barb shook her head. "Nope, it's been quiet aside from a disturbance over at The Trophy Room. Lodge volunteered to go take care of that."

Sam tapped his foot against the ground.

"Thought Lodge was working on CCTV and verifying Fry's alibis?" Kimberley raised an eyebrow. She knew he couldn't sit still and hated doing anything that required use of his brain. He was an ape with a short temper.

"He passed it off," Barb said. "Overheard him telling Burns to take care of it."

J.R. ADLER

Sam puffed out his cheeks as he let out a deep breath. "Alright, let's go rally the troops."

"I'll bring the pizza in when it arrives." Barb gave them a small smile.

Kimberley and Sam nodded and made their way to the office floor. All of the deputies were slumped over their desks. Some were reading reports. Others had their head in their hands. And others were typing slowly on their keyboards. It looked as though they had just lost a war or surrendered to an enemy. Their spirits were broken. The room smelled of a mixture of sap and body odor. Bearfield's hair was slicked back and greasy. Hill had grime on the back of his neck and his head was rested on his desk. The couple of night shift deputies that were pulling double shifts were leaned back in their chairs with their eyes closed. Burns was the only one that looked somewhat clean as he had been pulled off the search early to help in the office. He took notes on a pad of paper in between clicks on his mouse and his fingers banging against the keyboard.

Bearfield noticed Sam and Kimberley's presence first when he looked up from his desk. He stood immediately and tilted his head.

"Barb says the woods surrounding Black Heart Lane are clear." Sam rocked back and forth on his heels. It wasn't a question. He was just stating the obvious.

"That's right. We got nothing. Questioned a couple of hunters. They hadn't seen anything out of the ordinary." Bearfield pushed some of his stray hair back, tucking it behind his ears.

Sam folded in his lips and scanned the room.

"Burns, how's it coming along?" Kimberley asked.

Burns popped his head up. "Almost done with CCTV and security on Will. As of now, his alibis are checking out. I'll start on Benjamin Fry next." He immediately went back to work on his computer.

"What about the emails?"

"I'll get to those after I finish up with Fry," he said not lifting his head.

Kimberley inhaled, trying to keep her frustration contained. They had nothing. They had less than nothing. Just a couple of maybes that seemed to be turning to noes.

"What now, boss?" Hill stood from his seat. He sat on the corner of his desk and itched at his pointy nose.

"Why don't you help Burns? Go ahead and give Benjamin Fry's alibis a call. I also need you to give a call to Americold over in Oklahoma City. Verify that an Oliver Baker was working there yesterday when Miley went missing," Sam instructed.

"You got it." Hill retook his chair and picked up his desk phone.

Sam looked down at his watch for a moment. "Night shift, Lopez and Willetts, you are dismissed. You can report back for your regular scheduled shift but go on and get a few hours of sleep for now." The two deputies rose from their seats and nodded, thanking Sheriff Walker. They lumbered out of the office area, disappearing through the double set of doors.

Barb carried in a couple of large pizzas and set them down on an empty desk. "Hope you're all hungry," she said, opening the boxes to reveal a cheese and pepperoni pizza.

Hill and Burns beelined for the food, placing a couple of slices each on a paper plate. They thanked Barb and returned to their work.

Bearfield hesitated not knowing what to do, what to work on, how he could help. He ran his fingers down his chin as though he were weighing out his options.

"Bearfield, after you get some pizza, why don't you go back out on the road and patrol. We're still looking for Piper Chase's bicycle. Maybe, we'll get lucky there," Sam said, shrugging his shoulders.

Kimberley could see it on all their faces… defeat, but she hadn't accepted it yet. Two little girls in a small town don't go missing without someone noticing.

Bearfield nodded. "Not hungry, so I'll just get on the road. I'll let you know if I find anything." He walked past Sam and Kimberley with slumped shoulders. It wasn't how he typically carried himself.

"Is that it then?" Kimberley said to Sam. She didn't mean to but her words came out accusatory.

"That's it for now. We've got a couple of leads, which Burns and Hill are following up on. We'll see what happens with them." Sam shook his head and walked to his office, closing the door behind him.

Kimberley's phone buzzed with a new text from her mother.

Can we talk?

Her fingers hovered above the keys for a moment before she texted back.

No.

Kimberley looked back at Sheriff Walker's office. She could see through the window he was seated at his desk and leaned back in his chair with his hands propped up behind his head. He was just staring at the ceiling. How could he just throw in the towel right now? How could he just wait for something to fall into their laps? They should be out there talking to everyone and anyone. Someone had to know something. Kimberley glanced over at Barb who was putting a small piece of pizza on a paper plate. She loaded up another plate with another couple pieces of pizza.

"Barb." Kimberley walked over to her.

Barb looked up as she wiped her hands with a napkin. "I'm just making a plate for Sam. When he gets like this, you've gotta make him eat."

"Gets like what? Gives up?" There was a tinge of sarcasm in Kimberley's voice that she didn't mean.

"Oh, he's not giving up. He's taking a step back. It's all a part of his process. When he gets overwhelmed, he shuts down for a little bit, like how you'd fix a computer. Turn it off and then turn it back on again." Barb picked up her plates.

"We don't have time for him to shut down," Kimberley said just above a whisper.

"I'll talk to him." Barb gave Kimberley a small nod.

"Hey, Barb. Would you mind watching Jessica tonight?"

Barb turned back.

"Of course, sweetheart."

Kimberley watched her make her way to Sam's office. She set a plate down in front of him and took a seat. Sam leaned forward in his chair and looked through the window, making eye contact with Kimberley. His eyes were apologetic.

Kimberley pulled out her phone and brought up Caleb's phone number. She hesitated again, but then sent her message anyway.

Want to meet me at The Trophy Room for a drink at 7?

She watched the three little dots light up. He was texting her back. They disappeared, then lit up again. Finally, a text came through.

I thought you'd never ask. ;)

It was a little after seven when Kimberley walked into The Trophy Room. She was running late after picking up Jessica and dropping her off with Barb. She scanned the bar. It always looked the same. The regulars bellied up to the bar and the slot machines. A few of the farm boys playing darts and pool. A haze of smoke cast over the whole room. The dead animals hung all along the walls like they were something to be proud of. Their dark frozen eyes seeming to watch your every move. And greaseball Ryan standing behind the bar in a ratty T-shirt. Although, they had had their differences, he along with the rest of the town had started respecting Kimberley. Or perhaps they just had gotten used to her presence. He give her a small nod and a crooked smile.

She walked to the bar and threw down a five-dollar bill.

"What will it be?" he asked, slinging a rag over his shoulder.

"Whiskey on the rocks."

"Ooo, a strong one today," he started to tease but his face turned serious. Ryan leaned in a little closer across the bar. "I heard about them girls. Sorry you're going through that."

Kimberley gave him a small nod. He seemed sincere, and he went back to fixing her drink. She glanced around the bar again, looking for Caleb, but also noticing everyone was giving her the same look that Ryan just had. Apologetic or sympathetic, she wasn't sure.

"Here you are," Ryan said, setting the glass down. It was poured much stiffer than usual. "It's on me," he added, pushing the five-dollar bill toward her.

"Thanks, but keep it." She took a sip. It burned all the way down, but she liked that first burn. The rest of it would go down smoothly. "Hey, Ryan."

He looked up from cleaning dirty glasses in a sink. "What's up?"

"Have you seen a man named Caleb in here? He's tall, dark hair—"

Ryan interrupted, pointing to a booth at the far end of the bar, right behind the pool tables. It was the same spot she and Sam always sat. Caleb was sitting there, casually drinking a pint of beer. How had she missed him? He was wearing a baseball cap, and the farm boys playing pool kept walking in front of him when they took their shots.

"Thanks, Ryan."

He gave her a nod as she walked across the bar.

"Hey there, stranger," she said with a smile.

Caleb looked up, repositioned his hat, and delivered a smile back. "Thought you were going to stand me up," he teased. "Have a seat."

Kimberley slid into the booth. She had been excited for a night out, some time to forget about work, her problems with her mom, and to not be responsible for anything but having a good time. Now that she was here, she felt guilty and uncomfortable. She swirled her glass, busying her hands and took another sip.

"Sorry, I'm late. I had to pick up Jessica and drop her off at a friend's house."

"Oh shit. I forgot about Flynn." Caleb's eyes went wide, and he partially stood from his seat.

"What? Oh my God! Go," Kimberley said. Her voice full of disappointment.

Caleb retook his seat and let out a chuckle. "I'm just kidding. I had his babysitter pick him up. Think I would forget about my own kid?" He smiled widely, then filled the space between his lips with his pint of beer.

"No." Kimberley forced a smile, trying to laugh it off. She herself had forgotten about Jessica a time or two. Forgotten to pick her up from daycare. She swallowed hard. That feeling of guilt creeping up again.

"But I have forgotten to pick Flynn up before," Caleb said, almost as though he knew exactly what Kimberley was thinking. "We're parents, but we're also human. We make mistakes." He gave a small shrug of his shoulders.

"Thanks," she said. The forced smile turned real.

"For what?"

"For understanding."

"That's what I'm here for." Caleb let out a chuckle. He extinguished it with another gulp of his beer.

"How's the new job been?" Kimberley asked, changing the subject.

"Same as the old job. Construction is construction no matter what you're building or where you're doing it. You're still starting off with the basic materials, wood and concrete. I should be asking you how yours is going." He leaned forward a little more, propping his elbows on the table.

Kimberley looked down at her glass, watching the ice melt into the whiskey, diluting it a little more. "I don't really want to talk about work," she said, picking up her head and looking into Caleb's eyes.

Caleb nodded. "Understandable. I was surprised you asked to meet for a drink, since you had said you wouldn't until the case was wrapped up. Is it?" He slightly tilted his head.

"Is it what?"

"Wrapped up?" He took another drink of his beer, finishing it off.

Kimberley shook her head. "Not even close. I just needed to take my mind off of everything."

Caleb gave a sad look. "Oh."

"Not like that. You're not just here to take my mind off of everything. Sorry." Kimberley nervously drank the rest of her whiskey. She was so bad at dating, but she wasn't even sure if it was a date.

"No worries. I'll take what I can get." He shot her a wide grin and grabbed both their glasses. "This round's on me," he said, getting up from his seat and walking to the bar.

Kimberley rubbed at her forehead, willing her mind to shut off. Why couldn't she just sit there and enjoy a drink with a nice guy? Her head wasn't in it. It kept going back to the argument with her mother. The interviews with Linda, Arthur, Edna, Will, Chloe, Benjamin, and Oliver. It was like she was missing something, staring right at it, but it was just out of reach. She took a deep breath and exhaled, hoping the cluster of thoughts would go with it. The image of Piper, lying on top of a bed of moss, flashed before her eyes. Kimberley slightly shook her head and rubbed at her temples.

"You feeling alright?" Caleb asked, setting down the drinks and taking a seat.

"Yeah, yeah. Just a little headache," Kimberley lied.

"Do you want to go? No hard feelings if you do."

"No, I'm fine. Nothing a little bit of this won't cure." She held up her glass, swirled the cubes, and took a gulp of it.

Caleb followed suit, taking a drink of his beer. "So, tell me about you."

Kimberley set her glass down, hesitating for a moment. She folded her hands in her lap and leaned back. "Not much to tell. I lived in NYC most of my life. A year ago, I moved here."

"What did you do in the city?"

"NYPD homicide detective," Kimberley said without missing a beat. The NYPD seemed like a lifetime ago.

Caleb raised his brows. "Impressive, King. What brought you here?"

A slideshow of images played right in front of her eyes. One right after another, like the passing of a freight train. Loud and fast. The woman shackled to the mattress. The woman strung up by her neck in the attic. The woman in the bathtub. *"Who's the King now?"* written in blood across a mirror. The bloody sink. The bathtub. One after another.

She blinked them away. "Just needed a change of pace."

Caleb tilted his head as if he knew she was lying, holding something back, but he didn't press any further. "You and your mom doing okay?"

"Oh yeah, sorry you had to see that. We're not really talking." Kimberley took a sip of her whiskey.

"I get it." Caleb held up his hands. "I won't pry any further."

"Tell me about you, Caleb," Kimberley said, changing the subject. She realized she didn't really know anything about him.

She knew he was new to Dead Woman Crossing, had a son, and worked construction. That was it. She could find out more from a Facebook profile or a LinkedIn page.

He leaned back into his seat and sprawled out a little, getting more comfortable. "You know the basics. New to town. Single dad. Just trying to give my boy the best life possible as I'm sure you're doing the same with your little girl."

Kimberley smiled.

"King," a voice called out from across the bar. She turned her head to find Sam walking toward her with a drink in hand. He had clearly been drinking because his eyes were glossy and his walk was heavy. She gave him a tight smile and whispered sorry to Caleb. He took a gulp of his beer.

"Sam, what are you doing here?" Kimberley asked. Sam stood beside the booth. His eyes lingered on Caleb for a moment too long, narrowing. He relaxed them when he averted his attention to Kimberley.

"Just stopped in for a drink," he said nonchalantly.

"Seems like you've had more than a drink." Kimberley raised an eyebrow.

Sam shrugged a shoulder, swirled his scotch, and slammed the whole thing. "Ryan, another!" he yelled, turning back to the bar. "Mind if I join ya?"

"I'd rather—" Kimberley started.

"Sure, pull up a chair," Caleb interrupted.

Kimberley gave him a fleeting look. He returned a crooked smile, while Sam grabbed his fresh drink from the bar top and pulled a chair to the edge of the booth. He turned the chair around so the back of it was closest to the booth and sat on it like he was straddling a horse. He was making his presence as known as possible.

"So, you work with King?" Caleb said.

"Yep. Hired her about a year ago. Best decision I ever made." Sam smiled over the rim of his glass.

Oh God. He was clearly drunk, Kimberley thought. What was he doing? This wasn't a good look for the Sheriff's Department, especially when there was a pending case. She scanned the room to see if anyone was looking at them, but surprisingly everyone was minding their own business. Not the norm for a small town.

"Sam's just being nice," Kimberley finally said. "I give him hell." She took a sip of her drink.

"Caleb, is it?" Sam questioned as if he didn't know his name, but Kimberley knew he did.

"Yeah, it's Caleb."

"Where'd you come from? We don't get a lot of new people around here. Kind of odd if you ask me." Sam cocked his head.

"No one asked you," Kimberley challenged.

"It's fine." Caleb held up a hand. "I moved here from upstate New York. A little town called Ithaca, quite charming."

"You did construction there?" Sam leaned in a little closer.

"I did. Worked in Ithaca, Binghamton, Cortland, and Elmira. Basically, anywhere they needed me." He took another drink of his beer, scanning from Kimberley to Sam.

Sam nodded several times, took a sip of his drink, and was quiet for a moment as if he was deciding what to say next.

"Are you done with the interrogation?" Kimberley's tone was firm.

Sam let out a forced laugh. "Just getting to know your lad here."

Kimberley blew out a gust of hot air and took a long drink. She rolled her eyes as the liquid went down her throat.

"Hey, I've got no problem answering questions," Caleb added with a laugh.

Kimberley appreciated that he was being patient with Sam, but her patience was running thin. She understood he was having a hard time, that the past week had ripped open old wounds, but this was out of line.

"Good," Sam said, squinting his eyes. Kimberley couldn't tell if he was scowling at Caleb or his lids were heavy from the alcohol. Either way, she didn't like it.

"Kimberley mentioned you have a son," Sam said.

"Yup, his name is Flynn. He's a good boy. What about you? Got any of your own?" Caleb's face lit up, while Sam's eyes went dark.

Kimberley closed her eyes for a brief moment. She should have warned Caleb, but then again it wasn't her place to disclose that information and she had no intention of the three of them running into one another again. She looked at Sam, watching the grief run over his face. He swallowed hard. His eyes became a little glossier. He brought the glass to his mouth and drank nearly the entire thing. Sam set the glass down hard.

"Nope," he said.

Caleb took a gulp of his beer. "I don't know what I'd do without my boy. He makes this life worth living."

Kimberley could see Sam's jaw tightening. "How did your conversation with Barb go?" she asked, hoping to change the subject.

Sam picked up his glass, tossing the rest of his drink into his mouth. He set it down hard again. "It's funny." He looked right at Caleb. "You showed up just a couple of weeks before those girls went missing." He flared his nostrils and raised his chin.

Caleb gave him a blank look. "What are you trying to say, Sheriff?"

"I'm not saying anything. Just making observations. Makes my life worth living." Sam shrugged his shoulders.

"Alright, that's enough." Kimberley's voice was full of irritation. She stood from her seat sharply. "I'm sorry, Caleb. I'll text you later, but I'm going to get him home."

Caleb nodded.

"I'm fine," Sam said.

Caleb put his hand on Sam's shoulder and looked him in the eye. "No hard feelings, man. I know you're having a hard week."

Sam's eyes bulged as he pushed Caleb's hand off of his shoulder and stood from his seat. His lips flattened and his face reddened. Before he could say anything, Kimberley grabbed him and pushed him toward the entrance.

"Let's go, Sam," she said. Kimberley turned back, mouthing sorry to Caleb. He gave her a small smile and showed his palms, saying it was alright.

"Come on, Sam!" She put one arm around his back and got under the crux of his arm, supporting most of his weight.

"You should run a background check on that guy," he slurred.

Kimberley rolled her eyes as she walked him out of the bar. Most people didn't notice, but the ones that did, gave sympathetic glances.

"He rubs me the wrong way," Sam added.

Kimberley was certain Sam was jealous and that was why Caleb rubbed him the wrong way. She didn't understand why, though. Sam had never shown any real interest in her. Sure, there may have been some light flirting, but it never went beyond that.

"Caleb. What kind of name is that anyway?" Sam scoffed as Kimberley got him in the passenger seat of her vehicle. "And Caleb what? What even is his last name?" Sam added just as Kimberley closed the door on him. Her eyes went wide. He was right. She didn't even know this man's last name.

CHAPTER THIRTY-THREE

After a failed attempt to bring Sam to his own house, Kimberley pulled up in front of Barb's home. Sam had forgotten his keys in his vehicle and locked himself out of his home. She considered going back to get his keys, but they were closer to Barb's house anyway, and she had left Jessica with her long enough. Plus, she knew Barb had a couple of spare rooms.

"We're here," Kimberley announced, shutting off the engine.

Sam woke from his slumber and rubbed his eyes. "Where?"

"Barb's."

"Thought you were taking me home?"

"Well, you locked yourself out."

Sam let out a deep breath and ran his hands down his face. He slid out of the passenger side of the vehicle and stumbled toward the front door. Kimberley caught up with him, straightening out his walk and ensuring he didn't fall. For how he acted, she should have left him on his front lawn, she thought. No matter how mad she was at Sam, she wouldn't do that. Kimberley could see the living room light on in the front window and the television lit up. She was sure Jessica was probably fast asleep and Barb was watching the Hallmark channel.

Kimberley opened the front door quietly and helped Sam inside. Barb was seated on the couch, knitting something out of green yarn. A glass of red wine was on the end table beside her and the Hallmark channel was indeed on the television. She set her knitting needles and yarn aside, jumping up from her seat.

"Oh heavens, what did he get into?" she asked, walking to Sam.

"A bottle of scotch," Kimberley said sarcastically.

"Ugh, I can smell it on him." She waved a hand in front of her nose.

"It's not what it looks like," Sam said, unconvincingly.

"I've got him," Barb said. She got underneath his shoulder and walked him through the living room and down the hall. "Shhhh," she added when Sam started to talk.

Kimberley pulled off her boots and took a seat on the couch, watching the colors bounce around on the Hallmark channel. It wasn't even Halloween yet, and Barb was already watching Christmas movies. Kimberley didn't blame her. What they were experiencing was scary enough. The person responsible for Piper's death and Miley's disappearance was still out there. For all she knew, she had spoken to this person, walked past them, maybe even bumped into them. Her mind went back to Sam's drunken words. *And Caleb what? What even is his last name?*

Barb walked into the living room, carrying a glass of red wine and a plate of cheese and crackers. She handed the glass of wine to Kimberley, set the plate down on the coffee table, and took a seat next to her.

"He's asleep in the back bedroom," she said, taking a sip of her wine.

"Good. How was Jessica tonight?"

"Better behaved than Sam," Barb said with a chuckle.

Kimberley smiled and took a drink of her wine.

"What happened tonight?" Barb glanced at Kimberley and then back at the television.

"I was having drinks with Caleb, and Sam showed up. He was already a little drunk, and then Caleb asked him if he had any kids. It all went south after that."

"Poor Sam." Barb shook her head. She leaned forward and put a piece of cheddar cheese on a cracker.

"He also kind of accused Caleb of being involved in Piper's death and Miley's disappearance." Kimberley rolled her eyes.

"Damn Sam," Barb added, popping the cracker and cheese in her mouth. "He's not always like this."

"I know," Kimberley said.

"Honestly, he used to be like this all the time, but he's changed ever since you came around." Barb raised an eyebrow and nudged a shoulder into Kimberley.

"Yeah?" she asked, giving her a quizzical look.

"Oh yeah. You're good for him. You just gotta be patient with Sam. He's like a ten-thousand-piece puzzle without the box for reference. It just takes a little while longer." Barb took another sip of her wine.

Takes a little while longer for what, Kimberley thought. She'd been more than patient with Sam, and she wasn't even sure what she was being patient for.

"Your mom called," Barb added.

Kimberley rolled her eyes. "What did she want?"

"Wanted to talk to you."

"I already told her I wasn't interested in talking to her." There was a bite to Kimberley's tone. She didn't mean to talk like that to Barb.

Barb and Kimberley sat in silence for a few minutes. They watched the lead actress run to the lead actor, professing her love for him on screen. Barb smiled widely as the cheesy film concluded.

"Well, you should get to bed," Barb said, turning off the television.

Kimberley finished her glass of wine. "Where should I put this?"

"Just set it down. I'll take care of it."

Kimberley set the empty glass down on the coffee table and stood from her seat.

"Thanks for watching Jessica tonight," she said, lingering for a moment.

"It was my pleasure." Barb stood from her seat and started collecting the dishes.

Kimberley called over her shoulder as she started off out of the living room and to her bedroom. "Goodnight."

"Kimberley."

She stopped and turned to Barb.

"Parents don't always make the best decisions. They're human too." Barb tilted her head.

Kimberley let the words digest before she moved a muscle. She knew what Barb was trying to say, but she wasn't willing to accept it. She gave her a slight nod and a small smile before leaving the room.

"Momma, wakey," Jessica said, climbing on top of Kimberley. She had climbed out of the crib Barb had in the corner of the bedroom for when her grandchildren were much smaller. Jessica was too big for a crib, which was why it was so easy for her to escape. Kimberley rubbed her eyes and sat up. She smiled at Jessica.

"You know you're not supposed to climb out of that crib," she said, tickling Jessica's sides. Jessica fell backwards onto the mattress, lying beside her mother. Her feet and legs and arms kicking all over. She was wearing pink pajamas with the footies. Jessica squealed and laughed.

"Sowry," Jessica said in between fits of giggles.

"Your punishment is a thousand kisses," Kimberley said, planting kisses all over Jessica's cheeks, head and neck. Her door squeaked open, and she stopped, glancing up.

Sam stood in the doorway, holding two cups of coffee. He was dressed for work already, minus the utility belt. Kimberley could tell he was hungover, thanks to his bloodshot, flat eyes, but he sported a smile as he watched her with Jessica. He held out a mug of coffee. It was a peace offering.

"Coffee?" he said.

Kimberley sat up in the bed and nodded.

"Sam," Jessica squealed.

He handed the mug to Kimberley and she took it with both hands, letting the cup warm them. Jessica sat up in the bed, reaching her arms up to Sam. Jessica always lit up when Sam was around. He had a way with kids. He set his cup of coffee down on the dresser and picked up Jessica.

"Heard you were good last night," he said with a smile, lifting her up in the air. Jessica squealed with happiness as he tossed her up a few inches and caught her.

Jessica nodded. "I was." She smiled wide and giggled.

"Sam was bad," Kimberley teased.

Jessica's mouth went wide. "Uh-oh," she said.

Barb stopped in the doorway. "Oh good, you're all up. I've got eggs and bacon on the stove. They'll be ready in ten minutes."

"Barb," Jessica squealed, reaching out for her.

"Hi, sweetie. Here let's get you ready for the day," she said, taking Jessica from Sam.

"You don't have to do that," Kimberley said.

"I know, but I want to." She smiled. She left the room with Jessica in tow, bouncing her on her hip.

"Can we talk?" Sam asked. His stance was closed off and he hung his head.

Kimberley hesitated, looking up at him. She stared into his green eyes, and when he couldn't meet her gaze, she took in each part of him, from his strong jaw to his broad shoulders. She scooted over in the bed and patted the open space next to her.

Sam slowly walked toward the bed and took a seat on it, while Kimberley kept her eyes on her mug of coffee.

"I'm sorry for last night," he said.

"Do you remember what you did?"

"Kind of. I was out of line. What you do in your personal time is none of my business, and I shouldn't have acted that way toward your friend, Caleb." He looked at Kimberley as if he had finally worked up the courage to. Or perhaps he was trying to gauge her reaction to him saying Caleb was a friend. She wasn't sure, but she met his gaze.

"Don't ever do that again, Sam."

"I won't."

She didn't want to let him off the hook that easily, but she had a hard time staying mad at him.

"Did you mean what you said?"

"About Caleb?"

"No, about me..." Kimberley said, taking a sip of her coffee.

Sam's face went blank. He clearly didn't remember telling her 'she was the best thing that ever happened to him' and it hurt.

"Umm... what did I say?" Sam tilted his head. His eyes begged her to tell him.

"It doesn't matter." She shrugged her shoulders letting her chin drop.

Sam put his hand to her chin, lifting it slightly, staring into her eyes. "Tell me, Kimberley."

She stared back at him for a moment. She'd never noticed before, but he had a small freckle on his left iris. Kimberley focused on it, but then pushed his hand away.

"I've gotta get ready for work." She slid out of bed and left the room.

If he felt that way about her, she didn't want to have to remind him of it. If he didn't remember, then he clearly hadn't meant it. Kimberley padded out of the room toward the bathroom.

CHAPTER THIRTY-FOUR

Miley, Miley. What do I do with you? I can feel them closing in on me. Or maybe that's the outside of my own brain, closing in on itself. No, they're out there. They're looking for you… and for me, but they don't know who me is. I know they're done combing the woods and Black Heart Lane. I see them driving around town, hoping you'll miraculously appear. Like you'll run out in the road and be returned home safe. But that's not going to happen. It's so hard to think. I need more time. More time to figure this out. More time with you. More time to decide what I should do with you. You're so quiet now. No more screams. No more pleading. You're just quiet. Motionless and silent. I like you that way. I liked Piper that way, too. I know I'm going to keep you forever, because the only things you can keep forever are things that can't run away from you. And you can't run away, Miley.

CHAPTER THIRTY-FIVE

The sky was gray and the day dreary, which matched Kimberley's mood as she walked out of Happy Trails Daycare. She had barely spoken another word to Sam after their talk. She had decided that from that point on, she'd keep it professional, speaking only about work. Kimberley didn't like the fine line she and Sam were dancing around or perhaps she was the only one dancing around it, because he seemed oblivious.

Up ahead, she spotted Caleb carrying Flynn. When he noticed her, he waved and quickened his pace, stopping right in front of her.

"How's Sam today?" he asked.

"Hungover." Kimberley shook her head.

"I can imagine."

"I'm really sorry about last night. He's been having a hard time what with the case and what not." Kimberley let out a deep breath.

"Understandable and no worries at all. Maybe, we can grab dinner or drinks another time… without your boss there," Caleb teased.

Kimberley smiled. "Yeah, I'd like that."

"Good, it's a date." He nodded. "Well, I better get this little guy to daycare." He tickled his neck and Flynn giggled.

"Alright. Bye, Flynn." Kimberley made her voice light.

"Can you say bye?" Caleb asked.

Flynn waved his hand and said bye.

"I'll text you," he said, walking past Kimberley.

Kimberley turned back. "Hey, Caleb."

"Yeah." He stopped looking back at her.

"What's your last name? I realized I never caught it."

Caleb tilted his head and gave her a wide smile. "It's Roberts."

Kimberley smiled back. "Nice to meet you, Caleb Roberts."

"Likewise, Kimberley King," he said, disappearing into the daycare center.

Caleb Roberts, she thought. See, she knew his name, his full name. It brought her a small amount of comfort. Sam was wrong about him. Right? He had to be.

"*Great*. Just what I need right now," Kimberley said as she looked through the windshield of her car. Her mother stood outside the Custer County Sheriff's Office with her arms folded in front of her chest.

Kimberley turned off the engine and paused, staring at her mom, willing her to get back in her car and leave. This was the last thing she wanted to deal with. She grabbed her bag and got out of her car.

"What are you doing here?" Kimberley asked.

"You won't return my calls, so I had to track you down myself." Nicole raised her chin and readjusted the purse on her shoulder.

"I'm not in the mood," Kimberley said, walking past her mom.

"I came to bring you these," she said.

Kimberley stopped. She let out a deep breath and turned around. "Bring me what?"

Nicole opened her purse, shuffling things around and pulled out several pieces of folded up paper. She held them out.

Kimberley looked at her mom and then at the papers. "What are they?"

Nicole took a step closer, and Kimberley begrudgingly took them. She unfolded them and quickly flipped through them.

"They're divorce papers," Nicole said.

She read them over quickly. At the top was her mother's and David's names. She folded them back up and handed them to her mother. "Okay."

"So, will you come back home?"

"We can talk about that when the divorce is finalized." Kimberley folded her lips.

Nicole's eyes and mouth went wide as she looked at the papers and then back at her daughter.

"That could take months."

"Then it takes months. You had a year to file them. You made your choice, Mom." Kimberley turned around and walked into the sheriff's station. Nicole stamped her heel, punctuating her frustration. She shoved the papers back into her purse and wiped away the tears that had slid down her cheeks. Kimberley wanted to forgive her mom right then and there. She wanted to tell her everything was fine, and they could be a happy family again, but she couldn't get over the betrayal, the lies her mother had told her for the past year. She was tired of giving everyone the benefit of the doubt.

"Hey, Barb," Kimberley greeted.

Barb stood behind her desk, dusting it with a disposable Swiffer duster. She picked her head up and smiled. "Did you get Jessica to daycare alright?"

Kimberley nodded. "I did. Is Sam in?" she asked before she even realized she was asking. It was her go-to question most mornings.

"Actually, no. I dropped him off at The Trophy Room where his vehicle was. He said he was going to run home for a quick shower and then he had a lead to follow up on." Barb picked up her plants, making sure to dust all around and underneath them.

"A lead? Did he mention who the lead was?" Kimberley tilted her head.

Barb shook her head.

Kimberley pulled out her phone and sent Sam a quick text.

What lead?

She looked down at her phone screen for nearly a minute, hoping he'd text back. When he didn't, she stowed the phone away. Kimberley walked to the office area, finding Burns sitting at his desk. The rest of the desks were empty.

"There you are," he said, standing up.

"Got something for me?"

"Oh yes." His face lit up.

Burns picked up several pieces of paper and held them out.

"What is it?"

"Well, first, neither Benjamin Fry nor Will, the camp counselor, did it. I was able to verify Will on security footage at a number of locations on the day Miley went missing. I can't entirely verify his whereabouts on the night Piper was murdered other than the alibi he provided you that he was with Chloe."

Kimberley nodded. "And Fry?"

"His alibis check out for the day Miley went missing. I spoke to his lawyer and his therapist. And the night Piper was murdered, I got him on several CCTVs driving back to Texas. He wasn't even in the state."

Kimberley let out a deep breath. "Okay. Do you know what lead Sheriff Walker is following up on?"

Deputy Burns gave her a puzzled look.

"Never mind. What else you got?" she asked.

"The emails you mentioned with the accusations about Will. They were all sent from the same IP address. See?" He pointed at the IP address at the top of each of the pieces of paper at a long string of numbers.

"So, the same person sent all four complaints?" Kimberley tilted her head.

"That's correct and better yet." He set the papers down on his desk and pulled a sticky note from his desk. "I was able to link them to a location. They all came from this address."

Kimberley glanced at a handwritten address. She looked at Burns. "Who lives here?"

Deputy Burns gave her a small smile. "Martin and Rebecca Welch."

"Welch… Welch. Why does that name ring a bell?" Kimberley tapped a finger against her chin, trying to conjure up where she had heard it before. She went through every person she knew in the area, like a Rolodex.

"They have a daughter. She works at—"

Before Burns could say it, the answer popped in her head like she had flipped a light switch and the answer had lit up in front of her eyes. "Chloe. Chloe Welch. Works at Camp Beaverbrook."

Burns nodded. Kimberley's eyes went wide as the pieces of the puzzle started falling into place.

CHAPTER THIRTY-SIX

"Chloe Welch, this is Chief Deputy King," Kimberley yelled, knocking hard on the front door of the home address Burns had provided. The home was two stories with clean light blue siding and dark red shudders. The lawn was well maintained with rose bushes lining the front porch. She knocked again and finally heard footsteps pounding down a set of stairs.

Chloe's face went blank and her eyes widened as she opened the door. Despite being tan, her skin drained of its color. She twirled her long blonde hair for a moment before tossing it over her shoulder. Letting out a deep breath, she quickly composed herself and forced the faintest of smiles. Kimberley could see the corners of her lips twitch.

"Chief Deputy King. How can I help you?" she said. She tried to make the words come out nonchalant and normal, but there was a tinge of panic and guilt to them.

"I'd like to ask you a few questions, Chloe. Do you have a minute?" Kimberley put her hand on the door, signaling to Chloe she didn't have a choice in the matter.

"I thought I answered all of your questions." Chloe's eyes darted from Kimberley to inside the house.

"I have more, and it'll only take a moment."

Kimberley could see Chloe visibly swallow hard. She hesitated, but then slowly opened the door up. "Come in," she said shakily.

The home was like any normal middle-class family home. A dining room off to the right, a staircase that led upstairs to a second story and a living room that opened up to a kitchen to the right. Although, the house was large, it was cozy thanks to décor in shades of reds and browns. Chloe led Kimberley into the dining room slowly. She kept looking back almost as if she were checking to make sure Kimberley was still there.

They took a seat across from one another. Chloe fiddled with her fingers nervously. "Do you want something to drink? I can make a pot of coffee." She half stood, ready to leave the room and escape Kimberley's presence.

"No, Chloe. Please sit down." Kimberley's voice was firm.

She nodded slightly and took a seat.

"Are your parents home?" Kimberley asked, throwing out an easy question. It was how she got people to talk. Start with a couple of simple questions to ease them into talking, then hit them with the hard ones.

Chloe shook her head. "No."

"This is a nice house." Kimberley glanced around the dining room. An antique china cabinet sat along the far wall filled with expensive cutlery and dishware. Off to the side of it, several family photos hung on the wall, including Chloe's senior photo. "Did you grow up here?" Kimberley averted her attention back at Chloe.

"Yeah," she said just above a whisper. Although she was eighteen years old, the girl across from Kimberley had shrunken down to almost childlike. Her shoulders hung and her voice had become quiet.

"You must have had a nice childhood, Chloe." This time it wasn't a question, just a statement.

Chloe nodded.

"Do you know why I'm here?" Kimberley made laser eye contact with Chloe, carefully watching for any tells.

"No."

Kimberley pulled out several pieces of folded up paper from her utility belt. She slowly unfolded them, while staring at Chloe. She slid the pieces of paper across the table.

"Do you recognize those?"

Chloe looked down at the papers, reading over the first one. She then flipped to the next and the next and finally read the last one.

To whom it may concern
acted inappropriately with Beaverbrook campers.
experienced it and witnessed it myself.
I do not feel safe with him here.
Sincerely, a concerned camper

The phrases jumped out at Kimberley. She should have known. It was too formal, too grown up, for one of the campers to write it. It was also too vague. But why would Chloe write those things about her boyfriend?

She took her time or maybe she was just giving herself time to come up with an answer.

"No," she said not looking up.

"No?" Kimberley tilted her head.

Chloe didn't speak this time. She just shook her head.

"Chloe." Kimberley's voice was calm yet demanding. "I know you recognize those emails."

She didn't say anything. Instead, she wrapped her long blonde hair round and round her pointer finger. They sat there in silence for a minute, Kimberley giving Chloe a chance to confess. She unwrapped her finger from her hair and tapped it against the table for a moment.

"I don't recognize those emails," she finally said, looking up at Kimberley with defiance in her eyes.

"Why did you write those emails?" Kimberley leaned forward in her chair, filling some of the space between her and Chloe.

"I didn't," she said, shaking her head, but her eyes betrayed her as they looked off to the left and became glossy.

"There's no sense in lying. We traced the IP address from where the emails were sent, which matched your parents' house. If you didn't send them, then I'll have to bring your parents in for questioning," Kimberley threatened.

Chloe's lip trembled. She squeezed her eyes shut and when she opened them, tears poured out. "I'm sorry. It was stupid. It's just everyone wanted Will. All the younger girls had crushes on him. All the other counselors had crushes on him. He's *my* boyfriend."

"Did something happen between Will and one of the campers? Like Piper or Miley?" Kimberley furrowed her brow.

"What? No." A look of disbelief crossed over Chloe's face. "Nothing happened between Will or anyone. It's just... I felt insecure. I hated seeing so many girls fawning all over him all the time. So, I just sent those emails."

"Why?"

"I thought it was best if he didn't work there anymore, so he wouldn't be around all those girls."

"So, you got him fired?" Kimberley leaned back in her chair.

"Yeah." Chloe's voice cracked. "Please don't tell him. He'll break up with me. He was so mad when he got fired. He loved that job. I just couldn't deal with all the attention he was always getting." She threw her face into her hands and sobbed. "I hate myself for what I did... but the jealously was eating away at me."

Kimberley closed her eyes for a moment and leaned forward in her chair. "Chloe, I need you to look at me."

It took a few moments for her to lift her head up. Her face was red and blotchy and crumpled. She sniffled over and over.

"Where were you Sunday, August the second, between the hours of five fifteen p.m. and midnight?"

Chloe's eyes went wide again and her mouth dropped open. "Wait, do you think I had something to do with that?"

"Were Piper and Miley a little too close to Will?"

"What? No. Well, not Piper. Piper was young and immature. Miley was a little more sophisticated and was always hanging around him." She narrowed her eyes.

"What did you do to Miley?" Kimberley asked.

Chloe shot up from her seat, sending her chair backwards. It hit the ground with a thud. "You think I killed Piper? You think I had something to do with Miley going missing? That's insane!" she yelled.

"Then tell me where you were the night Piper was murdered," Kimberley said firmly.

"I told you. I stayed over at Will's place."

"And where were you on Wednesday between six a.m. and eleven a.m.?" Kimberley raised a brow.

"I was working. You can call Joy," Chloe yelled.

Kimberley made a mental note to double check with Joy on Chloe's alibi. There wasn't anything else she could do now. She didn't have enough evidence to bring her in yet. Kimberley stood from her seat and pushed in her chair.

"I can't believe you would ever think I'd hurt either of those girls," Chloe seethed.

"It doesn't matter what I believe, Chloe. It matters what I can prove," Kimberley said. "I'll see myself out."

Chloe folded her lips and crossed her arms in front of her chest, stomping behind Kimberley. Once outside, she pulled her sunglasses down over her eyes.

"Chief Deputy King," Chloe yelled out.

Kimberley turned around. Chloe stood in the doorway, fuming. "If you want to throw around accusations, you should point them toward Miley's mom. She's the one that's fucked up."

Chloe was about to slam the door, but Kimberley put her foot in front of it. She pushed her glasses on top of her head and looked her in the eyes. "What do you mean by that?"

She opened the door a little wider and swallowed hard. "I overheard Miley talking to Piper at camp. She said her mom was often out of it and that she didn't give a shit about her. She only cared about her dead sister, Sophie."

Kimberley nodded, thinking it over for a moment. This was the second person in twenty-four hours that said there was something wrong with Linda. Oliver had said something similar, that Linda was crazy, but she hadn't taken it seriously, since that was Linda's ex-husband. Exes never had good things to say about one another.

"Thank you for your time, Chloe," Kimberley said and removed her foot from in front of the door. "I'll be in touch."

She left the house, walking down the driveway back to her vehicle. Pulling out her phone, she dialed Sam. It rang over and over and finally his voicemail picked up.

"Hey, Sam. I'm heading over to Linda Baker's house. Just want to check on something. Give me a call when you get this." She paused for a moment unsure of what else to say after what happened between them. Kimberley sighed and clicked the end call button.

CHAPTER THIRTY-SEVEN

Linda Baker's house looked just as it had the last couple of times Kimberley had visited – a small, gray, ranch home with a patchy lawn, chipped paint, and broken shutters. The gloomy day matched the house. It looked like a fitted gray sheet had been stretched across the sky, blocking out the golden sun. She paused before knocking. Leaning her ear against the door, she listened. It was dead silent. Kimberley hesitated, pulling her head away. Her knuckles hovered an inch from the door. A moment or two passed before she finally knocked. It was met with silence. She knocked again. This time louder. Silence. Kimberley took a step back, looking around the neighborhood, the houses lining the street, it wasn't an area people were clamoring to live in. It was a ghost town with not a person in sight. She leaned over trying to peer into the window that saw into the living room, but the thick, heavy shades were drawn.

Kimberley looked at her watch. It was early afternoon. Perhaps, Linda was at work—but surely not with Miley missing. She considered leaving and coming back as she still had to verify Chloe's alibi. She weighed out her options, but Chloe's words stayed in her mind. *"If you want to throw around accusations, you should point them toward Miley's mom. She's the one that's fucked up."* She couldn't shake them, and then Kimberley thought of her interview with Oliver. His words echoed in her head.

"After Sophie passed, Linda got loopy. She started drinking heavily and taking painkillers. She started lashing out at me and Miley."

"Wasn't sure what Linda was saying about me. For all I know, she was telling you guys I did it."

"Because she's goddamn crazy, that's why."

Kimberley took a deep breath and scanned the road once more. She walked off the stoop and took a sharp left around the side of the house. There were a couple of small windows on the side and she tried to look in each of them. One had frosted glass, impossible to really see through and the other had the blinds drawn. It seemed Linda liked to keep the house closed up. Kimberley had only seen the living room, kitchen, and Miley's room in her previous visits. They had never searched the house inside or out. Perhaps that was a mistake. She reached the back of the house. The yard was large with a clothesline, a swing set, and an old wooden shed off in the back corner. The wind whipped, causing the door of the shed to bang against the frame. It wasn't latched and sat partially open. Kimberley retied her ponytail, taming the flyaway hairs. She looked back toward the house, and then focused her attention back on the shed. The door creaked as it opened a couple of inches and then closed and opened and closed. Kimberley imagined it was calling out to her, telling her 'to come have a look.' The wood had faded to a gray, and it looked as though it had been built before the house. Several planks were haphazardly nailed to it, going in all different directions.

Kimberley's footsteps were slow. The dried grass crunched under her boots. She stood a foot in front of the shed and placed her hand on the handle. She noticed a couple of holes in the door where the wood had rotted away. Kimberley readjusted her hand to get a look through one of the holes that was a foot below eye level, but a wood splinter got her and she pulled her hand away, inspecting her palm. It has a half inch in length with the thickness of a sewing needle, burrowed just below her skin. She put her thumbnail underneath it and pushed on the end of it, wincing. It slowly slid out, leaving behind a red streak and a tiny trickle of blood. Kimberley put the wound to her mouth and sucked on it for a moment, giving a little bit of relief. She shook her hand out and carefully placed it on the door handle. Opening the door, she saw it, leaned up against an old wheelbarrow. A shiver ran down her spine. Kimberley recognized it immediately. It's what they had been looking for. Piper's pink bicycle. But it was charred in some places as though someone had tried to burn it. She stepped over a couple of pieces of wood and paint cans to get to the bike. She ran her hand over the handles. This was it. She pictured Piper riding it freely down Black Heart Lane on a hot summer day. Her blonde hair flowing in the wind. Her smile wide and her laughter infectious. But why was it here?

The door slammed behind her, and she heard something lock into place. Kimberley scrambled to the door, banging on it, but it wouldn't budge.

"Hello," she called out, slamming her hands against the door. The top corner of it gave way only a couple of inches.

She was met with silence when she stopped banging. Kimberley bent down, lining one of her eyes up with the hole that was the size of a golf ball. She scanned the area as best she could but saw nothing but the back of the house and an empty yard.

"Hello," she called out again. Her voice a little panicked. Her pupil dilated taking in the light from the outside.

A dark eye appeared looking back at her. Startled, Kimberley lurched backward, falling onto the pieces of wood and paint cans. One of the paint cans with a loose lid tipped over, a thick red paint spilling from it. Kimberley scrambled to her feet.

"Linda!" she called out.

She looked at the hole. The eye had disappeared as light from the outside was pouring through. Kimberley took a couple of deep breaths and walked to the door. She bent down, looking through the hole again. Ten yards away stood Linda Baker. Her black, stringy hair was matted to the top of her head. Greasy thick strands slightly blew in the wind. Her eyes were dark and unsettling, staring directly back at Kimberley. Even from ten yards away, Kimberley could see areas of her face where her makeup was caked on too heavy. She was wearing a loose-fitting black top and dark jeans. The look on her face wasn't one Kimberley had noticed before. She had seen sadness, guilt, anger, and frustration in Linda prior. Now, it was sinister.

"Linda, what are you doing? Let me out of here now," Kimberley yelled, banging on the door again.

She went to click on her radio, but her hand touched the front pocket of her shirt. Shit, she thought to herself, remembering she had taken it off on the car ride from Chloe's to Linda's as the battery was dead. Since she had been staying at Barb's, she had forgotten to charge it.

Kimberley grabbed her cell phone from her utility belt, clicking it on. The battery blinked red at the top and noted two percent. She was sure Jessica had unplugged it again. She pulled up Sam's contact.

"I wouldn't do that if I were you," Linda said, her eye reappearing in the hole. Kimberley looked at her and then down at her phone.

She heard Linda's footsteps shuffle and glanced through the hole again. Linda stood just a few feet away holding a red gas can. Kimberley clicked call and dropped the phone in the dirt. She glanced down, seeing the call was connecting. The sloshing of liquid pulled her attention from the phone.

"What are you doing, Linda?" Kimberley's voice was full of panic.

She followed the sound around the shed, looking through small holes and openings where the wood had rotted away or where it hadn't been repaired. Linda walked around the shed, casually tossing gasoline all over it. It coated the wood, running down it in trickles.

"Linda, don't do anything stupid," Kimberley warned.

The sloshing stopped. A manic laugh escaped Linda's mouth. "I have nothing left to lose. One of my daughters is dead, and the other one doesn't love me."

Kimberley's ears perked up. *And the other one doesn't love me.* Miley had to be alive, she thought.

The sloshing sound continued as Linda poured the rest of the gasoline around the shed. She retook her position several feet in front of the door. Kimberley quickly scanned around her, looking for something to help get her out of this. There were paint cans, pieces of wood, a wheelbarrow, Piper's bicycle, a ball of tangled Christmas lights, a propane tank, and a couple of bags of unopened potting soil. She looked down at her gun, considering pulling it from the holster and shooting through the golf-sized hole in the door. Did she have a shot to even shoot Linda? She'd be shooting blindly, not being able to see where the gun was aimed. She could fire off a shot through the door and hope it hit her or scared her enough for Kimberley to try to bust down the door. She bent down looking through the hole again. Kimberley saw something in Linda's hand. It was silver, smaller than a deck of cards. Linda flicked it open, revealing a flame. It was a lighter. She couldn't risk trying to shoot off her gun. Even if she was lucky enough to hit her, Linda would have time to light the whole shed on fire. Kimberley took another deep breath, realizing she was at her mercy. She glanced down at her phone that was lying in the dirt. The screen was black.

"Linda, we can talk about this. Just unlock this door and let me out," Kimberley said in her calmest voice. She kept her eye on Linda who kept flicking the lighter open and closed. She was playing with Kimberley like a cat with a mouse, deciding its fate.

"I understand you better than anyone, Linda. I know what deadbeat men are like. I know what it's like to be a single mom." Kimberley was trying to get through to her.

"I know how hard it is," she added. "I know how easy it is to fall apart when everything around you falls apart."

Linda closed her eyes tight. When she opened them a couple of tears fell down her face, creating streaks through her heavy makeup. She stopped opening and closing the lighter and held it in her hand. It was working. Kimberley was getting through to her. She thought carefully of what to say next as she knew the wrong thing could set Linda off and make her fly into a rage. Kimberley could see it on her face. Red had crept up her neck. She was a ticking timebomb ready to explode.

"Linda, what happened to Piper? Was it an accident?"

Kimberley was met with silence.

"I saw how you left her. You clearly didn't mean to hurt her. She was clean. Her hair was brushed. You placed her in the most beautiful spot in the woods," Kimberley said.

She remembered how peaceful Piper had looked, how the person that murdered her had taken their time to make sure she was comfortable in her resting place, how they had straightened her clothes, folded her hands over her torso, and positioned her hair in a way to cover her wound. Kimberley remembered thinking Piper looked as though she was sleeping, not dead.

"It looked as though she had just laid down for a nap." Kimberley was trying to paint a vivid picture for Linda. "Where's Miley?" she added apprehensively.

Linda flicked the lighter open again, staring at the shed. Her dark eyes focused on the door.

"I know you didn't mean to hurt Piper. Tell me what happened."

Linda closed the lighter.

"You *never* recover from the death of a child. No matter what anyone says, you don't." Linda's voice cracked. She looked up at the gray sky as she spoke as if she were explaining herself to a higher power. "A part of me died when Sophie did, the good part of me. I could barely live with what was left of me. But when Miley brought

Piper home after summer camp, a small piece of me came back. The two of them spent a lot of time at my house. I wasn't strict and boring like Piper's grandparents. I was what the young ones call a cool mom," Linda said, letting out a high-pitched laugh.

She was quiet for a few moments, staring up at the sky. Kimberley glanced around the shed again, hoping something like a shovel would appear. She considered pushing on the door again but decided against it as it could set Linda off. She returned her eye to the hole and watched Linda, waiting for her to continue her story. She smiled up at the sky like she was seeing something. Kimberley's eye followed her gaze up. It was just a sheet of gray above her.

"That must have been nice having two little girls in the house again," Kimberley said with caution.

"It was. Except Miley wasn't my little girl anymore." Linda's lips flattened. "I struggled to relate to her. She was ten going on eighteen." Linda shook her head slightly. "She didn't want to be around me anymore. I was now embarrassing to her. She was interested in being around boys and friends, not her mom. But Piper was different. She was young for her age and innocent. Probably because she was brought up in an old-fashioned, sheltered way by her grandparents. Piper was exactly how a daughter should be. Sophie would have been the same way if she had lived." Linda smiled up at the sky.

Kimberley didn't know what to say, so she stayed silent, waiting for Linda to continue. There was more of the story left. How did Piper die? How did the loss of Sophie years ago have anything to do with Piper's death?

"Life is cruel though. I didn't get to see Sophie grow up." Linda dropped her chin and narrowed her eyes, looking at the shed. "I just wanted my little girl back. Having Piper around gave me a glimpse of that, but she wasn't always cooperative. If she had been, things would have been different."

"What do you mean by that, Linda? What happened?" Kimberley asked.

"I just wanted Piper to stay a little longer that day. That's all. She agreed. I made her chocolate chip cookies, Sophie's favorite, and I asked her to call me mom. I wasn't asking for much. It was just a three-letter word. But she freaked out. Started yelling at me, telling me I was sick, saying I needed help, telling me I wasn't her mom. A daughter shouldn't talk to her mother like that." Linda tilted her head, flipping the lighter open again. Her eyes flickered with anger. The flame on the light was steady, a half inch in height, a yellow and orange hue. Kimberley looked at it as if she was looking down the barrel of a loaded gun.

"That must have been hard, Linda," she said. Kimberley kept using her name, saying it as much as possible to create a connection, a familiarity with her. "If I lost my daughter, Jessica, I don't know how I'd continue on, if I even could." Kimberley reminded Linda that she herself was a mother, that she had a daughter of her own.

Linda closed the lighter again.

"If Piper would have just called me mom, played the part, things would have been different. But no, she had to be defiant." Linda closed her eyes and exhaled through her nose. She reopened them staring directly at the hole in the door. It nearly made Kimberley look away, but she had to keep an eye on her.

"She didn't even eat one of the chocolate chip cookies I made her. She became hysterical, and when she tried to leave, I couldn't let her. I wasn't going to lose another little girl. I grabbed her by her arm and pulled her to the basement door. I just wanted her to stay with me. She fought back, trying to force her way out. But… she fell down the stairs, smacking her head on the concrete at the bottom of the steps. She didn't move. Just laid there. And then the blood poured from her head, like a halo of red."

Kimberley put a hand to her mouth, covering her gasp. Tears escaped Linda's eyes as she stared up at the sky again.

"It was an accident. I didn't mean it," she cried. "I'm sorry."

"Where's Miley?" Kimberley asked. Her voice full of apprehension.

"Miley had witnessed the whole thing. She cried for hours, and she let me hold her like she was my little girl again. I made her promise not to tell anyone. She was frightened and agreed to keep my secret. But like I said about her earlier, she wasn't my little girl anymore. I found her sneaking off to Arthur and Edna's, drawing them pictures, and writing them stories. I was terrified she was going to tell them. Then one day, when I got home from work, Miley wasn't there. I drove over to the Chases' house, and I saw…" Linda lowered her head and narrowed her eyes at the door of the shed. "You and Sheriff Walker outside of the Chases' house. Miley's bike was off to the side of the house. I knew she was inside. I panicked. Was she confessing? Was she telling you and the sheriff what happened to Piper? I nearly left town, but instead I waited, parked a block away, watching the house."

Kimberley thought back to that day. She was surprised to see Miley visiting with the Chases. Miley had been so shy, not saying a word to her or Sam. The little girl couldn't even look at them. Within minutes of their arrival, Miley had scurried off.

"I didn't have to wait long. She was out the door and on her bike a few minutes later. I picked her up and took her home, knowing she could never leave again."

"What did you do to her?" Kimberley yelled. "Did you hurt her, Linda? Did you kill your only living daughter?"

Linda gritted her teeth. "Of course not. She's all I have left in the world, but I couldn't trust her to keep her mouth shut."

"Where is she, Linda? Where is Miley?"

"She's fine, just taking a long nap."

Kimberley's lip trembled. Linda was so far gone that a long nap could mean dead to her. Would she kill her daughter?

"Is she alive?" Kimberley yelled.

Linda didn't say a word. She just stared at the wooden door. It was like she was in a trance.

"Is Miley alive?" Kimberley yelled again. Her voice trembled. "Tell me, goddamn it!" She screamed, banging on the door. It rattled, and she realized then, Linda had padlocked it.

"Tell me where she is. We spoke to Oliver, Linda. He wants to know where Miley is," Kimberley said, trying to get Linda out of her silent trance.

As soon as she saw her face distort, Kimberley knew she had made a mistake by mentioning Oliver. Her lips flattened. Her face flushed. A vein in her forehead became engorged, forming a ridge above her left brow. She tightened her eyes and one of her fists. Kimberley scanned the shed again. Shit. There was nothing. Her eyes went to the propane tank, then flicked back to the lighter in Linda's hand. The color from Kimberley's face drained as she realized her fate if Linda set the gasoline soaked shed on fire. Beads of sweat formed on her forehead, and she blinked rapidly.

"*Oliver*! Oliver hasn't shown an interest in Miley since Sophie died. I've done it all!" Her tone had deepened, and her words were coming out like a firehose, fast and hard. "Now, he acts like he gives a damn about her. Ha! He can't just show up like some sort of doting dad. It's too fucking late. He won't get anywhere near Miley, and I'll make sure of that." Linda narrowed her eyes and flicked open the lighter. The small flame looked like a bonfire to Kimberley as she knew what it was capable of.

"Linda, please. You don't have to do this," Kimberley pleaded.

She walked a few steps toward the shed, so she was just a few feet away. Bending down, she looked at Kimberley through the small hole in the door. "I won't let him have her. She's mine!"

"Linda, put your hands up!" Sam commanded.

Kimberley looked off to the right where his voice came from. She couldn't see him, until he walked into her line of sight. His gun was drawn, and he walked carefully across the yard toward Linda. She didn't move a muscle.

"Put your hands up now or I'll shoot," he said again.

Kimberley watched Sam, then looked to Linda who was frozen in place, staring just above the hole in the door. Then she glanced at the flickering flame.

"Sam!" Kimberley cried out. She tried to keep her voice light, but it came out panicked.

"King, I'm coming. Don't worry, I got you."

"Linda, this is your last warning. Put your hands up or I'll shoot."

Kimberley could hear the apprehension in Sam's voice. She knew he'd shoot if he had to, but she also knew he didn't want to.

She looked at Linda's face and watched it go blank as she tossed the open lighter into a puddle of gas just in front of the shed door.

CHAPTER THIRTY-EIGHT

I can't keep Miley, but I can be with you again, Sophie. Remember the nursery rhyme I used to read to you. *Humpty Dumpty*. It was your favorite. I told you, unlike him, we'd put you back together again. But I was wrong, Sophie. I couldn't save you. I couldn't keep that promise, but I promise I'll be with you again soon. Just like you, all the king's horses and all the king's men won't put Mommy back together again.

CHAPTER THIRTY-NINE

The flames immediately engulfed the shed door. Kimberley scrambled backward to get away from the heat. Smoke began to fill the inside of the shed. A shot rang out followed by a scream. Kimberley quickly undid her sheriff's button-down shirt and used it to cover her face. The smoke was already becoming thick and heavy. She coughed several times, watching the flames dance their way around the gasoline-soaked shed and pressing the shirt against her mouth.

"Sam!" she screamed. "Sam."

Her heart raced so fast there was a sharp pain in her chest. She got down low, trying to escape the smoke, and kept to the middle of the shed as far from the flames as possible.

"Kimberley!" Sam yelled.

He called her name over and over again. She heard it come from all around the shed. He was clearly circling it, trying to find a way to get her out, but the whole thing was engulfed in flames. She heard him speak into his radio for emergency backup. Then he called out for her.

"I'm going to get you out of there," he said, but it didn't come out confident at all.

"Sam, there's a propane tank in here." Her lips and chin trembled.

"Move it to the center if you can," he instructed.

Kimberley held her breath and crawled to it. When she went to grab it, it was already hot. It burned her leaving a nasty red mark. She grabbed her shirt and wrapped it around the handle, then dragged it to the center. She crouched down, covering her face with her shirt again. She could feel the heat from the fire on her bare arms and on the back of her neck. Sweat trickled down her forehead and chest. The smoke burned her eyes, so she squeezed them shut. Images flashed in front of Kimberley's mind. Jessica as a baby, cooing in her arms. Jessica feeding the ducks in Central Park. Jessica rolling around in the grass at the cottage, trying to catch fireflies. Her mom holding her granddaughter telling her how smart she was. Nicole sitting on the couch having a glass of wine with Kimberley, talking about their day. Dozens of images of Barb with her infectious smile handing Kimberley baked goods, each one sweeter than the last. And then Sam. The day they met. All the days they worked together. The nights they had drinks at The Trophy Room. The moments he gave her grief and the moments he told her he was proud of her. She blinked rapidly clearing her mind. She wasn't going to die in this stupid shed.

"Sam, hurry," she yelled, but he didn't say anything back.

She couldn't hear him, just the crackling of the fire. A piece of burning wood crumbled from the ceiling, falling on to her leg. She screamed and kicked it away. Kimberley looked up. The fire had spread to the roof. The whole structure was going to collapse on top of her. She flinched when something hit the back wall of the shed. Kimberley's muscles tightened as she turned to face where the noise was coming from. Another thud hit the wall, but this time she saw the head of an axe split through the wood.

"I'm coming, Kimberley. Sit tight."

"There's not much else I can do," she yelled, her attempt at lightening the current dire situation.

Another piece of burning wood fell from the ceiling, hitting her shoulder. She screamed, kicking it away and holding her burned skin.

"The ceiling is coming down."

"Fuck," Sam said. Although she was sure he didn't mean to say it aloud.

The axe slammed into the shed again, this time ripping a big chunk of the wall out, enough that she could see Sam's face. She had never been so happy to see him. His strong square jaw, his military cut, ash brown hair. His perfect facial stubble. She wished he'd smile in case it was the last time she ever saw it, but she could see how tense he was as he swung the axe over and over. Although, he was wearing his uniform, she could see his muscles bulging in his arms from swinging tirelessly.

"Get back," he yelled as he swung the axe, making the hole bigger.

Pieces of burning wood flew into the shed. Kimberley held her arm in front of her face and scrambled backward. She rammed her shoulder into the opposite wall, not realizing how little space she had. Her skin sizzled as she pulled away, and she screamed in pain as her shoulder blade turned an angry red.

"Kimberley." Sam's voice was full of concern. He choked on the smoke as he swung the axe. The hole was nearly big enough to get through. Kimberley coughed deeply. She was dizzy from the smoke. The ceiling started to rain fire and she used her shirt to cover her head. Sam dropped the axe and bent down grabbing a folded-up blanket he must have grabbed when he found the axe in the garage. He undid his utility belt and dropped it in the grass and then wrapped it around himself and looked to Kimberley.

"Are you ready?" he asked. His eyes were glossy and bloodshot but his face was determined.

Kimberley looked up at him and nodded. She stood, glancing at the ceiling that was ready to collapse and then back at Sam.

Sam nodded and charged through the hole, breaking away the burning wood around him to get through. He grabbed Kimberley, wrapping his hands around her waist so she was safely under the blanket too.

"Stand behind me," he said. "Put your arms around my waist."

She slinked around him and wrapped her arms around him, her hands resting on the ridges of his abdomen.

"Don't let go of me," he said.

Kimberley nodded.

They walked quickly through the hole, choking on the smoke and staying as close as possible underneath the blanket to escape the heat. The blanket caught on fire, and as soon as they were outside, Sam threw it off of them. He grabbed Kimberley's hand, pulling her with him. They sprinted away from the burning shed. The ceiling collapsed into a pit of fire and the walls fell into themselves. Sam and Kimberley made it twenty yards before the propane tank exploded, blasting splinters of flaming wood. He pushed Kimberley to the ground and jumped on top of her, shielding her from the debris. It scattered all around them, some of it hitting Sam on the back. He flinched, shaking it off, but he kept his eyes on Kimberley. She cradled into his chest, her long brown locks covering her face. Sirens blared in the distance as the sky stopped raining fire and debris. They laid there for a couple of moments before either of them moved. Sam brushed the hair out of Kimberley's face. She opened her eyes and looked up at him. His face was just a few inches away from hers.

"You're safe now," he said, delivering the wide smile she had yearned to see just minutes before.

She couldn't help but smile back. He brushed his hand against her cheek, inspecting her, making sure she was okay and taking her in as if he was scared this was the first and last time he'd see her up close. Her vivid, big blue eyes. Her heart-shaped face. Her pouty lips. Kimberley didn't know what to say. She just laid there in the grass, wrapped in Sam's arms. Her heart still raced, but she wasn't sure if it was beating out of fear anymore. The sirens roared as they pulled up to the house. Kimberley heard people yelling, but she couldn't move a muscle nor take her eyes off Sam.

"How'd you know I was here?" she finally asked.

"I went to catch up with Oliver before he left, and I just had this bad feeling in the pit of my stomach about Linda after questioning him again. I realized he didn't talk about her like he hated her, he talked about her like he was afraid. And then I missed your call and saw you left a voicemail earlier, saying you were heading here," Sam explained.

"Wait, where's Linda?" Kimberley scrambled, but her body was stiff and had taken a beating.

"Sheriff Walker. Chief Deputy King," Bearfield called out. "You two alright?"

Sam slowly sat up and got to his feet, helping Kimberley. She was dressed in just a white tank top and her uniform pants. Sam and Kimberley could see a crowd of deputies and paramedics surrounding something off to the side yard. Paramedics loaded Linda onto a stretcher. One of her wrists was handcuffed to the side of it.

"Get a paramedic. King needs medical attention," Sam yelled.

Linda screamed as they rolled her off. Her words were incoherent. Hill and Burns held down her legs as she kept kicking and flailing.

"I'm fine," Kimberley said.

Sam touched the top of her shoulder where the skin had begun to pucker. "You got a nasty burn here." His fingertips lightly brushed the top of it.

"I'll see someone when we find Miley," she challenged.

"Is she alive?" Sam's eyes went wide.

"Yeah, and I think I know where she is."

CHAPTER FORTY

Despite the stinging on her shoulder blade where her skin was burned, Kimberley swung the axe against the padlocked basement door. She ignored the pain, swinging over and over again, until the wood was busted away around the lock. Bearfield and Sam called out Miley's name as Kimberley pulled the splintered door open. The old wooden staircase led to an unfinished basement. It was dark and quiet as Kimberley went first down the stairs. They creaked beneath her. Something bumped her arm, and she looked to find Sam handing her a flashlight. She turned it on and used it to light the stairs. Cobwebs stuck to her face and she fell back slightly as she tried to wipe them away. Sam caught her.

"Are you okay?" he asked.

She nodded, got her footing, and planted her feet firmly on the dirt floor. Kimberley shined the flashlight to the right. There were rusty metal shelves lined up against the wall, filled with cardboard boxes labeled 'Sophie' in black marker. An old sink was off to the side. Drops of water fell from the faucet one at a time every ten seconds or so. Kimberley matched her breathing to it. Inhale. Hold for ten. Exhale.

"Miley," Kimberley called out.

She was met with silence and the drip, drip, drip from the sink. Maybe Miley wasn't here, Kimberley thought. She shined her light to the right lighting up a large-cluttered room. It was full of everything from boxes to old furniture, all stacked into a pile in the center.

"Miley," she called out again. Panic had returned to her voice.

If she wasn't here, then where would she be? They'd have to go to the hospital and try to get it out of Linda. In the state she was in, it might take a while, days maybe. She had had a full-on mental breakdown, and they didn't have time to waste interrogating her. Kimberley took a few steps toward the pile of junk, shining her light all around it. It was a tangle of metal and wood and plastic. A crash from behind startled her. She whipped around shining her light at Bearfield who had knocked over a stack of boxes. Coffee mugs spilled out onto the dirt floor.

"Sorry," he muttered.

Kimberley turned back and walked around the pile of miscellaneous objects that was stacked nearly to the ceiling. Behind it, something caught her eye. The corner of a stained mattress. She held her breath as she took another step. She was scared as to what she would find. Maybe, it would just be a bare mattress. Or maybe, Miley would be sitting there alive and well. Or perhaps, she'd find Miley like she did Piper. An old, stained mattress in a dirty, unfinished basement would be her final resting place. Kimberley shook the thought away. She moved closer. More mattress. And then, she saw it. A child's foot hanging outside of a blanket. A shackle around the ankle with the chain hooked to an old gas grill. She moved the light up the child's body. Miley lay on the mattress. Her long black hair covering her face.

"Miley," Kimberley called again, quieter this time as her voice was stuck in her throat.

The child did not move.

Kimberley swallowed hard and took another step. Her lip was already starting to tremble.

"What is it?" Sam asked. He was still standing on the other side of the pile of junk.

"Get a medic down here," Kimberley said as she took another step.

"Bearfield, go now," Sam said.

Bearfield's steps up the stairs were thunderous as he took two at a time. It shook the staircase and then the floor upstairs as he sprinted through the house.

The child still hadn't moved. Kimberley focused on the girl's chest waiting for it to rise and fall, but the flashlight shook in her hand, so she couldn't tell if she was breathing or not. One more step brought her close enough to crouch down beside the little girl. She pushed the greasy, black hair out of Miley's face revealing pale skin, sunken eyes, and dry, chapped lips. Kimberley ran her hand down Miley's cheek. It was cold or maybe Kimberley's skin was cold, she couldn't tell. A teardrop ran down Kimberley's face landing on Miley's forehead.

Miley flinched and her eyes shot open. Her mouth opened to scream but all that came out was a hoarse sound.

"Miley, you're okay. You're okay now. I'm here to help." Kimberley put her hands up to reassure the little girl that she wasn't there to hurt her.

Sam walked around the pile of junk to find Kimberley crouched down by Miley who was looking at her like she was someone from another planet. She was clearly in shock, severely dehydrated and disoriented. Kimberley helped her sit up. The blanket fell off her shoulders into her lap and Kimberley could see the bruises on Miley's arms and wrists. Miley rubbed at her eyes.

"Oh, thank God," Sam said with a sense of relief that she was alive.

"I'm sleepy." Miley let out a big yawn.

"I know, baby." Kimberley rubbed her arm. She could see small puncture wounds in the crease above her forearm. Linda must have been injecting her with some sort of drug to keep her asleep. "We're going to get you to a hospital. You're going to be just fine."

"Where's my mom?" Miley's voice shook, yet there was an edge of concern. Like she was worried about her.

"She's getting help."

Miley shivered, rubbing the sides of her bare arms. Sam unbuttoned his shirt and removed it, handing it to Kimberley. She wrapped it around Miley, helping her put her arms through the massive sleeves.

"Do you want to come upstairs, Miley?" Sam asked.

"I can't." Miley's bottom lip pushed up and quivered. She pointed her arm to the shackle on her ankle.

Sam tilted his head and glanced around the floor and at the pile of junk. He pulled a piece of wire from beneath a box and started twisting.

"I'll set you free," Sam said in a cartoon-like Superman voice. He puffed out his chest and it made Miley laugh.

He bent down, inserting the twisted wire into the keyhole. He moved it around for a bit, until it finally clicked. Sam removed the shackle and tossed it aside.

"See." Sam smiled at her.

Miley slightly smiled back, but she winced as her lips were so dry and cracked.

"Let's get you upstairs," Kimberley said.

She tried to help Miley stand, but her legs were wobbly as she'd been chained up in this basement for days. She let out a small cry and pushed out her bottom lip.

"Want me to help you?" Sam asked.

Miley looked up at him, wiped her wet eyes with the oversized sleeve of the shirt she was wearing, and nodded. Sam bent down and picked her up. She wrapped her legs around him and rested her head on his shoulder.

"I've got you, Miley. You're safe now," he said, carrying her through the basement.

They met two paramedics and Bearfield at the top of the stairs. Sam and Kimberley told Miley they'd be right behind her as the paramedics took her away.

"Well, we did it," Sam said, patting Kimberley on the shoulder. She winced and bent forward.

"Oh God, I'm so sorry," Sam stammered. "I forgot you were injured."

"It's fine," Kimberley said, standing up straight and letting out a deep breath.

"If you weren't so tough, Sheriff would have remembered you were hurt." Bearfield let out a husky laugh. It was more of a compliment than anything else.

"Thanks, Bearfield," Kimberley said with a smile.

The three of them walked outside and watched the ambulance speed off. Sheriff's vehicles and a firetruck were blocking off the road. Deputies roamed the outside of the house collecting evidence and taping off the area, while firefighters ran a hose to the back of the house where the burning shed was. Kimberley glanced down the street, seeing neighbors come out of their houses and stand on their porches, watching the scene unfold. Dead Woman Crossing was safe again.

"Bearfield," Sam said. "Bag and tag any evidence and wrap up the scene. King and I are going to head to the hospital, so she can get some medical attention." He eyed Kimberley.

"I'm fine." She rolled her eyes.

Bearfield raised an eyebrow. "It looks like someone just took you off a grill." He pointed to the nasty burn on her shoulder blade.

"Yeah, yeah, yeah," Kimberley said, waving a hand playfully.

"You're going, King. Plus, we should check on Miley. Bearfield, keep things quiet for a bit until we can tell Arthur and Edna what happened to Piper."

Bearfield nodded. "You got it, sir."

A young nurse with round cheeks and kind eyes finished bandaging up the burn on Kimberley's shoulder. Kimberley sat on an examining table still dressed in her white tank top and her uniform pants. She had a few other less severe burns on her arms that were lightly covered with an A&D ointment.

"Just try to reapply an ointment a few times a day for the next week or so and keep the area clean," the nurse said. She gave Kimberley a sympathetic glance.

There was a knock on the door. Sheriff Walker peeked his head in. "Is she going to live?" he teased.

The nurse smiled. "It was touch and go for a minute there."

"Ha-ha," Kimberley mocked.

The nurse looked over to Sam. "The burn is in a hard to reach area, so you'll want to help her reapply her ointment, especially after showers."

Sam cleared his throat and gave a half smile.

"Oh, we're not together like that. We just work together," Kimberley corrected awkwardly.

Sam's smile faltered.

"My mistake," the nurse said with a laugh. She tossed some bandages and wipes and removed her gloves. "You're all set then." She smiled and left the room.

"How's Miley?" Kimberley asked, scooting off the table.

"She's doing better. She was dehydrated, so they're pumping her with fluids. Nutrition wise, she was fine, so Linda was feeding her." Sam folded his arms in front of his chest.

"Good. Did you talk to Arthur and Edna?"

Sam nodded. His smile turned downward. "They were devastated. Blamed themselves for not keeping a closer eye on Piper and wished they would have known about Linda."

Kimberley shook her head. "It's such a shame. You just never know what's going on in someone else's home."

"Do you want to go and see Miley?" Sam asked.

Kimberley nodded. The two of them walked side by side down the long hallway of the hospital. Nurses ran back and forth between rooms, tending to patients. They entered Miley's hospital room. She was sitting up in bed eating mac and cheese from a bowl and watching cartoons on a television that hung on the wall opposite her. An IV drip was hooked up to her arm, but she didn't seem to notice it. The color had returned to her face and her hair was clean, tucked back behind her ears. A middle-aged woman with shoulder-length black hair sat in a chair in the corner, flipping through papers in a folder. She was dressed in a blazer and black pants. Kimberley already knew she was from child protective services.

When Miley noticed Sam and Kimberley, she smiled widely and nearly squealed.

"Jodi, these are the people that rescued me," she said in a high-pitched voice.

The woman looked up and smiled.

"Hi, Miley. How are you feeling?" Kimberley said. Her voice was a little hoarse from smoke inhalation.

"Much better now. The nurse gave me mac n' cheese." She held up her bowl.

"That's great, kiddo," Sam said.

The two of them stood by her bed, looking down at her. They couldn't believe the change in her. The first time they had visited Linda's house, Miley was like a shell of a person, lying on the couch, unable to make eye contact or even speak. Kimberley could understand her behavior now though. She had just lost her best friend, she was keeping her mother's dark secret, and she was frightened.

"Hello," a man's voice called out from behind them.

Kimberley and Sam turned around to find Oliver standing in the doorway. He was holding a stuffed teddy bear, a box of chocolates, and a get well soon balloon. His eyes were glossy and his mouth quivered like he was on the verge of crying. Sam and Kimberley nodded at him and moved aside, so he could see his daughter, Miley.

"Dad!" Miley squealed.

That did it. Tears streamed down his cheeks. His face crumbled. "You remember me, Miley?" he asked.

"Of course. How could I forget my own dad?" Miley said with a laugh.

"You don't hate me?" Oliver wiped at his eyes.

"How could I hate my dad?" Miley asked.

Kids were forgiving, resilient and forgiving. It was what made them so innocent. Oliver had been away for years, but she didn't care. That bond is like rubber. It stretches, but it doesn't always break. Kimberley knew it would be a long road for them, though. Since he walked out, he'd have to prove he was fit to parent her. Hence why the social worker was in the room. He'd also have to earn her trust. And Miley had a long road of recovery ahead for herself after what she had witnessed and endured, at the hands of her mother.

Oliver walked over to Miley. "I got you some presents."

Her eyes lit up as he handed over the teddy bear and chocolates and tied the balloon to the hospital bed. Miley reached out her arms and Oliver hugged her. Kimberley and Sam looked at each other and nodded. Their work was complete. They left the room and continued down the hallway. Sam smiled at Kimberley.

"What?" She tilted her head.

"Thought you said you weren't going to call Oliver." He gave a small smirk.

"Who says I called him?"

Sam looked forward, smiling. "Okay, King."

Kimberley smiled as they walked side by side. She had called Oliver and told him that they had found Miley alive as soon as she arrived at the hospital. After hearing that Linda had told Miley that Oliver was responsible for her sister's death, she knew he was stuck between a rock and a hard place. He deserved a second chance to be her father again. When she saw the look on Oliver's face as he entered the hospital room and Miley's reaction, she knew she had made the right decision.

CHAPTER FORTY-ONE

Kimberley walked across the parking lot toward the Custer County Sheriff's Office. On her drive into work, Dead Woman Crossing seemed different, more relaxed, more at peace. She saw children out and about, people running and tending to their yards. The sun shone a little brighter, the sky was a little bluer, and the wheat was a little more golden. Her shoulder ached, but it was a price worth paying to find Miley alive and safe. She considered taking the day off to rest, but that wasn't her style. Sam had urged her to take the next day off, knowing full well she wouldn't.

Barb was seated behind her desk. She stood as soon as she saw Kimberley.

"Did Jessica make it to daycare on time?" she asked.

Kimberley nodded.

"You know you and Jess can stay with me as long as you want. I enjoy the company." Barb smiled sweetly.

"You're too kind." Kimberley smiled back.

"No such thing." Barb waved a hand at her.

"Is Sam in?"

"In his office," Barb said with a sly smile as if she were in on a secret of her own.

Kimberley walked onto the deputies' floor. Burns, Lodge, Hill, and Bearfield were all at their desks. They had a lot of paperwork to wrap up now that the case was closed.

Bearfield smiled wide when he saw Kimberley. "Pay up, boys." He chuckled.

Burns, Lodge, and Hill looked up from their desks and let out a collective groan as they fished their wallets out of their pants. Kimberley smirked, folding her hands in front of her chest.

"You all bet against me again?" She tilted her head.

"Why are you here? You've got severe burns..." Hill groaned as he flopped a twenty in Bearfield's large palm.

"Think she was going to miss a day of work from a burn? She got thrown through a wall last year and showed up the next day." Bearfield let out a deep belly laugh.

"Shit. I forgot about that," Burns said, placing a twenty-dollar bill in his hand and retaking his seat at his desk.

"I underestimated you, Chief Deputy King," Lodge said, paying up and retaking his seat.

Bearfield fanned his money in front of his face in a mocking way. "Gonna get me a steak dinner and a beer tonight with these winnings."

Kimberley laughed and walked past the deputies toward Sam's office. The banter between them continued as she knocked on the door and popped her head in. Sam was seated at his desk.

"Come in," he said.

Kimberley closed the door behind her and took a seat across from him.

"You didn't get in on the bet?" Kimberley teased.

Sam shook his head. "No, I knew you'd come in. It wouldn't be fair for me to bet."

"How ya feeling today?" she asked.

"I should be asking you that." Sam raised an eyebrow.

"I'm fine. A little sore, but fine." She shrugged her shoulders. Her eyes lingered on his face, taking him in. "I wanted to say thank you, Sam," Kimberley said sincerely.

"For what?" Sam leaned forward in his seat.

"For saving my life."

"Just returning the favor." The corner of his lip perked up.

Kimberley's brows knitted together. "What do you mean?"

Sam hesitated for a moment, then looked directly into Kimberley's eyes. "You saved my life the day you walked into this station a year ago."

Her cheeks became warm and her heart started to race. She could feel it beating all over her body, the side of her neck, her hands, everywhere. Kimberley didn't know what to say.

When she didn't speak, Sam continued. "And the other night at The Trophy Room, I do remember what I said about you, Kimberley."

She raised her eyebrows. "You do?"

"Hiring you is the best decision I ever made," Sam said with a smile.

Kimberley's eyes lit up and her mouth slowly curved into a wide smile. Was this it? Were they finally admitting that there was something between them? Should she jump up from her seat and run into his arms? Should she ask him out on a proper date? She didn't know what to do, especially since she was at work. It made it, whatever it was, all the more complicated.

There was a quick knock on the door and Barb popped her head in. "Sorry for interrupting. Caleb's here to see you, Kimberley."

Sam's smile immediately faltered. Kimberley cleared her throat. "I'll be right out, Barb."

Barb nodded and walked away, leaving the door partially open.

"You were saying…" she said to Sam, trying to keep the conversation going. Kimberley wanted to sit there and keep talking, keep going down whatever path they were on. She wanted to see where it would lead.

Sam had a look of sadness and defeat on his face. She wanted to wipe it away, making it happy and bright again like it was a minute before. He exhaled deeply before he spoke.

"I was saying good work, King. You're fantastic at your job and an invaluable member of this team," he said with a nod.

Sam pulled a couple of folders from a stack and started flipping through them.

Kimberley swallowed hard. All the words she wanted to say were stuck in her throat.

"You better get going. Don't want to keep Caleb waiting." Sam looked up at her and forced a strained smile. He let his head drop, looking at the folders on his desk again.

She nodded and slowly rose from her seat. "Okay… thanks, Sam." Kimberley walked toward the door, but before leaving, she turned back, glancing at him.

Staring hard, she wanted Sam to meet her gaze, to tell her not to go. She wanted to go back in time a few minutes and say all the words that were stuck in her throat. She wanted to tell him that he was the only man she'd ever been able to trust. That he was the first person she wanted to see every morning and the last person she wanted to see every night. She wanted to tell him all of those things and so many more. But most of all, she wanted him to look at her because she knew she'd have the courage to do it if he did. She waited a few seconds. They felt like minutes.

Sam didn't look up, and when Kimberley closed the door behind her, she knew she was closing more than just a door. She took a deep breath and forced her mind to think of Caleb. He had been wonderful to her and Jessica. He had been patient and kind, and he was clearly interested in getting to know her. He had put in the effort. That was what she needed to remind herself.

As she walked away, Sam glanced through the window of his office. His eyes were glued to Kimberley, and he couldn't pull away until she disappeared through the set of doors.

"Shit," he muttered to himself.

Sam took a deep breath and leaned back in his chair. Rubbing his hands over his face, he let out a sharp exhale.

A LETTER FROM J.R. ADLER

Dear reader,

I want to say a huge thank you for choosing to read *Last Day Alive*. If you enjoyed it and want to keep up to date with all my latest releases, just sign up at the following link. Your email address will never be shared and you can unsubscribe at any time.

www.bookouture.com/jr-adler

I hope you loved *Last Day Alive* and, if you did, I would be incredibly grateful if you could write a review. I'd love to hear what you think, and it makes such a difference helping new readers to discover one of my books for the first time. If you loved what you read, be sure to check out the first book in the Detective Kimberley King series, *Dead Woman Crossing*. I also wrote *The Perfect Marriage* under the name Jeneva Rose, which has been optioned to be developed into a film or limited series. Feel free to get in touch with me on my Facebook page, through Twitter, Goodreads or my website as I love hearing from and connecting with readers. Once again, thank you so much!

Best,
J.R. Adler

JRAdlerAuthor

@sJRAdlerAuthor

www.jenevarose.com

ACKNOWLEDGEMENTS

First and foremost, I want to thank the entire Bookouture team for believing in my writing and bringing me on for this incredible journey. To my fellow Bookouture authors, thank you for being so supportive. To my editor, Lydia, thank you for being a pleasure to work with. You've pushed me to make *Last Day Alive* the best book it could possibly be, and I can't thank you enough.

Thank you to my friends and family for supporting me throughout this crazy author journey, through all the highs and lows, from rejections to book deals.

Thank you to my Ithaca critique group who I've been a member of for nearly three years. Thank you for bringing me joy and much needed constructive criticism. I'm a better writer because of all of you.

Finally, I want to thank my readers. Thank you for taking the time to read my work. I hope you enjoyed *Last Day Alive*, and I hope you'll continue on this journey with me and Detective Kimberley King.

J.R. Adler

CPSIA information can be obtained
at www.ICGtesting.com
Printed in the USA
LVHW031512190421
684905LV00025B/709